Ian Watson was born on Tyneside in 1943. He studied English at Balliol College, Oxford. His first speculative fiction stories were stimulated by his three-year stay as a lecturer in Japan. In 1969 *Roof Garden Under Saturn*, a short story, was published in *New Worlds* magazine, and since then his stories have appeared in various magazines and anthologies. They have been published in book form in four collections, *The Very Slow Time Machine*, *Sunstroke*, *Slow Birds* and *Evil Water*.

Ian Watson's first novel, *The Embedding*, was published in 1973 and received enormous critical acclaim. His second novel, *The Jonah Kit*, became a British Science Fiction Award winner as well as confirming his position in the front rank of contemporary British writers. He has been features editor of the journal *Foundation* since 1975 and a full-time writer since 1976.

By the same author

IAN WATSON

Queenmagic, Kingmagic

GRAFTON BOOKS

A Division of the Collins Publishing Group

LONDON GLASGOW
TORONTO SYDNEY AUCKLAND

Grafton Books
A Division of the Collins Publishing Group
8 Grafton Street, London W1X 3LA

Published by Grafton Books 1988

First published in Great Britain by
Victor Gollancz Ltd 1986

Copyright © Ian Watson 1986

ISBN 0-586-07414-7

Printed and bound in Great Britain by
Collins, Glasgow

Set in Times

For Matjaž Šekoranja
and Matjaž Šinovec

Contents

PART ONE
Queenmagic, Pawnmagic

'What you see on the board is only the outcrop of a much larger world, like mountain peaks above mist.'

– Bishop Lovats the Perceptive

Do you spy the palace of Queen Isgalt?

Magnificent, eh? Yet what a medley! Part fortress, part fantasia.

Hewn into the curtain walls were mullioned windows of stained glass; invaders could practically leapfrog their way in. Isgalt's predecessor, Queen Alyitsa, had those windows sawed through the stone – to let in light, she said, for light is the foe of dark and night. Alabaster statues of soldiers (from Queen Dama's reign, before) stood on the palace parapets: a perch for pigeons. The white onion domes were so pierced by quatrefoils that they resembled peasants' lacework – or curious colanders for draining salads. Rain poured through them to spout out by way of demon gargoyles. The impression was of roofs which moths had feasted on.

As for the cupolas topping the towers, on festival nights bright blaziers were lit in those. Often updrafts swirled sparks aloft so that the royal flags caught alight, burning high in the night and skidding down the spires to the roofs below like bloody, tattered shirts.

But of course, no common-or-garden siege would decide the outcome of the war . . .

Our lovely, wistful Queen Isgalt only possessed half the magic force of Queen Alyitsa; quarter of the power of Queen Dama. King Karol spent much of his time high in the central tower devoting himself to bubble-art. Prince Ruk, who guarded the King, could race along two lines of magic. But the prince had long since used up his ability to shift instantaneously to another place through the body of a pawn-squire. (He used it to rescue King Karol from the suicidal attack of the Knight of Night, Oscaro.) Bishop Veck, who practised crosswise magic, continued to minister to the queen and to brace her courage. As did chevalier Sir Brant, who jumped askew through magics. Our city of Bellogard had survived longer than some of us imagined it might.

And I?

My name is Pedino. I was a pawn-squire.

At times how I envied the ordinary lives of burghers and menials of Bellogard, of farmers and peasants throughout the Dolina valley and the rest of the kingdom; even though those people had no full souls which might migrate to another life when our kingdom finally fell, when all houses and barns tumbled into chaos, and the palace burned like white paper.

How proud I was, as a lad, to have my soul divined as a full soul by the late Bishop Slon. How can I forget that day?

Queen Alyitsa was still with us. Isgalt was only one of a quartet of princesses. Despite the loss of Queen Dama, the struggle against the ebon city of Chorny seemed remote, inconsequential to our lives; not so much a total war to the death, by magic, as a mischievous dispute, a cantankerous scrimmage. There had been sorrow at the death of the long-reigning queen – she was killed when I was only an infant, and my mother told me about the pang people felt. There had been a whole fortnight of mourning; but no sense of doom. (Ah, but Prince Ruk and Bishop Veck knew the truth. They realized how vulnerable – in the long run – Dama's loss had made us.)

My father was a pipe-maker in Chalk Street near the Spomenik Monument, and my mother ran the tobacconist's shop which occupied the front of our premises. My sister Drina, a year older than me, was blonde and slim and tall, though with blobby features which gave her an air of whimsical babyishness; whereas my own hair was dark as walnut, my features were open, and I was broader of build but always somewhat shorter than Drina. She was a long clay pipe with a little bowl of a head; I was a burlier, briefer briar.

My childhood was interesting and happy. Both parents were at home all of the time and there were constant visitors to the shop, sometimes quite exalted ones. Shop and workshop provided fascinating hideouts.

In the workshop were tool-strewn benches for cutting, whittling, drilling, and polishing wood, for crafting silver lids to cap expensive long pipes; clay moulds and an oven; a deep cupboard where chunks of wood matured for up to two years. As kids, we sometimes took clays which had been rejected because of some trivial bobble or air-pit, and dipped them in soapy water to try to blow magical bubbles. Naturally we always failed, producing streams of quivering airy spheres which quickly popped.

Dad was purveyor of pipes by appointment to the palace; perhaps we weren't such total commoners. His royal warrant looked grand, carved on the sign which hung outside, but this by no means implied constant consultations with the king. Dad had crafted his most recent bubble pipe masterpiece for His Majesty in the year of my birth. Equerries occasionally purchased ordinary smoking pipes, and flunkies frequently called to buy Mum's special 'royal cut mixture'; but that was a more mundane matter.

Mum's shop! – with its heady, nostril-teasing jars of shag and rum-shag, mellowleaf and ambershred; the plugs and pigtails laid out like knots of rope; the boxes of cheroots; the snuff of all scents from mint to strawberry. Dad's pipes on display: racks and trays of clays and chibouks, briars and lulus. Boxes of lucifers illustrated with views of Bellogard, blooms from the botanic garden, fish of Lake Riboo.

Every year during our childhood we holidayed in the countryside at the village of Duvana, where the tobacco plantations were. Mum did not personally buy tobacco wholesale, but she liked to keep an eye on the quality of the crop and the standard of curing in the sheds. Duvana was close to the Shooma Forest and uplands; Dad would make excursions with the woodcutters to choose his branches for maturing in the cupboard back home and subsequent carving into pipe bowls and stems. The area around Duvana was a well-known beauty spot dominated by snow-tipped Mount Planina. The Vodopad Waterfall was half a day's journey by horse and trap. Ruined Zamak Castle offered a stiff climb up from the base of the falls. We enjoyed our holidays.

Then there was Bellogard itself to explore: sprawling Piazza Market with its flower and fruit and vegetable stalls, the cool catacomb of the fish market underneath, slippery smelly stone steps leading down to the fish quay on the River Rehka, and behind Piazza the blood and sawdust arcades of the meat and offal shops. There was smart white Terga Square with its outdoor cafés and cake-icing buildings, the carved stone and plasterwork seeming piped from a master pastrycook's tube – and the astrology observatory on Bresh Hill overlooking the botanic gardens . . .

Drina and I were forbidden to explore the Seveno district with its sprightly, disreputable bar–restaurants, 'theatres', casinos, dancing halls, and 'house of ladies'. Since Drina usually tagged along with me and since I didn't entirely trust her to keep a secret, on the whole Seveno remained for years as much outside my ken as the queen's own palace. Take Drina through Seveno, even by day? She might be dragged inside one of those 'houses of ladies' by a burly doorman for some unknown but embarrassing purpose.

A couple of incidents stand out from my boyhood, the second one marking its end.

The first event was an outing by my Gymnasium class to the Samostan, Bishop Slon's town residence, with its wonderful topiary gardens where peacocks shrieked and stamped in circles, flaunting their blazoned tails, quills rattling like sticks on railings. Bishop Slon was Chairman of Governors of the Gymnasium.

All of us had visited the Samostan gardens numerous times; yes, and chased the big, stupid, glorious birds hoping to snatch a plume unobserved. On this occasion we were special guests of the bishop, who had arranged for a picnic of stuffed pancakes and lemonade on the main lawn.

There we all were, guzzling away of a bright, breezy afternoon under the benevolent gaze of the bishop. Swathed in white dalmatic and tunicle, with pearl-trimmed buckled shoes on his white-socked feet and a white biretta on his head, he sat enthroned in a high-back wicker chair with parasol attached. Our austere, dun-suited teacher, Master Samo, was chatting to him deferentially. Head-bobbing peacocks and hens pecked at crumbs which we flicked their way.

Slon was a tubby fellow. His cheeks were ripe apples, almost tomatoes. His hands, however, were big and bony. I remember noticing his hands because he began crackling his finger joints, producing crunchy little explosions which reminded me of a hound chewing over a marrow-bone, or far-off crepitations of thunder.

Presently Slon's gaze unfocused, so that it seemed as if Master Samo was boring him considerably.

In view of what was to happen, might it have been more sensible and considerate if Slon had fled, skirts flapping, inside the residence while he still had time? Vulnerable children sat all around him.

Yet what were the lives of a score of striplings – most of whom might only have the hundredth part of a soul – if protecting them from harm distracted the bishop's concentration from a far more important task?

And perhaps he did shield us.

Abruptly, to everyone's astonishment, Slon leapt up, knocking his wicker throne over. He adopted the stance of someone holding a quarterstaff – or invisible crozier – with which to do combat. He stared up. So did we.

Amidst otherwise scudding billows of clean woolly cumulus, one tiny compact black cloud moved at an eerily slower pace. This cloud didn't obey the wind at all. It swung gently from side to side like the bob of a pendulum, always coming closer. Soon it was overhead. Its shadow fell upon the lawn, drinking the sunlight. Momentarily the cloud seemed to be flying up and away, shrinking as it receded. But no. It was descending, compacting, growing denser as it sank.

Slon skipped diagonally through our midst, scattering boys like pins. He danced diagonally a different way, kicking a peacock. Sweat-dew flew from his cheeks. He shouted words which I didn't understand but some of which – alas – I memorized.

'*Opasnost po Zhivot!*'

Lightning flashed from the coaly cloud which was only just overhead. Slon swung his pretend crozier this way,

16

that way, as the dazzling blue bolt struck. Electric fire shattered and flew aslant across the lawn.

When my vision blinked clear, I saw Slon still standing erect. The stuff of the black cloud – no longer above us – had gathered tarrily on his hand. He jerked the evil material to the ground, where it bubblingly evaporated. Kneeling, he furiously wiped his skin clean on the grass, which withered into brown threads.

Peacocks were rushing around, tails erect, clattering with colour. Peacocks have such tiny heads that it took me several moments to realize that all the birds had been decapitated – their heads sliced off by the lightning.

The headless birds paraded madly for a couple more minutes, displaying passionately, thin pulses of blood squirting from their severed necks as they cavorted. Their claws raked the hands and cheeks of sprawled, stunned pupils until one by one the peacocks fell over and lay still.

The bishop had resumed his previous pose of alertness, though twice he massaged his wrist.

A young man in a sober black suit staggered out from between huge box-bushes clipped to the shape of spinning tops. Bloody saliva dribbled from the stranger's mouth, beneath a trim black moustache. His suit jacket was torn. A limp hand held a dagger loosely.

The young man advanced waveringly. He raised his dagger. In a flurry of white, Slon dashed forward. Hoisting his skirts, he kicked the weapon from the stranger's grasp. The young man moaned, sighed, sank to his knees. Slon placed a pearly shoe against the would-be assassin's shoulder and toppled him on the turf.

By now our whole class was watching, agape. Absurdly, Master Samo was scurrying to pick up all the scattered heads of peacocks and hens. He loped to a flower-bed and pressed his gruesome collection down tidily, beak

17

first, into the soil to hide them. Had it occurred to Samo that he might as easily have been collecting the severed heads of boys for delivery to their parents? Supposing that Slon had parried the lightning *thus*, rather than *that way*?

Slon laughed grimly. 'You may plant 'em. Those corms won't grow new birds.' He wiped a tear from his eye; or was that a bead of sweat?

Scrawny, respectable Master Samo shook his head in confusion. He blushed as if caught in some childish prank or act of lubricity. His body had been doing things of which he was hardly conscious. His undermind had been operating him.

The black-clad stranger lay twitching. Perhaps near death, perhaps already dead, his weak spasms those of a dissociating soul.

Samo jerked a questioning finger at the body, gestured at his flock of boys. How much was it advisable to say? Would the bishop be so kind?

Obliging, Slon spread his arms. 'Beloved boys! Behold here a man from Chorny. A magical pawn. What do we have to fear from such feeble bumblers?' He scooped up the dagger and cautiously sniffed the point. 'Well, even a bumbler has a sting! I detect poison as well as magic – which is why I used my shoe to disarm him. Do not fret about this disruption which mars your picnic. But do not neglect to reflect in one corner of your mind upon the basis of reality, namely the magical enmity which dark Chorny holds for our beautiful Bellogard.'

'Boys, be watchful,' Samo instructed. 'Ever watchful.'

The bishop frowned. 'No, that would be paranoid, and would spoil our town. I've no doubt that in Chorny everyone watches everyone else. They must, there where blackness reigns! Ours is a land of light and openness and pleasure. Let us fear no evil.'

18

He rubbed the hand which had been soiled by black ooze, and smiled approvingly. With a mischievous grin at us boys he stuck two fingers in his mouth and emitted a piercing whistle.

Flunkies came running.

'*Remove* this creature. Convey him speedily to the queen's dungeons. Summon chirurgeons to inspect him. Farewell, and bless you, boys.'

Obviously we gossiped amongst ourselves, and at home, about this incident. My classmate Alexander Mog (whose death I shall come to shortly) claimed that when Slon spoke of summoning chirurgeons he really meant torturers. Given the assailant's moribund condition this seemed unlikely, a product of Mog's unwholesome imagination.

A. Mog's mind wasn't entirely healthy. He was handsome and tall for his age, but he was also a bully with a cruel, nasty streak. He bred rabbits, confining them in tiny hutches. He liked to pick them up painfully by their long ears to show how they should be killed, by a chop on the neck. He especially enjoyed demonstrating this skill to girls, and pressured any classmate with a pretty sister to bring her round to his home for a visit. He boasted how he would hypnotize a girl, like a weasel fixing a bunny, then he could leap on her and bite her neck with kisses and play with her indecently. The rabbit which he killed before her eyes would do the trick. A girl's slight, shy, yielding soul was like the soul of a rabbit. (Irrespective of the virtual certainty that A. Mog himself would only have a partial, microscopic soul!) Within six months of the magical assassination attempt A. Mog was leaning on me to persuade me to bring Drina his way; for what I perceived as a baby-face

19

perched upon a willowy frame he viewed as someone vulnerably desirable.

But I anticipate.

To infill for a moment, we all talked about the magical skirmish, speculating in particular about the workings of the lightning which lopped off the heads of the bishop's prized peacocks (a feature of the incident which strongly appealed to A. Mog!). I kept quiet regarding the exact words which Slon had shouted, and which I alone appeared to remember. (I was specially receptive to the magic language but I didn't know that at the time.)

The official paper, *Noveeny*, carried a statement from the palace dismissing the attack as a trivial impertinence; and my parents and neighbours soon lost interest. Nothing was said about the fate of the attacker. Maybe he was already in Grobbny Cemetery or buried in a lime pit inside the palace grounds. The life of Bellogard, and my own boyhood, flowed on. The event seemed of no more ultimate account than a stone tossed into the Rehka. It made a splash then sank out of sight.

Now we shift forward almost a year. It had been a cold winter with much fluffy snow to toboggan on, long icicles spearing down from gutters, and small floes speeding along the swollen Rehka like families of dingy ducks.

The spring arrived, hot and sudden. All over town Jew's–mallows, quinces, and magnolia trees burst into bloom: golden pompons, waxy cups of blood, milky goblets. A. Mog had begun browbeating me the previous autumn but winter cooled his ardour. A few idle threats to whip up a gang to bind me with rope on the way home and plaster me up as a snowman amounted to nothing.

Come spring, with its sudden heat and restlessness, its frustrated excitement and sweet fragrance in the air, and the doffing of heavy clothing, he resumed his onslaught. I must bring Drina to visit his rabbits – who were mating vigorously till the bucks lay flopped out, heaving and panting – or he would punish me.

Coincidentally – if it *was* a coincidence – A. Mog's more amiable crony Boris Slad proposed a swimming expedition. Boris's sister Dana attended the same academy as Drina. A dozen of us, plus any sisters, should visit the thermal baths.

These baths were at the south end of town beneath the looming Razval Rock which housed picturesque ruins of an ancient fortress, or perhaps a folly, the origin of which was something of a mystery. A fortress situated on that eminence would splendidly command the river; yet who would ever attack upstream? Anyway, an attack was a magical affair, not a jaunt by boat or barge.

Hot mineral water bubbled up from the deep guts of the rock. The outer, marble bath was a cold one fed by river water. The inner bath – carved into the limestone itself, though open to the elements – was hot, steamy, and sulphurous. Breezes ventilated the excess of rotten-egg vapour.

During the winter the baths were only used by the sort of stern old men who believe that an extreme contrast of hot and cold on their bare bodies – a simmering by mineral soup interspersed with icy plunges and soft flagellation by snowflakes – is salubrious.

Come the spring, the baths became much more popular as a way of steaming the winter out of one's pores; not to mention accumulated dirt, if one was poor and had no home plumbing. Later, summer's heat would render the inner bath intolerable; attendance would fall off; those spartan curmudgeons would come back into their own.

Boris declared as an added inducement that we were all invited to call at A. Mog's afterwards for a wine and soda and a home-made rabbit pasty, since swimming

21

always leaves such an enervating hole in the belly. Alexander Mog leered at me.

'Come on now!' Boris insisted. 'An opportunity not to be missed. Everyone must turn up without fail. Anyone who lets us down is a fish-head. He'll be forced to eat a dozen fish-heads cooked in piss.'

Personally, the prospect of the outing worried me sick. It even worried me into a dream that night. Otherwise I doubt I would ever have stolen – or borrowed – Dad's perfect pipe. Otherwise A. Mog wouldn't have drowned.

I dreamt of A. Mog slicing heads off rabbits with single lightning chops of his hand, then using their long ears to tickle my sister's long legs, higher and higher, while she stood paralysed, giggling feebly.

A big buck bunny arrived. Standing up on its hind thumpers, it blew bubbles from a long clay pipe held in its little front hooves. The animal could easily blow bubbles because a rabbit's mouth is only a tiny opening like a fish's mouth; and fish blow bubbles in water. (Watch a rabbit when it yawns.)

One huge bubble flew at A. Mog's head and enclosed it without popping. Inside the bubble Alexander Mog soon began to gasp for air, and his face turned blue. My sister ran away, and I woke up.

The pipe which the bunny blew in the dream was the very same clay that my Dad had made a few weeks earlier, and which he had pronounced to be an impeccable pipe. It was the very ideal of a Dutch-style clay as regards the curve of the stem, the oval of the bowl, the little nub on the underside – the acme of master craftsmanship.

'King Karol ought to blow this one himself,' Dad said. 'Except, I doubt if a king would ever blow a mere clay.'

He placed it inside a glass case in the shop, instructing Mum never to sell it, though to her eyes the perfect pipe looked much like any other clay specimen.

The visit to the Razval baths had been set for a Sunday afternoon. Before Drina and I set out (both wearing our costumes under our clothes so that we wouldn't have to get changed anywhere near A. Mog) I sneaked into the closed shop, opened the case, and slipped the perfect pipe inside my towel – along with a little bottle of liquid soap.

Our route to the baths took us by way of the wooded Vertovy Gardens, overlooked by white stucco walls and steep red dormer-studded roofs of prosperous burgher houses, one of these being the Slad residence. Slad Senior was a banker.

We had set out earlier than need be, so I suggested that we ring the bell of the Slad door. Boris and Dana were still at home; soon they were accompanying us.

I felt as much at ease with Dana as did Drina, whilst Boris was cordial when not in bad company. I opened my towel to show them what lay inside.

'My father made a magic pipe for the king,' I said. 'A fortune pipe.'

'But, Ped,' protested my sister.

I hushed her. 'Listen here, Boris and Dana, I intend to blow a fortune for Alexander Mog. By way of a jape! We'll pull him down a gentle peg or two – without imperilling our pasties, of course.'

'You?' scoffed Boris. 'Blow a magic bubble?'

I winked. 'If my bubble shows nothing and bursts right away, will you two swear that you saw something absolutely *awful* in it?'

'Such as what?' asked Dana gleefully.

'So dreadful that you can't tell. Keep him guessing.'

'No fear! He'll duck me. He'll twist my arm.'

'I'd stop him,' declared Dana's brother.

'There'd be a fight.'

'Hmm,' said Boris.

'Let's pretend,' I said, 'that the ghastly thing you saw was Mog's nose starting to twitch, and his ears suddenly growing long and hairy – and him becoming a big black rabbit. All because of some magical attack from Chorny which goes askew. Let's hold off from telling him for as long as possible; preferably till we get back to his house and have our pasties. But beforehand we'll spread the word to everyone we trust. When you do finally tell him, everybody who's in the know can stick their fingers up above their ears and hop up and down together and laugh at him.'

'He won't like it,' said Boris. 'He'll be furious.'

'He won't *do* anything. Bullies shrink when everyone else gangs up on them. He might even cry.'

'And *you'll* be the leader of the class,' Dana told her brother, 'as you ought to be.'

I'd been intending to suggest the very same thing myself.

'Better,' she went on, 'a banker's son as leader than a butcher's boy – with banker's son dancing attendance all the time.' Mog Senior was indeed a butcher; hence his son's habits with rabbits.

'Damned impertinence,' muttered Boris. I couldn't be sure whether he was referring to his sister's criticism of him, or to the supremacy of A. Mog. He walked on with us in silence for a while, then suddenly said, 'Right! That's what we'll do.'

An hour later our whole party was disporting in the hot, effervescent, smelly waters. This great stone inner bath was contoured so that a shallow shelf led to a sloping middle area with a very deep pit of water beyond. The limestone roof was vaulted so that condensation mostly ran down the slope of the vault to slick the walls instead of falling directly in cool, stinging drops upon the pink-flushed bodies below. This, too, deterred stalactites from

24

forming. The walls were embossed with enormous fluted columns, crusted with deposits.

Most of us were capering in the shallows. Our voices clattered back at us from roof and walls like cascades of breaking crockery. Word had been passed surreptitiously. Meanwhile A. Mog was showing off to Dana Slad, who had volunteered to be his audience. Down at the deep end he was performing backward flips into the water, scrambling out and flipping again.

I scampered to the stone bench where I'd left my towel, and returned with pipe and soap bottle.

'Alexander Mog!' I shouted. All my fellow conspirators stood stock-still in the water and chorused his name, then became quiet as mice, watching intently.

From the edge of the deep end A. Mog glared across the water at me. I shouted my lie about the magic pipe. I unstoppered the bottle, poured soap in the hot water, and scooped the pipe through.

'This is your fate!' I cried. For good measure I shouted these words in the language of magic which I remembered the bishop uttering: '*Opasnost po Zhivot!*' I put the pipe to my lips.

To my surprise I blew a perfectly enormous, shimmery bubble.

I continued blowing. The bubble did not burst. It swelled and swelled till it was a full metre across.

The bubble detached itself from the bowl. Bobbing on hot air and rising mineral gas, it floated away over the water in the direction of A. Mog. Everyone stared in wonder. The bubble showed no scenes, only an oily sheen, but it was still a marvel.

'*Opasnost po Zhivot!*' I shrieked, intoxicated with myself. The bubble picked up speed.

A. Mog decided that he'd had enough of this; he wasn't

going to wait till the bubble popped all over him. He clove the water in a swan dive.

The giant bubble also dived. When it touched the water, it spread out; became an iridescent, frail dome. Swiftly the dome shrank and vanished.

A. Mog failed to surface.

'Look!' Dana was pointing down into the deep water.

I padded hastily around the side of the pool. Classmates were hauling themselves out and rushing along to join Dana.

A. Mog was balled up tight against the bottom. His knees were drawn up to his chest, his head was bowed over. His palms were pushing and his knees were jerking as he tried to kick. He looked like an engraving I'd seen of a foetus in the womb.

His womb was a sphere of water, a sphere which stayed heavily in the depths irrespective of his struggles. He couldn't break free, no matter how hard he thrust. The bubble had sunk down, enclosed him, and become that deathtrap.

A crowd of us gazed in horror, yet no one volunteered to jump in. A. Mog's submerged flailing reached a climax of desperation, then ceased. He hung motionless, a big limp foetus in a blue-striped bathing costume. My classmates turned to stare at me as I stood there with the perfect pipe in my hand.

'I'll fetch him out,' I said. 'I'll try to revive him.' Obviously he was stone-dead by now. I passed the pipe to Drina for safe-keeping.

I made four exhausting trips down into the pit. The depth was too great for me to grab the equivalent of a sack of potatoes, get my feet on the bottom, and kick our combined weights back up. Water blurred my vision, though since I could feel Mog's limbs I knew that no magic bubble of water surrounded him – now that he was a corpse.

Eventually the bath attendant brought a rope and tied a noose with a slip-knot. Boris dived and secured one of A. Mog's wrists. Thus the bully, dead by magic, was pulled back up to the surface and heaved out on to the stone surround.

I heard Dana say to Boris, 'Wonder what'll become of our rabbit pasties now?'

A. Mog lay in the soil of Grobbny Cemetery. The affair stirred a deal of gossip and a somewhat inaccurate paragraph appeared in *Noveeny*, but now that the threat of Mog was gone no classmates rallied to praise the dead bully; nor did his family receive more than two-faced sympathy. On the contrary, people began grumbling about the amount of fat and even bone which Mog Senior had ground in with their mince on a certain occasion, or how, another time, some belly of pork was folded around thick suet. I seemed unlikely to be accused of magical murder by Mog the butcher; such an accusation would only stick if popular feeling could be roused.

As to Dad, he was angry at my deceit; but he also cried, 'I knew it! I knew it!' and put the impeccable pipe back in the same glass case, to which he now added a lock. He bolted the case to a wall in the shop and hung underneath a neatly lettered sign: *The Perfect Pipe*. Business blossomed better than ever. People from over the river deserted their regular purveyors of baccy to visit our shop and gaze at the white clay pipe which had killed.

Two days subsequent to the drowning, Master Samo had a word with me after class.

'This, er, tragedy, Pedino.' Tucking his dominie's gown around his dull brown suit, Samo perched on the edge of his long oak desk. Everyone else had departed.

27

'Sir?'

'Obviously it was not your fault.' (Obviously?) 'However, a teacher is occasionally a butt for practical jokes, Pedino, such as a pin on his chair or a book balanced on top of a door. Other boys might, hmm, egg such a joker on.'

Samo wasn't meeting my eyes. Was he scared? He was looking beyond me at the rows of scholars' desks, stained with ink, carved as if beetles had bored them.

On the rear wall hung a framed painting of King Karol and Queen Alyitsa. Both were heroically dressed in amberglass armour, though the queen's long legs – also of golden hue – were bare to the thigh, so that we boys had best have our backs to her while we laboured at our lessons. Both monarchs were crowned with jagged forks of lightning as though their hair was standing on end, having been washed and dried by a maniac. Under Alyitsa's foot a slaughtered raven held a scroll in its beak lettered thus: *The Curse of Chorny*.

Next to the portrait hung a map of the kingdom, from the rocky goat pastures of Zima in the north to the southern vineyards of Letto, from eastern Istok province to westerly Zapad – with Bellogard at the heart. Crowded along the bottom were those border marshes where our kingdom melted into Chorny.

'In the past,' observed Samo, 'you've brought snuff into school. I've smelt it. I've turned a blind eye.'

And one good turn deserves another.

'Honestly, Dominie, I wouldn't dream of bringing a *pipe* into school.'

'Good, hmm, good. Glad to hear it. But a pipe is just a tool, don't you know? – the same as a pen is. What it does depends on the person. If the person can't write, then a pen can't help. If he *can* write, he can write equally powerful words with his finger dipped in soot. If

28

he has the capacity. So: be watchful – of yourself. Will you?'

I promised Master Samo that I would keep my mind in chains.

'Though it's hard,' I added, 'with Her Majesty on the wall.'

'Our queen has magic,' he cautioned. 'She may know when anyone is concentrating on her.'

'In that case she must be blushing all the time. She ought to commission uglier portraits, don't you think, Dominie?'

He sighed. 'Ah, Pedino, such pubertal bravado. Yet you are privately rather relieved that the killer of rabbits can no longer pester one's own princess, eh?'

I gaped. 'How did you know . . . ?'

He tapped his nose. 'I'm not such an imperceptive fogey, such a prematurely dry old stick.'

(Indeed not! A couple of years later, when I grew familiar with Seveno district, I was to run into Master Samo under quite other circumstances.)

'At some time in our lives,' he continued, 'we all experience magic moments. To some degree or another. To the extent that we each possess a little piece of soul! Usually those are *only* moments. A shaft of magic, to us – a mere triviality to a lord or lady of the land from whom true magic flows. I suppose a mighty magic may shaft its way through a commoner due to a chance concatenation of circumstances. So, Pedino, don't be disappointed if it all amounts to nothing; if you spend the rest of your life selling snuffboxes. I'm sure that will be a happier life, while it lasts! There are many ways to amuse oneself in Bellogard. Now, be off with you.'

'Thank you, Dominie. Thanks for speaking to me like this.'

'A man, to a man.' He smiled wryly; and I did not

understand the depth of his sadness, but I left the class-room admiring him.

Bishop Slon sighted along the stem of the perfect pipe, unlocked from its case specially for him. It was a week later. He had arrived just as the shop was closing.

'An arc of a hyperbola,' he commented.

Dad nodded, gratified.

'And the bowl a fractional ellipsoid with exactly seven twenty-secondths of it absent, I'll be bound. This truly is an *excellent* pipe – a wonderful happenstance where tacky, finickity, cheap, common clay is involved. Or,' he conceded grandly, 'a master creation combining eye, hand, alchemistry of the chosen matter, temperature, time, and temperament.'

'More likely that,' agreed my mother.

'Much more likely. May I purchase this pipe for my collection, sir?'

Dad hesitated. A conflict of urges characteristically made him suck in his cheeks and pop his pursed lips with the sound of a dripping tap.

'Thus we'll keep it out of harm's way, eh?' added Slon.

The interval between drips lengthened as Dad arrived at a decision. 'Let it be a gift, my Lord Bishop.'

'Oh no! Very generous; but no. My sense of obligation might interfere with divination.'

'Divination?' Mum queried quickly.

'Of your son, madam. Do set a price, sir.'

The tap started dripping again. This time it didn't stop.

'I see your problem, sir. You value this pipe highly, yet to price it at that value might seem excessive. Shall we say twenty crowns?' Dad had stopped drip-popping. Slon fished inside his dalmatic, found a purse, and pressed silver coins on my delighted mother. 'Will you wrap the pipe carefully, madam, so that I shan't crack it?'

Slon produced a little bundle of his own and unwrapped a magnificent antique briar. 'And if you could bring a bowl of soapy water?'

This was soon done.

The bishop whisked the water with his fingers. 'If you will kindly look into the bowl, Pedino? Select a bubble; concentrate.' Slon spoke a spell in the magic tongue. He dipped the briar in the bubbly water – 'Watch the pipe bowl now' – raised it to his lips and blew.

A bubble swelled to the size of a basketball. Jerking his head away, he barked a magic command. 'Now Pedino, lift the bubble gently in both hands.'

The bubble was firm to my touch, and heavy – it might have been thin glass.

A shape appeared within: my image, dressed in a smart white uniform with brass buttons. I sported a little moustache. I looked older. In my right hand I held a poniard slackly; some blue lightning flickered at its tip.

'This is you, as you will be,' said the Bishop. 'I declare that you possess a full soul, Pedino!'

'A full soul,' my mum echoed. 'Oh my.' (I shall come to the matter of souls, and their sizes, soon.)

'I invite you to train as a pawn-squire at the palace.'

'A royal page,' said my father. 'That's an honour, lad.'

'No,' said Slon, 'it's a *consequence*. The boy has little choice in the matter. Untrained, yet possessing a full magical soul, he would be bound to come to the notice of Chorny eventually; even if he spent his whole life hiding down a drain.' (This wasn't quite true, but no matter.) 'He might be attacked, or possessed.'

'I could cry *Opasnost*!'

'Boy, *boy*!' The bishop chuckled. 'No sooner do I say you have a soul, than you are the equal of Sir Brant or Prince Ruk! You must be trained. Now drop that bubble.'

I obeyed. The bubble promptly fell to the waxed oak

floorboards and shattered, like the skin of ice on a puddle of a wintry morning under a schoolboy's boot. The glassy shards melted till there was only a patch of moisture, drying.

'You've *killed*,' Slon said to me. 'That may come in useful. You're one of the guardians of Bellogard now, Pedino.'

And so my true education began.

I soon took up residence in the pages' quarters of the palace, in one of those high towers with a white onion dome atop.

Does this suggest that I was high up the tower? I wasn't. My room looked through mullion windows upon a cobbled courtyard at the rear of the kitchens. Trays of cabbages were my view, sacks of potatoes, churns of milk, crates holding honking geese. The prospect above was of steep towers, and only then the sky.

When I became more proficient I would earn a room higher up, with an outlook over the town. There was sound sense in my initial immurement down by the kitchens. The bulk of the palace protected me, while I was still naïve.

But nor was I housed in a miserable cell. My chamber was spacious, with a grand stone inglenook. The walls were walnut-panelled, and numerous paraffin sconces backed by mirrors lit the room as brightly as desired. I had a big four-poster bed, a carved chest to keep my belongings, a marble washbasin with silver taps, and other creature comforts – not least a maid, Margarita, to tidy, collect laundry, trim wicks, and such. It was Margarita who soon saw to it that I lost my virginity, in that same four-poster bed. More of this in a moment.

We pages (or pawn-squires) numbered six, of whom I was the last to 'make a move on the board', as a palace saying went. (One pawn-squire had been lost due to Prince Ruk's 'castling' defence during Oscaro's attack. A second had been 'swept off the board' when Princess Alyitsa was promoted to queen.)

We were a mixed bunch. King's Page, Beno, who took me under his avuncular wing, looked to be in his late fifties, though undoubtedly he was much older. A pawn-squire with full soul could live as long as the kingdom itself without showing undue signs of ageing. (Equally, a pawn might at any time be squashed like a fly.)

In descending order of apparent age were: Castle Page, Josip, who had lost his own lord when Prince Carl was killed in magic combat – Josip generally attended Prince Ruk who had been forced to sacrifice his squire. Then: grim Henchy, Bishop Slon's page, who often visited the Samostan. And: Iris, a forceful and handsome woman apparently in her thirties, who was the only female squire. She served Bishop Veck, Queen's chaplain. Finally: Knight Page Pyeshka, who squired Sir Brant. Pyeshka was just twenty to look at, jaunty and debonair.

Though nominally a Knight Page, I had arrived too late to serve slain Sir Vlado; I would be expected to serve the queen herself.

Which brings me to the matter of my sexual initiation in Margarita's arms, and in her loins . . .

I'd been living in the royal household for about three weeks, and so far the transition had passed off painlessly. I knew that I couldn't visit my old home on Chalk Street again until I'd been judged competent – which might take a couple of years. Exposed in town I might be in peril from any infiltrating Chorny magic. However, I wasn't homesick; I had no fits of the weepies. My fellow squires numbered no A. Mog amongst them. They went out of their way to be accommodating. Even Henchy, who looked so dour, took me on a guided tour of the upper towers. Nobody teased or japed me. I found no dead slugs floating in my soup in the refectory. No one sent me on a mock errand to the dungeons and clanged the door behind my back. Already Beno was my long-lost uncle, and Pyeshka my older brother.

I hadn't yet been presented to Their Majesties but I'd met Prince Ruk, who would coach me in forward magic, and Bishop Veck, who would show me the diagonal kind. Pyeshka had spent days leading me around the halls and galleries, courts and gardens and parapets, stables, kitchens and servants' quarters, then testing me on my newly acquired knowledge. ('What's the fastest route from White Garden to the Buttery, *not* going by way of the Corridor of Charm?' 'Name the route from Top-mizzen to Glass Shield Hall, via the Beehive Well?') And I had seen the princesses at their play.

I'd become reasonably acquainted with the palace in physical terms. I was still a newcomer in other ways, bound to get lost upon that other invisible plan – of relationships, psychology, intrigue.

Intrigue? My fellow squires certainly didn't intrigue against me. Nor did the surviving noble lords plot against one another. They would be stout in each other's defence and in defence of the realm. In furtherance of this it might become direly necessary for one lord to expose and sacrifice another; but that would not really be intrigue. True, the princesses schemed, whilst conducting their gavottes of amusement and cousinly interplay. They were all rivals to eligibility. Skilful attainments mattered to them as rosettes to a champion horse rider.

The real intrigue to which I refer was the way that the hidden war between Chorny and Bellogard inevitably impinged upon everyday life at the palace. Not upon life in Bellogard, oh no! Far from it. This was a war which only immediately menaced and destroyed those people who were magical. A few soldiers on the southern frontier might be killed in brawls. A village in Letto province might suffer conflagration or pillage. However, it was members of the royal household who would be destroyed by any serious attack, while the ordinary people of the kingdom went about their normal lives. So yes, the war touched the palace with long fingers. There might be years of peace, but when a move took place it happened abruptly, sometimes murderously, sometimes inconsequentially. (Or seemingly so. Thus the sense of intrigue at the palace.)

Of course, in the end all would amount to the same thing. If the lords and queen and squires were destroyed and the king 'checkmated' then the kingdom itself would blaze into ashes, fall to pieces, crumble to dust. The hearts of farmers and townsfolk alike would halt, their brains would cease to think. The river Rehka would dry up. The sun would vanish, and the stars. The whole land would be black and empty.

Margarita, additionally, was maid to Iris and Henchy. She was dark and slim, soft-voiced, yet also fierily graceful in a gypsy kind of way. Her smile was magic (though strictly speaking, unmagical!); and her dark eyes too, and her bobbing curly hair. I didn't really know enough to say to myself that she was desirable, though I don't doubt my body told me so. She was taller than me, as of then, but I would outgrow her.

Margarita . . . oh why should I detail each separate moment of my delicious initiation? Imagine it, rather! Imagine her amiable skill, her tenderness and enflaming caresses, the taste of her tongue, touch of her nipples, the (unmagical) moist magic between her legs which I soon made so much moister, more than once. I was still a boy, after all; these were naked mysteries. I shall keep

35

them mysterious. Surely it is the aftermath, when the seduction was *explained* to me, that is most germane.

I'd wondered initially whether what Margarita and I were up to in a palace bedroom was licit or illicit; soon I'd decided that I didn't care.

Subsequently Margarita lay back yawning. 'Boys are so potent at your age! Men go downhill.'

'Do you often make love to boys?' I hoped I sounded nonchalant.

'Oh no. Never before. I've heard that said of boys, and it seems true.'

I put my hand on her breast. 'You wanted to check the truth of it?'

She shook her head, smiling.

'Why then? Why me?'

'I was asked to, Pedino. Bishop Slon asked me.'

'He asked you to take me to bed? Why?'

'He told me to explain, if you asked me.' She knit her brow in concentration. 'You are to be Queen Alyitsa's squire, aren't you, my vigorous young lover? Well then, what is your attitude to women? Thus far: idealism!' She sounded as if she was reciting. 'You have a sister, whom you idealized; whom you wished to safeguard as a creature without sex. You directed magic violence at another boy who would, in your eyes, violate her blasphemously. The success of your magic reinforces this idealism, carving an emotional channel which in essence denies love and the body. Adolescent frustration would emphasize this pattern – of magic and denial. In your classroom there was a picture of the queen, which you lusted after . . .'

'So Master Samo has been gossiping!'

She ignored my interruption. 'The queen would become your new idealized, forbidden elder sister. In your under-mind you would resent King Karol for bedding her. This would make you erratic, unreliable. You mustn't protect the queen out of frustration, but out of knowledge. Equally, you might need to defend the king – since the king's survival is crucial. The lava-plug must be drawn from your volcano, so that it gives up its power steadily, flexibly, and consciously – not impetuously and explosively. Therefore I have given you knowledge, of woman's body and your own.' She laughed. 'Don't look crestfallen. Show me once more what you've learnt! If you can!'

Oh, I could.

Next morning, I was presented to the king and queen in the Ex-Chequer Chamber high up.

Sun streamed through great leaded-light windows. The thick, wide-spaced strips of lead cast a network of shadow bars across a long white marble floor, dividing it into phantom diagonals. In twin ivory thrones sat King Karol and Queen Alyitsa, flanked by muscular soldiers wearing mostly clear glass armour as though each man occupied a contoured, transparent box. These guards held spears of glass with crystal tips, another fashion favoured by Alyitsa. Flunkies attended behind. Brass-bound doors, wide open, led to a further, sunlit room: the Chequer Chamber proper.

The king, puffing at a meerschaum pipe, was contemplating a glassy bubble balanced on his knees. He wore a white silk dressing-gown, woolly pantoufles on his feet, and a golden coronet. King Karol was stout, ruddy, whiskery, and looked to be sixty years old, though I knew he was as old as Bellogard. He was smoking fruity shag rather than the more suave 'royal cut mixture'.

Queen Alyitsa's long yellow hair tumbled from under a helmet of milky glass. She wore a breastplate of the same material, white leather boots, and a skirt of thonged white leather exposing golden knees and a glimpse of golden thighs. Across her lap she held a sword of glass.

As Beno led me forward she regarded me intently, though the king continued to admire his bubble. This enclosed a vision of a crazy river looping through space, describing a twisted figure-eight so that the surface became the bottom, the bottom the surface. Yachts upon that river became fish; fish changed into yachts.

Beno presented me. I knelt. The guards shuffled, clanking and tinkling, to attention. Alyitsa tapped me on the skull with her sword then descended from her throne. She raised me by the hand, kissed me briefly on the brow.

'Welcome, Pedino, faithful squire. May your magic multiply and magnify. Will you escort me to the Chequer Chamber? Come, Karol,' she called.

Her husband harrumphed but handed his bubble-prisoned mad river to a flunkey and followed us, pantoufles sliding over the marble.

In the Chequer Chamber clear glass windows occupied five out of six walls, affording a fine view of Bellogard and the surrounding countryside. I could make out Lake Riboo in the distance. Within a perimeter of white tiles was an eight-by-eight chequerboard of white marble and black jet slabs, each large enough for a person to stand on with plenty of elbow-room. Queen Alyitsa stepped upon a black slab. She directed me to a white square: the queen's knight's squire position.

'Now,' she told me, 'you will see some queenmagic.'

The king had moved over to one of the windows and was staring out while chatting to Beno, as if reluctant to watch the queen's display or involve himself. His hands described the vista, enfolding, twisting it.

The queen began to sing in the magic language. Ghostly figures appeared on several slabs. The bishops, Slon and Veck. Sir Brant. Prince Ruk. The king himself. My fellow squires. These apparitions seemed as oblivious as sleep-walkers; perhaps I should say 'sleep-standers', since none took as much as a step.

'Stand steady now, Squire.' The queen's song quickened and changed key.

Other figures appeared. Of a king – yes, plainly a monarch. He was as portly and antique as our own King Karol, but of cruel countenance and squeezed into a tight black uniform decorated with red sash, red sunburst.

Of a red-headed queen in long black silken robes, who looked lascivious, sensual. A black-cassocked bishop. A bearded knight in black iron armour. A sly, wiry prince. Two squires in black suits with obsidian buttons.

I glanced at my queen. 'Are these actual positions in the war?'

'No. The eidolons only show the number of fighters. Chorny is better positioned.'

'They only have two squires. Have all their squires not yet, er, made a move on the board?'

'Chorny are ruthless with their pawn-pages. But one is still invisible.'

'Is it possible to predict the outcome, your Majesty?'

'Yes. Probable defeat for Bellogard, unless Chorny blunders. That may be many moves from now. Many, many years.'

'Unless a stalemate's reached, where no move ever leads to a result?'

'Move to the square before me, Pedino.'

I felt a sense of the bizarre to be moving sideways . . . almost a nausea. The queen beckoned, drew me. I persevered, arrived.

'There'll be no stalemate,' she said in my ear.

'Isn't stalemate better than victory by either side? If there's stalemate, life continues. Shouldn't we be trying to force a stalemate? Can't we make a pact with them?'

The queen ruffled my hair. 'If only it was so simple. How could we trust them? How could they trust us? Their souls are black, and ours are white. Bishop Veck says we must always aim for victory, even if we vanish as a result. Otherwise, in the next cycle of existence . . .' She fell silent, then resumed. 'We must never resign ourselves to defeat; still less adopt the futile impotence of a stalemate policy.'

'If only there was some magical means to monitor their actual moves,' I said.

'Bellogard has spies. So has Chorny. But spies only learn part of the truth. Spies can be trapped and corrupted.'

'There are spies in Bellogard?'

'Oh yes. Spies don't fight. They don't assassinate; though perhaps they may sabotage. And they spy.'

'Stalemate might happen by accident? By luck?'

'Unlikely. Human nature finds a position of stalemate hard to tolerate for long.'

'How did we first start losing ground, Majesty?'

'Queen Dama dared a rash move, to try to protect Bellogard totally, for ever. She had some such idea as yours. So she exposed herself without a squire. She became vulnerable. There's no total defence, no wall of adamantine.'

Alyitsa sang again, and the eidolons faded. The chequerboard was soon empty.

'Off to your lessons, my page and pawn!' And the queen smacked me on the rump.

Souls and magic . . .

The war, of course, was waged by means of magical attacks and magical defences; and magic belonged to people with full souls. However, no one in the kingdom was entirely soulless. Soul diffused outward from the palace and refracted among the whole population. Yet a woodcutter in the Shooma Forest might only possess a hundredth part of a soul (and perhaps the A. Mogs of this world only owned a ten-thousandth!). After death he would be a mere mote in the soul-pool, at best a fractional ghost, according to the bishops.

A king had his own characteristic kingmagic. Likewise, a squire possessed pawnmagic. Alyitsa had once been a princess without any magic; now she had half of the magical power of former Queen Dama. When Dama was killed, the princess was promoted through the sacrifice of the previous queen's squire. *His* full soul adhered to Alyitsa, though since his magic was lesser her new queen-magic was diminished accordingly (while remaining queenly in character).

This I learned from Bishop Veck; I suppose I should present a vignette of one of his tutorials.

Veck was a gaunt, not unkindly man with close-cropped silvery hair, starveling birdlike features, and a perpetual sore on his cheek where he had suffered a magical injury years earlier. He wore a flesh-tinted patch to hide whatever raw deformity lay below. I suspected it pained him to eat, which accounted for his meagre diet. Maybe it hurt him to talk, resulting in his usually careful choice of words.

So here I am, meeting this bishop in the palace Bibliotek.

What a strange room that Bibliotek was. I had marvelled at the quantity of volumes lining the dusty mahogany shelves. Dusty, indeed! No servant was allowed inside with broom or feather-duster. Bare floorboards recorded every footprint. Tables and leather chairs were coated. So was the window glass, which looked out upon battlements with some alabaster soldiers on statue-guard.

Veck warned me to step gently so as not to stir up dust

41

unnecessarily; I imagined he would have found sneezing painful.

'What a multitude of books, sir!' I recalled the one bookshop in town which mainly sold school texts and volumes of engravings, one whole section being locked away from young lads and lasses. 'I never knew there were so many.'

'There aren't,' Veck said mysteriously.

'Who wrote them all, sir? Have you read them all?'

'Read?' A laugh, or a cough? Nodding me to join him, he pulled out a leather-bound tome, and leafed through. Every page was blank. Yet there was a title tooled on the spine, in the magic language.

'*Kneegu*,' I pronounced.

'It means "book", Pedino. The title will become more specific once the book starts to fill up.' He blew dust from the volume before replacing it. 'The dust is words, and words are dust. The dust of time seeds these books and slowly fills them one by one. It records the life of the kingdom: births and deaths, harvests, floods, simple events and strange events. This is a part of magic which I myself still don't properly understand. Everything that has been, is here somewhere. Here is everything – and nothing. All, in its essence, is dust.' He gestured. 'Do you mark how the books become smaller and smaller towards that furthest, topmost shelf of all? Up there are books so tiny they are indecipherable even with a glass. I believe those contain records of earlier wars. When our present war is finally lost or won, all the big books in this Bibliotek will collapse into one single book the size of a thumbnail, just like one of those.'

'Earlier wars, sir? We've never fought anyone else.'

'Wars in earlier ages of the world, boy. During previous cycles of existence. Do you imagine that this is the first such cycle? Or that it will be the last?'

'If Bellogard and Chorny could reach stalemate . . .'

'Pah! It's impossible. A vain dream; which will destroy the dreamer.'

'What is this room, sir? How did it come to exist?'

'Perhaps it *has* to exist. The whole of the kingdom is reflected here, as surely as souls diffuse outward. I've always been acquainted with it, since the start of existence itself. It does change – despite the dust, or because of the dust. More books fill up slowly. More dust settles out of thin air.'

'Can you actually remember the start of existence?' I asked.

'No. When I began to exist, and knew that I existed, my mind already contained memories; just as Bellogard itself had a history of sorts. As witness the Spomenik Monument or the ruins on Razval Rock. You, of course, were born to parents subsequently. All of your memories are genuine.'

'Those previous cycles, sir: what do you suppose happened during them?'

'Why, I think that a white city fought a black city. Sometimes the white palace won, and sometimes the black. Whether those cities were named Bellogard and Chorny, I've no idea.'

'Why should they fight over and over again?'

'*They* do not necessarily fight. An ideal fights an ideal, yet each time the embodiment is new. Perhaps. And perhaps one cycle does influence the next.'

'But why *fight*?'

'That's how the world is powered, as a stream powers a water-wheel. Without the war there would be no energy to sustain existence. That is why there can never – *must* never – be stalemate; or the world would become crippled, dim, and sick, stale as a month-old muffin . . .

'What wheel does the stream of war power? Why, it

powers this fine city of ours and the whole realm. Thousands of human lives – loves, hopes, creations – are the flour which is ground out by that wheel from the grain of time. Thousands of beasts and birds and buildings, villages and vines and fields, ox-carts and fishing boats: those are the bread from that flour. We are at war so that the kingdom can live. Fruitfully, busily, richly.' He touched another book with his finger. 'Before the dust comes again.'

We adjourned to the bishop's apartment, where he began to teach me diagonal magic; for when a pawn-squire attacks, he does so crosswise . . .

On other days old Beno coached me in the magical language. I've already mentioned one potent phrase and a stray word or two, and I don't intend to utter many more. I might burn a hole in your ears!

Some, I can't help but mention. A lot of our place names were actually words in the magic language, sometimes altered a bit by popular usage. Thus: the Dolina valley, the Vodopad waterfall, the Samostan, our own river Rehka . . . many such names. I hadn't realized this till Beno explained, but it made – if you'll forgive the pun – sound sense. If our kingdom was sustained by the magical war, magic place names were the nails by which parts of the world were fastened into place.

On other days Prince Ruk taught me straightforward magic, the normal technique for a pawn-squire. A prince could take many magic steps at once, a pawn only one. Still, a squire in the right place might prove as devastating as a prince.

Ruk was high, handsome, and haughty, with wavy blond hair and ice-blue eyes. He was a tower of strength and ungrudging in his training of me, yet with him I never felt the sense of zany imagination that I did with Veck. Veck showed me how to skip mentally aslant and view the world askew; with Ruk there was always the blunt, unswerving thrust of power. Could a squire forget that Ruk had once destroyed his own squire by thrusting through his body?

Time flashed by. I grew fully familiar with palace ways, and accustomed to what passed for peace – no magical event had occurred since I arrived.

The king continued to absorb himself in art, conjuring up and imprisoning weirdly warped scenes within bubbles upon which he set a seal of permanence. The queen commissioned new stained-glass windows and glass garments, and occasionally considered her eidolons. The four princesses grew taller and more womanly, though still as mischievous. About once a month Margarita made my body sing in tune with hers.

A year was soon up, then before I knew it, two. At last I was put through my paces before the queen. Alyitsa sang up her eidolons and I moved amidst them. Veck partnered me in a mock magical attack upon Prince Ruk. Finally I defended the queen herself against a joint attack by Veck and Ruk. Having passed all the tests, I transferred my few belongings to a higher room with a vista across palace roofs and town beyond.

A week later Veck summoned me to the Bibliotek and told me that I had Her Majesty's permission to go home for a fortnight. Whilst in town, though, I must do a service for the queen. I must acquaint myself by night with the Seveno district; then on the tenth night I should visit the Zupsko Tavern. An agent of Bishop Slon would contact me and point out a suspected spy. From there on I should use my initiative, to misinform the spy or trap him into revealing information.

'Such as what?' I asked. 'Misinform how?'

'That's up to you, Pedino. If I guide you, you'll merely be a puppet acting out a role.'

'If Bishop Slon believes this person's a spy, why doesn't he take him on? I mean, Slon's much more powerful than me.' In the past two years I had grown taller and filled out, yet I was still only a youth – to be pitted against a spy. I had pawnmagic on my side, but the spy had expertise.

Was this a final test? Was the spy only a pretend one, who would report back to Slon on how I acquitted myself? I discarded this idea. I had to behave as though the suspect was an actual spy.

Veck smiled faintly. Or did he wince? 'Bishop Slon is *too* powerful to deal with a possible spy. He's too consequential. He can't be seen haunting Seveno. A squire can.' Veck produced a dagger from under his dalmatic. 'For you, from the queen. Your own magical dagger, at last.' (I had been loaned a blade for training, and for the tests.)

I weighed the weapon in my hand. I spoke a magic word and blue fire sparkled.

'It has ordinary uses, too, in brawls and tight corners,' Veck reminded me.

'Am I supposed to . . . *kill* this spy? If he is a spy.'

'You must make your own mind up. Sharpen your instincts.'

'A spy might think to sharpen his wits on my ribs.' I remembered the queen saying that spies did not assassinate. Maybe not by habit. What if a dagger-fumbling squire challenged or tempted a spy?

The queen surely wouldn't be willing to sacrifice me so lightly, to so little advantage? Unless . . . my own humble manoeuvres masked some fiercer move against Chorny by herself or Ruk or Brant.

46

Veck touched his cheek-patch as though he had just felt the prick of a poniard.

'Don't be nervous,' he said. 'No harm will come to you. Be insouciant and easy; that's the best way to behave. You're a squire on holiday. Wear ordinary clothes, incognito. Enjoy yourself. Learn to drink. Be a little wicked. Margarita must have shown you how.'

I believe I blushed.

The bishop trailed his index finger through dust and anointed me upon the brow.

I sneezed. Not because I had got some dust up my nostrils, but because of the thought of Margarita, and of other Margaritas who might haunt Seveno by night. Sudden strong sexual thoughts sometimes made me sneeze explosively. This sneeze raised dust from half a shelf of books. Veck wafted it gently away from us.

'Maybe you just sank a boat on Lake Riboo,' he joked. 'Or caused an avalanche down Mount Planina.'

Did Isgalt, at this stage, possess much by way of a soul? Was there something special which marked her out from her cousins? Her chums, confidantes, and competitors. Perhaps!

The four royal princesses – Isgalt, Ysa, Aseult, and Izold – were lovely, wilful, naughty creatures who had flitted about the palace giggling and tinkling like exotic crystalline birds, like enchantress sprites from some wood-cutter's tale of the Shooma Forest.

As they matured they grew more distinct. Isgalt was wistful; Ysa was fiery and short-tempered; Aseult, cheerful and capricious, impulsive; Izold, cunning and capable of cruelty.

Originally they had seemed more like four humours of the same person, than independent individuals. One was at a loss on her own. The others couldn't bear any of their number to be separated, or secretive, for too long. Their favourite game of all – which stimulated the most urgent emotional tension, as well as the sweetest, sharpest release – was hide-and-seek. The hectic concealments and chases through all the courts and corridors and little gardens were a physical analogy of what went on constantly in the cousins' minds: a braid of hidings and confidings, conspiracies and heart-barings, fleeting quarrels and assuagements. Woe betide any kitchen boys or junior flunkies foolish enough to be lured into choosing sides in a prank, dazzled or charmed by one or other of the cousins. Their patroness would soon enough desert them, letting the outsider fend for himself against three peeved princesses.

Yet Isgalt did seem genuinely to be drawing apart from her cousins, becoming her own person, resisting teasing, blandishment, and cloying reconciliation. Was the reason simply her native wistfulness? Was she losing ground against their ardour, buoyancy, and clever calculation? Or was she rising above the kittenish humours of the others?

On the eve of my holiday I met Isgalt loitering alone in the Turquoise Gallery. This gallery was tiled in blue, and the domed ceiling was painted sky-blue; the paint had flaked, exposing white cloud shapes. The skylight was a giant eye with a tiny pupil and huge blue iris. The wooden frame formed eyelids. A few hanging cobwebs imitated eyelashes.

Display stands resembling large wooden eggcups held various bubbles blown and fixed by King Karol. Within, lakes curved into waterfalls and hills rolled upward to become thunderclouds. One 'scape always caught my attention. It was a view of Bellogard from Izlozba Hill to the north. However, the palace and town buildings were stretching up into the sky as though roofs and walls were made of baker's dough; of glue which an invisible foot had just trodden in. Withdrawing, the offending foot pulled the substance of the city after it, attenuating every edifice into dissolving blobs and threads. A divination of our apocalypse, this? Or merely a random fancy on the king's part? It was this bubble which Isgalt was contemplating.

'Squire Pedino! You surprised me.'

'Apologies, Princess!' Something in her look – haunted and wide-eyed – impelled me to add, 'Does that bubble disturb you?'

'Death disturbs me.' She tapped the bubble with silvered fingernails. 'Can Bellogard dissolve and disappear like this?'

'Ah, once you have confronted death,' I said brightly, 'then you are truly alive, and human. What does a dog know of death? Or a bird, or a horse?'

She smiled. 'So you view my cousins and myself as fillies? Or is it peahens, or bitches?'

'Peahens are dowdy,' I protested.

'That narrows the field! Bitches or fillies.'

To distract her I quoted something which Veck had said. 'Our world is a fluctuation in a void, Princess. Out of nothing it comes. Back into nothing it goes again. In the interval we exist. Subsequently another world appears.'

She surprised me by an earnest reply. 'Yet our actions determine the length of that interval, do they not?'

'Aye, they do, I suppose. If we try to prolong the interval merely by procrastination . . .'

'The elastic sinews of the world grow slack? As in this bubble here?'

'I never thought of that! This bubble might warn of slackness, eh? You could be right. Our city losing shape

49

and form . . . In a way that's worse than the death of dust.'

'Than what?'

'Have you ever hidden in the Bibliotek?' I asked on impulse.

'That awful dirty place! Certainly not. Princesses would soil their dresses there.' Her smile was wry and mocking. Yet if she was mocking me, I felt that she was mocking herself more. 'Hmm, why shouldn't I soil my dress?' (She was wearing a cloth of embroidered Madonna lilies hung with glass medallions.) 'And my hair, and face, and hands?'

She touched her hair which was yellow, ringleted. She touched her soft downy cheeks as though for the first time she felt her own existence. She licked her rose-petal lips. Tears moistened her blue eyes.

To me, now somewhat experienced in Margarita's caresses, there was an innocence to Isgalt's touching of herself; and also a sudden horrid knowledge. Isgalt was feeling the skull beneath the softness, the raw bleached canvas under the pastel picture.

'Have you ever opened a book in the Bibliotek?' I asked recklessly.

'A book? No. Why should I?'

'Because . . . because she who would be queen must know the emptiness; so that the kingdom can be firm.'

'Hmm, my cousin Izold would be a firmer queen than me. Hard, and clever.'

'And cruel?' I dared to add.

'Cruel as Chorny's queen; possibly. Surely darkness should be opposed by light, not by darkness of a different calibre! Yet I can't believe our own queen will ever fail.'

'She's weaker than Dama was.'

'I would be weaker still.'

'But kind. When the magic descends, maybe you could

50

hold more than Alyitsa? Perhaps you could reverse Bellogard's fortunes.'

'So, Pedino, you're a queen-maker as well as a squire?'

'I'm sorry, I presume. My tongue runs away.'

'No matter. Will you squire me to the Bibliotek? Will you show me those books of yours?'

So I went with Isgalt to that dusty chamber, took down one of many volumes entitled *Kneegu*, and showed her its blank pages.

'Here is the emptiness,' I said.

'If I'm ever queen,' she replied, 'I shall take a pen and illustrate these books. I shall fill their pages with beautiful pictures before the dust can fill them.'

I had spoken oh so boldly – brashly – to Isgalt about the maturity which staring death in the face conveys; as if by virtue of witnessing attempted assassination at the Samostan and causing death myself at the Razval baths I was an expert.

I had never confronted my own death.

This was to happen as climax to my holiday in town . . .

First, the holiday itself.

For a long time I'd been observing Bellogard from the palace heights, diminished by distance. Suddenly the busy buzz of town life surrounded me again – markets and rushing river, chatter and errand-boys, tradesfolk, the whole motley – and all that had been no more than a tiny, slow spectacle was accelerated and doused with noise and smell and savour, with vigorous sensation. It still seemed strangely toy-like, as though *I* had shrunk and strolled into a dolls' house, a dolls' town. I had altered my perspectives.

In my absence sister Drina had become a young lady. In doing so, she seemed to me to have exchanged one type of babyishness for another. She had adopted the more mature childishness of grooming herself for a suitor who would presently relieve her of responsibility for thinking, acting, working, or suffering any upsets.

Perhaps this was my fault! Even, my crime. When I thought back on how I had tried to protect Drina from the likes of A. Mog (bearing in mind Margarita's explanation) I realized the extent to which I must have oppressed my sister in many ways, robbed her of initiative, laid out a future course for her by which she would seek, as soon as possible, a brother-substitute.

Boris Slad, now a trainee banker in his father's counting house, was courting Drina; and my parents nodded glad approval at the prospective match, which shouldn't occur for two more years. Dana Slad, fast becoming a belle and source of broken hearts, smiled upon Drina as a would-be sister-in-law. It puzzled me why the rich Slads should be so eager to ally themselves with a pipe-maker's family. Then the half-crown dropped. I was the reason. Boris would ally himself royally, by association. So I had doubly decided Drina's destiny. This grieved me. Margarita might have bedded me at Slon's request, but *her* hands were definitely independent agents.

Viewed in another light, here was a further proof of how the power of life itself diffused outward from the palace, not in any obvious way such as by edicts, honours, patronage, or fashion – or, alternatively, apprehension caused by dungeons or executioners! – but in the most fundamental, 'existential' aspect.

Back in the house on Chalk Street I felt snugly at home amidst the aromas of tobacco only to the extent that an orphan lamb (so they say) is comforted by its dead mother's fleece being roped on a substitute ewe. The scene persuades, even if the touch is wrong. The familiarity of Bellogard, the pleasant regularity of life, made me feel awkward.

It wasn't *merely* to heed the queen's instructions that I quickly took myself off to explore Seveno. Formerly that area of Bellogardian life had been a mystery to me. Now, in its very unfamiliarity, it seemed authentic and desirable – a zone where the town redeemed, rather than belittled, itself. That may have been why nominally decent townsfolk patronized the district under cover of darkness. They felt substantiated.

It was early autumn, so dahlias dominated the public gardens. By day, flower borders looked like aquarium tanks crowded with big bright sea-anemones. My own eyes were more intent on the flowers of the night: the myriad rainbow lanterns strung outside Seveno's bars and dancing halls and casinos; the orange lamps hung in the windows of 'houses of ladies' to lure visiting male moths.

Here was I, admiring the *salle blanche* of the *Grand Salon de Chance*: white marble walls, water-lily chandeliers, ornate ormolu clocks, green lawns of baccarat and roulette tables. A wide spiral stairway wended upward to the *salle privée*.

I'd purchased a half-crown entry ticket from the commissariat. A cadaverous man wearing an impeccable cream suit and mulberry bow tie beckoned me discreetly aside.

'*Gospodin*.' To my consternation he addressed me quietly using a polite mode from the magic language. I was wearing ordinary trousers and jacket, a striped shirt, a floppy neckerchief, certainly not my palace uniform. My poniard was hidden in my inside breast pocket.

'Pardon,' he murmured, 'but you have magic. May I remind you that you must not play downstairs? A player with known magic must use the *salle privée* upstairs, by arrangement with the management. The odds are different there. Of course you may watch the proceedings here.'

'What makes you think I'm magical? I've never been here in my life before.'

The cadaver permitted himself a faint smile. 'I'm this casino's physiognomist, *Gospodin*. I know almost every face in Bellogard, and many country faces too. I know the gait of everyone. A certain dishonest farmer may visit town once a year wearing false whiskers, yet I know him. I walk about town every day, memorizing. If someone cheats here once, they are barred for ever. Not that I impute any such motive to you, you understand?'

'Actually I wasn't planning to place any bets – much less use guile! I don't happen to know the rules.'

'In another hour you may know them, and grow excited. However, I'm discretion incarnate. I needn't reveal your identity to the table supervisors, *Gospodin*. I merely make a subtle signal; and you fail to find a seat.'

'Is yours a magic skill?' (*How* did he know me?)

'No. A matter of observation and memory. You're the pipe-maker's lad. I used to notice you on your way to the Gymnasium. Later, I spotted news items in *Noveeny*: a certain episode at the Razval baths, your palace appointment.'

What an ideal fellow to spot a spy! Maybe the Physiognomist tipped off our agents in town. Yet I was sure that he wasn't the person I was due to meet at the Zupsko Tavern the following week. There was an obsessional pedantry about the Physiognomist which didn't fit my concept of an agent.

I watched the roulette and baccarat a while. More interesting to me than the activities of croupiers and the gambling gentry of Bellogard, with their fine ladies, was a certain fat woman. Dressed in rosy silks, ruby necklace and domino mask, she strolled the *salle*, inspecting play through a pair of opera-glasses mounted on a bamboo rod, and holding court between whiles on a sofa. A succession of solo gentlemen sat by her, chatting softly. They generally gave her presents of high-value chips or plaques.

I stopped a valet. 'Excuse me, but who is that lady?'

'She is the Prophetess, sir. Supposedly she recommends winning systems.'

'Supposedly?'

The valet cleared his throat. 'She makes arrangements, too. For the subsequent amusements of gentlemen.'

I thought of Margarita. I imagined myself sitting by the Prophetess describing my tastes to her – such as I imagined those to be, based on the slightest of experience!

Ah, but I had no plaques or chips to give her, nor any way to acquire them . . .

So here was I later that night in a less elegant, more typical casino, kibitzing a rowdy game where dice were tossed along green baize marked with lines and boxes for bets. No Physiognomist accosted me. Even so, I avoided joining any games of hazard.

Here was I in a noisy bar–restaurant devouring fried horsemeat steak and lovely lumpy potato salad, washed down with black beer.

And here was I, tipsy in Pozoristu Street, loitering over the way from one of its 'theatres'. I crossed and bought a ticket – for all of three crowns, but I'd received a large purse from the palace for expenses. I joined a small audience of men in a dark, smoky room to watch a dance–striptease while a jangly piano played waltzes.

Afterwards I walked down Groody Lane past windows with orange lamps. Women and girls sat in the lamplight wearing petticoats or négligées. Some were knitting, others playing patience. I thought again of Margarita. I thought of Princess Isgalt. I walked on home.

Next day towards noon I retraced my route of the previous night, but everything had become demure and orderly.

My commission from the palace: to steep myself in Seveno. Did this mean that I had a positive duty to patronize Groody Lane? I thought about this and decided, 'Why not indeed?'

'You're keeping late hours,' my mother observed as we sat at our family meal of dumplings, sausages, and mushroom. 'Is that what you've learnt at the palace? Unless you're out visiting a friend, it strikes me there's only one part of Bellogard where you could stay so late.'

'The boy has grown up,' observed my father mildly.

My sister toyed with her food. 'It wouldn't do to bring shame. To disgrace one's position at the palace.'

'My point exactly,' said Mum. 'I'm thinking of how the Slads might regard any sort of . . . scandal.'

So that was it. Hints had been dropped. Mother and Drina would rather I donned my squire's uniform with buttons well polished and promenaded my sister around Terga Square of an evening, pausing at one of the cafés for glasses of spritzer with lots of soda water to dilute the heavy Muskat wine.

'Mother,' I said. 'I have a reason for where I go, and what I do. A squire isn't an ornament. A squire is a soldier. I'm on holiday. I'm also on the queen's business.'

'Didn't I tell you as much?' said Dad.

'What business?' Drina asked excitedly.

I shook my head. 'I *do* have a full soul,' I reminded her.

Drina cried a little, then cheered up.

Later, cloaked in night, I passed along Groody Lane

peeping in at the ladies sitting by their lamps. I wasn't the only such window-shopper. Behind one window a slim young woman sat in her petticoat at a little table turning over playing cards. She had fine, delicate features framed by a cascade of crinkly black hair. I wandered on by, then halted. I felt compelled to hasten back. I tapped on the glass. She started, looked, nodded her head in the direction of the door, and extinguished her lamp.

She met me in the dark hall, a black ghost smelling of jasmine. A single candle flickered at the stairhead. She asked a few inconsequential questions – mainly about the weather – before naming a price; for the rest of the night? or only an hour? I chose the night and paid. She hid the crowns somewhere in the hall then locked the front door and led me upstairs, collecting the candle as she passed. She ushered me into a large bedroom, where she lit a second candle. The two candles combined yielded less light than her downstairs lamp, but the lamp had given her skin the look of orange peel. Her flesh now took on a buttery hue.

As she hoisted her petticoat over her head I sneezed violently three times.

Oddly, I'd expected that making love to her might feel radically different, as regards the main sensations, from making love to Margarita. I remember when I first saw another boy's penis at school, in the urinals, it had looked different to my own. This was because the other boy was uncircumcised. At the time I drew the logical yet absurd conclusion that every boy's penis was of a unique character, as diversely designed as faces are.

Likewise I somehow expected the act of sex with another woman to produce unexpected joys. The ultimate pang of pleasure might taste as different as peaches from pears.

Not so, of course. I felt that I'd travelled to a distant

province where all sights and scents were strange, only to taste, from an unknown bottle, a familiar delicious wine.

'What's your name?' I asked as we lay together later.

'Sara,' she said, and rubbed my nose with hers. 'What's yours?'

I hesitated.

'No need to tell! I shall call you Karol, since you're my king for tonight. Should I blow the candles out, Karol? Should we sleep?'

'I'll blow them out for you.'

'You might stub your big toe in the dark.'

She slipped naked from the sheets and went to extinguish the wicks. I watched her. Big toe, indeed.

The days – no, the nights – slipped by; and soon I knew Seveno pretty well. I also got to know Sara more deeply. Maybe it was unenterprising to revisit her time and again, but I found her sweet and friendly. I could hardly stay away. She liked to fantasize that I was a royal Prince Karol who had slipped from the palace at dead of night to her bed. She stroked my ego playfully.

Since this fantasy wasn't far from the truth I felt nervous at first, then happily acquiesced and invented bizarre tales of palace life.

I said that the alabaster soldiers on the ramparts were former lovers of Queen Dama, now enchanted by magic. I told her that the king imprisoned his enemies inside glass bubbles. I made believe that the four princesses dwelled underground in a huge maze which extended outward around the dungeons; its walls and floor were covered with luminous silver fur. I maintained that Queen Alyitsa was guarded by magic glass swords which flew through the air of their own volition. I described a 'water library' containing a marble pool of enchanted water and a single huge book of magic. The pages were blank until the book was held underwater, whereupon magic spells appeared, different each time. Fighting fish lived in the pool, and unless you wore special glass gauntlets, which were kept in a secret compartment under the queen's throne, your hands would be stripped to the bone. Whenever the kingdom was menaced, the book was consulted and it yielded up a fresh, efficacious spell which could only be used once. No one knew how many spells were available.

And other such nonsense as this.

I confess to another motive (or rationalization) for revisiting Sara. If anything went direly wrong with my adventure in Seveno maybe I could use Sara's house as a bolt hole.

Surprisingly, nobody else was ever with her when I called. We did not speak of other visitors. Ours was a grand, royal passion.

On the ninth night of my holiday I whispered to her in bed, 'I'll have to go away soon. Duties of state! I shan't see you, maybe for weeks and weeks.'

She kissed me on the shoulder. 'Let me see: you're really an underchef in the palace kitchens. You cook the king's feasts. Or a flunkey; you serve them. Or maybe a guard. You know all the secret passages.'

'What secret passages?'

'Aren't there any? Oh dear. A palace without secrets.'

She stroked me intimately, and I paid no further attention to royal palaces, only to the palace of her limbs.

I sat in one of the oaken booths of the Zupsko Tavern sipping light beer. A gypsy played a wailing, maudlin violin; his melodies wove in and out of the laughter and tipsy talk like a swallow darting through a storm. A buxom waitress was forever on the go with fistfuls of beer mugs, glasses of vinyak liquor, plates of the house specialities: pig's knuckle, cabbage leaves stuffed with mince and rice.

Who should slip in opposite me but Master Samo?

'Evening, Pedino.'

'Oh hullo, Dominie. What a surprise! You look well, sir. I'm, um, waiting for someone.'

His eyes twinkled. 'And someone has arrived!' He signalled the waitress, managing at once to catch her eye and to mime an order.

She rushed a glass of grape brandy to him. 'So, Sammy, how's the world treating you?' She didn't hang about for an answer. I gathered that he was a *habitué*.

'Treating me well enough, I suppose,' he told me, as though it was I who had asked. 'Although I'm only of slight soul, which must always cast a shadow over one's antics.'

The hastening waitress stopped to confide, 'He's a real card, this one. Watch yourself, young fellow-me-lad,' and off she went.

'As well as being a good motive for antics,' Samo continued. 'To drown the darkness, don't you know? But one still serves the palace loyally. The palace bestows life itself – however long *that* lasts. Better to serve as a shadow – offering Chorny no real target – than as a substantial soul. I tell myself so, anyway.' He drank his brandy. 'Don't look now, but the fellow in question is four booths down on your right, facing this way.'

'Our suspect.' I stared resolutely into my beer.

'He's been lurking all over – by the palace walls, the Samostan – painting little grisailles on glass panes. Supposedly some artist from Letto province. The queen, of course, is devoted to glass art.'

'What are grisailles, exactly?'

'Paintings done without colour; entirely in shades of

grey. Verges on the black arts of Chorny, hmm? The artist's name is Meshko. Good Lettish name.'

'Isn't his behaviour a bit public for a spy?'

'The perfect excuse! An artist has to arouse curiosity. How else could he sell his work?'

As the gypsy advanced towards us, sawing his violin, I had an opportunity to stare in Meshko's direction. The man was stocky, with broad open features. He might have been clean-shaven that morning, but by now his jowls were purple-shadowed with fast-renascent beard. He wore a leather jerkin, tough blue serge trousers, a wide floppy felt hat decorated with pheasant feathers. Black curls peeped out. His eyes were chestnut; his brows dark and woolly. He looked more sober than his drinking companions. Casually I transferred my attention to the musician.

'He might be drawing coded maps,' murmured Samo. 'Or magic ink pictures to provide a bridge back to Chorny. Or he might be a lure for our queen; a bait. Over to you, Pedino.' Samo prepared to leave.

'Hang on: has anyone tried to get reports from Letto on this artist fellow? The man can't have hatched out unnoticed under a vine.'

'Reports prove nothing. The Meshko you see here may not be the same Meshko who set out for the capital. He might have been magicked; his crumb of soul overwhelmed.'

'The Physiognomist – at the *Grand Salon*: is he one of our agents too?'

'The Physiognomist's skill lies with familiar faces, familiar gaits. He doesn't know everyone from the provinces.'

'But he might be able to tell . . .'

'If a man was possessed?' Samo chuckled softly. 'You should know more about that than me.'

Should I?

I didn't.

'No one at our court has ever invaded another soul – not so far as I know.'

'Maybe no one can,' said Samo, 'unless the victim-soul is willing – eager! Maybe magical possession's no more than a phantom we scare ourselves with. Something vile, of which we believe Chorny capable. A species of perverted love-magic; if there's any such thing. I'm sure I wouldn't know. On the other hand, how did Alyitsa become queen?'

How indeed. By the sacrifice of a squire, who loyally yielded his soul to the new queen, so that she possessed it.

'I must be on my way.' Samo departed with a cheery wave, leaving me to my booth and beer.

It wasn't hard to fall in with Meshko. He broke into a lusty song; which I applauded. I bought him a beer to wet his whistle. I said I'd spotted him down by the Samostan painting on glass.

'Can't say when for sure. I hardly know what today is!'

'You on holiday, then?' he asked.

'Exactly!' I lowered my voice. 'From the palace.'

And so forth. Soon he was inviting me to visit his 'studio' the following afternoon.

Now a lad like me was unlikely to be a prospective purchaser of glass grisailles. Why should Meshko give up some of his precious afternoon light to show me round unless he was rather more interested in my palace connections? I'd been indefinite about these – I hadn't confided that I was actually the queen's squire – but I'd dropped hints. I'd also told him that I was in debt at the *Grand Salon* and that I'd pawned a family heirloom to raise the crowns which I'd let him glimpse in my purse. I needed a decent win at baccarat to redeem myself. After a few drinks at the Zupsko Tavern that evening to steady my nerves I was bound for the *Salon de Chance* (upstairs or downstairs, I did not say); but no, I did not wish for company. Once there I must concentrate totally.

The studio proved to be an attic over an alley five minutes' walk from Pozoristu Street. It contained dozens of views of Bellogard meticulously painted on panes in shades of grey. ('Ashen, oyster, dove, pearly, smoky, charcoal, leaden, and special *seevo* grey,' Meshko explained.) Many were stacked. Some stood on narrow home-made easels. Others hung on the walls, though this did not show them to best effect since ideally light should shine through. A table bore tiny brushes, a palette, a pestle and mortar, jars of ingredients: oils and gloomy minerals. An unmade bed occupied one corner.

My host polished glasses on a hand towel and filled them from an already open bottle of Muskat.

'If only I could paint *inside* the palace!' he exclaimed. 'I've heard there are such enchanting courts and gardens.'

'Hmm,' I said. The red Lettish vintage was sweet and heavy, like sugary blood.

'Is it possible, I wonder . . . ?'

'You would need truly magic paint,' I said lightly, 'to capture yon palace.'

His hand shook; he spilled some wine. Then he laughed. 'My little brushes are my magic.'

'Of course.'

'Why do you carry a hidden dagger, Dino?' (I'd told him this was my name.)

My turn to spill a drop. 'Do I?'

'When you shift your shoulder, thus, there's a slight bulge.'

'Oh, that. I believe there's a war going on, isn't there?'

'The war with Chorny? That's surely fought with tools other than blades.' (Not *exactly*.) 'Do you fear cutpurses in Seveno? I suppose there are some. I find Bellogard a very safe town.'

'Compared with what?'

'Why, with Letto province. Bandits hide out in the marshes. There's military trouble on the borderland. Incursions. A village burnt. Would it be possible, do you suppose, to peep inside the palace? Naturally I wouldn't exhibit or sell any private palace views.'

'In that case, why paint them?'

'To pick up the atmosphere – in case of a future royal commission. My work's starting to sell modestly, to discerning local burghers. I could afford a few crowns to grease a guard's palm, if need be. That's wholly at your discretion, my friend. I would entrust the money to you, asking no further questions.'

'How many crowns?' I asked.

'Twenty? Maybe I could stretch to thirty.'

'You *must* have sold a few panes of glass!'

'Oh, I don't let them go for a song. I'd rather starve than cheapen them. Anyhow, I had the forethought to bring a small sum of savings with me. How did your own luck fare last night?'

'Rotten. I *nearly* pulled it off, damn it!'

He paced. 'Oh the beauty, the grace of grey. I find bright colours rather brash. Letto is a grey district. One grows sensitive to nuances, Dino.'

While Meshko rhapsodized to himself artistically and refrained from watching me too eagerly, I too wandered the attic apparently deep in thought.

I spotted an edge of paper under a discarded shirt, draped to hide it. Casually blocking Meshko's view with my body I shifted the cotton, found a sketch-pad. I turned a page. And my heart stood still.

Here was a charcoal drawing of Sara, stripped to the

waist. I flipped quietly; saw several other portraits of Sara. Hastily I shut the pad, pulled the shirt back.

I swung round. 'Thirty crowns should buy you entry.'

'Oh marvellous.'

'Just for a couple of hours, understand?'

'Fine. When?'

'Day after tomorrow?'

With Meshko's money in my purse, I hastened to the Samostan. I took a roundabout route to make sure I wasn't being followed. On the way I had time to think about what I'd seen in the sketch-pad.

Item: Sara's playful interest in the palace and its secrets, our little masquerade of prince and paramour. Item: whenever I visited Groody Lane she had been available, as though reserved for me alone. The first occasion might have been coincidence; not thereafter. Item: Meshko must be as besotted with her as I was. His sketches were so richly sensual. He hadn't spent a night with her recently. Yet he had money.

Maybe the money came from her. She was controlling Meshko, subsidizing him; permitting him to sketch her at her convenience in return for services. Such as painting strategic scenes and trying to breach the palace. Had she let Meshko bed her too?

What had Veck said to me once during training? 'Magic often gravitates to magic.' I hadn't really chosen Sara's door at random. She possessed magic; my undermind had sensed this.

If so, Sara was more than a mere spy. She must be the missing black squire. She hadn't yet made her first magic move; her eidolon couldn't yet be observed on the chequerboard.

I might be totally wrong: that was why I wanted to consult Slon. When I arrived at the Samostan, however, the bishop wasn't there. He and Prince Ruk had gone hunting. They wouldn't be back till late at night. I debated sending an urgent message to the hunting lodge. I debated rushing to the palace to ask the queen to sing the summoning of the eidolons. Both courses of action seemed hysterical, lacking in initiative. Should a squire hasten to his queen to confess that he has fallen in love with a whore down Groody Lane and suspects that her heart is black, not white?

Two days hence I had undertaken to smuggle Meshko into the palace; there was that to bear in mind as well.

I couldn't bear to think of Sara checked for years in the palace dungeons . . . Had she possessed Meshko, as Samo surmised? Or merely intoxicated him – as she had intoxicated me?

Could Samo advise? Hardly. He was only an agent.

Use your instinct, I'd been told.

So I used it. That night I went to Groody Lane.

Sara's orange lamp burned bright as a beacon, apparently for no one else but me. Hers was a clever cover for an enemy power (though how could I think of her as an enemy?). Who would query or distrust a whore? A whore who needn't be abroad by day when physiognomists were about. A whore who could receive any number of visitors at odd hours, visitors who wished to remain discreet. A whore, who wasn't quite a whore . . .

How *did* she deter unpromising customers? Did she have to apologize often? 'Sorry if you rapped on the glass, sir, but I'm waiting for somebody else.' Did she use some love-magic taught her by Queen Babula to make the majority of mundane men pass by?

I rapped. She immediately doused her lamp; admitted me. 'Ah, my prince has come!' She preceded me upstairs to that room which was haunted with my joy.

Had Meshko reported success in suborning a palace employee? Did Sara connect me with the employee in question? Maybe not, as yet. She might be playing two games which hadn't yet come together.

Would Sara have seen an eidolon of *me* in some black chamber in Chorny, and known me at once? Maybe not. She couldn't have travelled to Bellogard directly by magic. She must have come wanderingly on horseback or even on foot, a journey of weeks or months. She might have arrived a year ago, two years ago.

'Aren't you going to undress, Karol?' Sara had already done so, and was sitting on the bed. She held out her slim arms. I ached for her.

I shook my head. 'You hop into the sheets, love. As this is our last time I'd like to tell you who I really am.'

Naked, wrapped up in bed, she could hardly pose much threat to a reasonably muscular, fully clad, armed youth. Obediently she pulled a sheet up her body, though she let a breast poke out.

'It's a long story, Sara.'

'I'm all ears. Why not tell it in comfort?'

I grinned. 'If you were *only* ears, I might.' I too could keep up a pretence.

So I began to tell her the story of my life to date, much as I'm doing now, though omitting my commission to uncover a spy . . .

'You've been wanting to know all along how magic *really* works, haven't you, Sara?'

'Yes.'

'All your life you've been aware of magic as a distant background. What are the tools and techniques, eh? What does one actually *do*? The question a young virgin puts to her best friend.

'I've dropped hints: the magic language, weapons

67

(sometimes) which bristle with lightning – and body movements (forward, diagonally, a skip aside).

'I think the main point is that people like me occupy mundane space and also magical space. Mundane space is huge, the size of a couple of kingdoms. Magical space is smaller. Not simpler, oh no! A thousand million permutations of position and action are possible. Lines of force are forever opening up or blocking one another. Along these lines of force we can leap, to strike or counterstrike.' I paused.

'Go on, Prince Karol. Or should I say, Squire?'

'Of course you already know all this extremely well, don't you, Sara?' I slipped the poniard from inside my jacket. 'That's why I ought to kill you now. *Opasnost po Zhivot*, Sara!'

'You're mad!' she cried. 'You're one of those twisted men who hurt and kill women like me. They always need an excuse. A pretext to justify their filthy crime! They need to believe the woman is evil.' She threw the sheet aside. 'Look at me. Look. I shan't cover myself to make murder easier. To make it like stabbing a pillow.'

I almost believed her. Almost.

'I should kill you, black page,' I said, 'to save you from a miserable lifetime held in check in a dungeon.'

'To . . . save me?' Her voice faltered. 'I think that killing me might be a cruel kindness.'

'If only you could change sides! Chorny is evil and ruthless. Look how they've used you.'

'Haven't *you* used me?'

'Maybe at first – but not subsequently, Sara. You know that! And I no more used you, than you were using me, whatever your cajolery. The body tells the truth. The undermind knows.'

In one fluid movement she was out of bed, standing

poised beside it. 'We all do what we have to do, my lover.'

'No, we do what we *choose* to do.'

She no longer denied that she was from Chorny, I noticed.

'By winning,' I said, 'we lose. We lose the whole world.'

She shook her head. To dispel confusion?

Her hands stiffened. Those gentle hands took on a fighting, chopping edge. She chanted a few phrases in the magical language as spoken in Chorny. I held my dagger towards her and spoke words which made it flash and sparkle with blue fire. She took a pace towards me. Her hands were sheathed in crackling blue.

Thunder crashed shockingly outside again and again. Through her window I saw lightning dancing madly over Bellogard. I felt awful tensions in those lines of force that connected me to other white magics in the realm. I sensed hewings, dartings, slashings.

Surely a major assault had begun. Black Squire Sara had been exposed, was being sacrificed – and the royal powers of Chorny were attacking.

She took another step towards me; another.

Without signalling my intention I leapt aslant – to take her and stab her.

I didn't stab. At the last moment I reversed my dagger and clubbed her on the side of the head with the pommel.

She collapsed.

I rushed downstairs and out into Groody Lane. Soon I was sprinting along Pozoristu Street, where night strollers had taken refuge in theatre doorways in case lightning toppled chimneys. Goaded by intuition rather than by any rational plan I raced out of Seveno. Instinct told me not to leap magically, but to run.

I ought to have been checking the captured squire,

binding and gagging her with torn-up sheets. If I'd killed her, I would still have been in her room. Instead, I found myself in Terga Square, poniard in hand. I leaned against a pillar fronting a café, to recover my breath.

A figure in a black dalmatic ran diagonally across the deserted square. He trampled through a bed of dahlias. He rushed over the road in my direction – not that he had seen me. Soon he would run right away – all the way back by magic to where he had come from. He scattered café seats, left out for the night. He would pass right by me, unsuspecting.

I stepped out. I recognized the man's startled face, from his eidolon. It was Bishop Zorn of Chorny. I spoke magic and stabbed him through the heart.

The following day we survivors of that brutal nocturnal exchange gathered in the Chequer Chamber.

Queen Alyitsa was dead – murdered by Prince Feryava of Chorny. Bishop Slon was dead, killed by Bishop Zorn. Squire Iris was dead, protecting Bishop Veck.

The survivors were: the king, Bishop Veck, Sir Brant, Prince Ruk, and five of us squires. Henchy was injured; his wrist had been broken. It would stay that way for the rest of his life. Magical injuries did not heal unless you killed the person who inflicted them. Henchy's right arm hung in a white sling.

Young Pyeshka was perspiring nervously. So, for that matter, was I.

'We must crown a new queen immediately,' insisted Veck.

Ruk demurred. 'The new queen would only have half of Queen Alyitsa's strength. She would only be able to move two magic steps at once.'

'She might never need to move more than two! At least she would have the omnidirectional queenmagic.'

'It might be better to retain a simple squire,' Sir Brant said.

And I understood: it wouldn't be the youngest squire – myself – who was sacrificed to create a new queen. I had acquitted myself admirably, astonishingly, by killing the enemy bishop. Instead Pyeshka would be sacrificed; and Sir Brant was trying to protect his squire. (To all appearances I'd distinguished myself! I hadn't confessed the full events of the previous night or how I'd spared the black squire in Groody Lane.)

'I present two arguments against,' continued Sir Brant. 'If we don't crown a new queen, the squire could still give us a new knight *in extremis* – at a crucial moment when a knight's askew move might save the kingdom from catastrophe. A queen could never leap askew. Secondly, we need that pawn-squire simply for the sake of extra numbers. Thanks to Pedino an enemy bishop died last night. Did Bishop Slon or Squire Iris kill or injure anyone? We don't know. Did Chorny only lose one fighter? We lost three; and Henchy is disabled.'

'That's exactly why we must urgently examine the eidolons,' said Veck. 'Only a queen can sing the summoning of those.'

King Karol pulled out a pipe. 'I could blow a bubble which might divine the future numbers on the board.'

'How far into the future?' Veck frowned. 'How accurately? Divination is a matter of probabilities, not certainties.'

The king tucked his pipe away. 'Yet I deserve a new queen, do I not? To invigorate me; to help me carry on cheerfully.'

The argument circled round for a while, without us squires having much of a voice, though Veck was in vociferous vein. Finally King Karol clapped his hands and said, 'The queen is dead. Let there be a new queen.'

Prince Ruk and Sir Brant bowed their knees.

'Pyeshka,' sighed Sir Brant, 'oh my Pyeshka.' (Even though he was shaking, Pyeshka stood to attention.) 'Proceed to the square before the queen's square.'

Pyeshka did so.

'Now then, Beno,' said King Karol, 'go and fetch Princess, hmm, Princess, let's see, Princess. . . .'

'Isgalt,' I said.

'Hmm? What? Eh? Yes of course, Princess Isgalt. The best possible choice.'

Prince Ruk protested. 'Izold is more devious and forceful.'

'Isgalt'll be the better bride in bed,' said the king. 'In my chamber. That matters too.'

'Majesty, this concerns the whole kingdom!'

'*I* agree with the nomination of Isgalt,' said Veck. 'I believe that young lady has depths.'

'Beno,' repeated the king, 'fetch Princess, yes, *Isgalt*.'

So Isgalt was fetched.

She was excited, nervous, happy, horrified. To be queen – but so soon! To wed – King Karol, who smirked at her. To have queenmagic descend on her, and promptly become a prime target for the savagery of Chorny.

She darted a glance at me as if for assistance. After all, I would soon be her squire. I smiled encouragement, yet it was Veck who by rights took her by the arm. He led her to stand on the vacant queen's square.

'Wait,' said Isgalt. Veck raised an eyebrow.

Isgalt stepped round in front of Pyeshka. She laid a hand on his shoulder as if for mutual support.

'Be brave,' she said, 'then I will inherit your bravery, Pyeshka. Be true to the last; then I shall acquire your truth. Be strong without flinching; thus I shall be strong and never flinch. May you live in me until victory, until the whole world empties out.' She kissed him on the cheek.

That was a very pretty speech. No, it was more than pretty; it was remarkable. Veck nodded his approval as the princess resumed her position.

Promptly Brant drew his sword. Without hesitating he ran Pyeshka swiftly through. Poor Pyeshka's eyes opened ever so wide, and his mouth gaped, but he only uttered one terrible gasp, and died. Brant's sword had passed right through the page's vitals like a huge nail driven fearsomely through a fence post. The point stuck out, almost touching Isgalt. Blood had sprayed her flower dress in the belly region. Sir Brant was struggling. I saw how he was holding dead Pyeshka up by main force.

'Long live the queen!' cried Ruk.

Isgalt shut her eyes and rocked from side to side. She moaned then began to sing to herself; magic words.

'Long live!' we all chorused.

Beno and Josip hurried to support the corpse. They held it firm while Brant wrenched his sword free, then they hauled Pyeshka away by the shoulders, heels dragging, to deposit him temporarily in the Ex-Chequer Chamber.

When Queen Isgalt opened her eyes again, I moved closer to attend her. Veck sketched a magic blessing. Karol advanced and kissed his bride. Isgalt didn't flinch.

Karol emitted a hearty chuckle. 'Release all the news to *Noveeny*. I decree public mourning for three days, to be followed straightway by wedding festivities. Let there be royal banners on all spires, blaziers by night. Bells are to be rung. Notify the kitchens. Let Bellogard enjoy three days' holiday. A pageant at the Samostan. Wine running from the fountains. The usual.'

'Of course,' agreed Veck, 'but let's consult the eidolons first. That's urgent.'

Isgalt nodded. 'I can summon them. The knowledge wells in me.'

We stood back from the chequerboard. Isgalt sang, waveringly at first, then firmly.

Our own semblances took on phantom existence. Isgalt changed key, and the black forces appeared.

No eidolon for Bishop Zorn. And Prince Feryava's eidolon was injured! The black prince had been wounded in the leg. His image stood there crookedly, resting on a crutch.

'That'll shorten the bastard's moves,' growled Henchy.

My main attention was on a different eidolon, one which I'd never seen before upon this board but whose face I knew . . . intimately. She was my lovely Sara.

'New squire,' Ruk rapped out. 'Their eighth. Young, female. Why did that one make her move; and where?'

I said nothing.

Might Sara still be in Bellogard? Surely not in Groody Lane. She would have woken soon after I hit her. I didn't think I had injured her. She would be fleeing back to Chorny.

Maybe I would learn something if Meshko turned up at our rendezvous the next day. *If* he turned up. In the wake of a battle royal this seemed dubious, especially if Sara – his instigator and control – had disappeared. Did Meshko know that yet?

There was a fair chance that while Sara was busy playing me like a fish she hadn't confided in Meshko, had even ordered him to keep out of the way for a couple of weeks. Meshko mightn't have tried to report back to her yet.

Two more things occurred to me in rapid succession. One was that I had to tell Veck something about Meshko, and soon. I'd been sent into town to investigate a suspect.

Recent events had distracted everyone, but Veck would want a report.

When Meshko was questioned, as was inevitable, Veck might rapidly deduce that the new black pawn had made her move right here in Bellogard. What manner of move? An aimless, ineffective one? One which got sidetracked?

Would I be linked to Sara? Perhaps not. Perhaps not even by proximity, since I had turned up so soon after and to such good effect in Terga Square.

The other thing which occurred to me was that Sara had laid long-term plans, into which I happened to fit conveniently. Meshko had only been getting into the swing of spying. Chorny had not intended to attack so soon. True, they had succeeded in eliminating our queen and a bishop and a pawn. In turn they had lost a bishop, and their prince had been injured. Their attack must have been premature. Presumably they'd hoped to inflict a more crushing defeat – but *I* had precipitated last night's battle by challenging Squire Sara.

So much, so much that I ought to tell! If I hurried up about it, one of our nobles might still overtake Sara. Why should I wish to protect her? Was it because of some cockeyed notion that Bellogard and Chorny might reach agreement in favour of perpetual stalemate, for which my sparing of Sara gave the precedent?

Or was it because I loved Sara and thought that she might truly love me too, especially now that I'd spared her life and let her escape?

Yes. Yes. Love is absurd, irrational. Sara was magical to me in more ways than one.

If the truth came out, how would my colleagues regard a white squire who let a Chorny squire off the hook? Oh, they would have to applaud – because in passing her by I'd placed myself advantageously in the way of the more powerful and dangerous Zorn, and had trounced him. However, they might applaud slowly.

Ruk waved at the eidolons. 'This isn't too bad. In sum, Bellogard lost a queen but gained a replacement, albeit less puissant. We lost a bishop and two pawns, Pyeshka included, and sustained an injured pawn. Chorny lost a bishop and suffered an injured prince. It almost balances.'

Directly after, I excused myself from the queen and reported to Veck. I told him a highly censored version of events – about Meshko, only Meshko – and managed to deter him from dispatching guards at once into town to seek the painter. ('Let him come here innocently,' I argued. 'Maybe he *is* moderately innocent. If not, he'll be far away by now.') It wasn't easy, but deter Veck I did. This was my operation, my initiative. I found that I'd accrued a certain persuasive aura of success as a squire who had slain a bishop.

Next I sought the queen, who was settling in to her new royal chamber. 'May I speak privately?'

Isgalt dismissed the maids who had been busily clearing away Alyitsa's belongings and replacing those with Isgalt's.

When we were alone she smiled at me. 'I suspect, my squire, that I may have *you* to thank for the fact that I'm queen.'

How did she know – so soon – that I had nominated her at the conference? Impulsively, against all etiquette?

'You took me to the Bibliotek,' she explained, noting my apparent puzzlement. 'You showed me the emptiness at the heart of all. After that visit, during the past fortnight – of thinking and feeling – I believe I became queenworthy. I'm only uncertain as to whether I should thank you for this, or hate you.'

76

'If I might make a suggestion, it's preferable not to hate one's squire.'

She laughed. 'In that case, I must thank you. Ask for something that's in my power to grant.'

A boon, a reward, would naturally endear her to her henceforth faithful squire. Perhaps Isgalt did possess a streak of Izold's cleverness, though in much nicer style.

I swallowed a couple of times.

'As it happens, there *is* something . . .'

I told her everything.

I didn't gasp out my tale in confused or hangdog style like a naïve stripling. I flatter myself that I presented events in lucid order, together with rationale and motive.

Does this sound unlike the lad who set out from the palace on holiday? Well, I'd changed since my nightly sojourns in Seveno. I'd changed since I stabbed a bishop mortally. And since I'd fallen in love with a spy, who was pretending to be a whore.

At the end of my account Queen Isgalt mused a while; then said, with a curious blend of mischief and melancholy, 'I think I see a neat solution . . .'

Meshko did indeed turn up at our rendezvous, which to my mind at least established his naïve artist's innocence. Innocence of any really dark evil.

He was arrested by the queen's personal guards, who had put off the glass armour of the previous reign on her orders and donned leather and brass.

To Veck's chagrin, Meshko was questioned in camera by Isgalt then condemned by her to indefinite imprisonment – though not in any deep dungeon. His cell was to be an airy studio high atop a tower, with a special royal commission to fulfil. More of this, in a moment.

Meanwhile the queen sent me hurriedly back into town

escorted by two guards in mufti. I went first to Meshko's lodgings, searched these, and took away his sketch-book with the portraits of Sara. Next I went to Groody Lane, but Sara had skipped, leaving only her flimsiest clothes behind.

Later, Veck's men would turn Meshko's place over and bring back to the palace all his grisailles and painting equipment. At his lodgings they found a small supply of magic paint – as diagnosed by Veck – additional to the little bottle which Meshko had brought to our rendezvous. Sara must have managed to enchant the paint herself; unless she had somehow had this smuggled in from Chorny after suborning Meshko.

Meshko swore (the queen told me) that he had misused none as yet; he was reserving his supply for grisailles within the palace grounds. Certainly no magical grisailles were discovered in his attic. He may have already delivered any such grisailles to Sara, who had taken them with her when she decamped. Alternatively those had been used and smashed during the premature attack on Bellogard. Indisputably Meshko had painted inside the Samostan grounds – which is where Slon was ambushed as he returned from the hunt. But Queen Alyitsa had been reached directly and brutally by Prince Feryava using normal attack magic.

On balance it seemed unlikely that Sara had fled with any crucial magic grisailles; certainly with none which could provide subtle windows into the heart of the palace.

Isgalt graciously – and in confidence – let me keep the sketch-book for myself, after she had examined it for a day or so. As I was eventually to realize, she had a subtle motive for this act of generosity. At the time I merely rejoiced. The charcoal of those sketches mightn't in itself be magical but the studies of Sara certainly were.

So how about Meshko's royal commission? Let me

78

sketch a visit which I paid him subsequently in his locked artist's eyrie.

A guard admitted me to a decent enough, spacious room with big bright barred windows. An unmade bed. A table crowded with paints and inks, brushes and pens, not to mention a bottle of wine, half a loaf, a ripe cheese, the remains of a roast chicken.

Days of mourning, days of marriage festival were over many weeks since. The reign of Queen Isgalt had well and truly commenced. The palace was at peace, as was Bellogard and the whole domain. The peace might last a year, or a decade.

Mcshko sat at a desk, smoking a pipe of rum-shag. Before him lay an open book in which he was roughing out an illustration of vineyards from memory.

He laid down his pencil. 'I swear I'll go mad, Dino.'

'Isn't this the dream of any artist from the provinces? Well fed, well housed, working for the queen herself?'

'A bird singing its heart out in a cage! How many blank volumes *are* there in that damned Bibliotek? No one will let me go to see for myself. I've hardly filled up one yet!'

'Several thousand,' I said, and he groaned.

'I'm sure the queen doesn't expect you to fill them all. Even if it were possible, that might be dangerous. Yet to fill up a few dozen . . .'

'A *few* dozen?' he repeated hopefully. 'Thirty-six? Forty-eight?'

'. . . to fill up a few dozen will lessen the emptiness, she feels. It may help strengthen the kingdom; so long as the artistic standard is high enough.'

'It is, it is. I know she'll inspect each volume when I finish – before she puts it back on its shelf in the dust!'

I crossed to the desk. 'May I?'

'Why not?' He paced to the bars and stared out.

I turned pages which were beautifully illuminated with landscapes, villages, farms he had seen in his travels; though showing a certain preference for grey tones. A figure in one rural scene caught my eye. I peered closer. Surely that was Sara. I turned a page. Sara's face! This time her features occupied most of the foreground, with a waterfall cascading behind her hair, white behind black.

On most pages Meshko had controlled his passion. Sara still put in some kind of an appearance on about one page in eight. She featured as reaper and milkmaid, horse-rider and goatherd, dancer at a village fête.

I felt a pang of jealousy that he could so readily re-create her image. I also experienced a certain stifled satisfaction that this 'rival' of mine was safely locked up, far from any chance of meeting her again.

'You seem to have a limited repertoire of faces,' I remarked. 'Is this your sister from Letto?'

'No,' he croaked. He didn't bother to turn. 'No.'

So he didn't know about my own relationship with Sara.

'I think you ought to vary your models.'

'How? By using people down in town? They're a bit too far away. I can't quite make them out!'

'I'll persuade some people to pose for you,' I promised. 'Only as minor figures in a scene, understand?'

It might amuse – and distract – the three unsuccessful princesses to have their portraits included in a magical volume. Fiery Ysa, mercurial Aseult, sly Izold . . .

No. I knew who I would prevail on. Margarita. Margarita might persuade our artist to forget about Sara.

I wished that Margarita could similarly induce me to forget.

However, Sara had surely magicked me. Not with any pawnmagic – only with her person.

PART TWO
Knightmagic, Nightmagic

On the evening when I accompanied Henchy to the astrology observatory, his broken wrist was hurting. Naturally this made him grumpy. Henchy was grim of demeanour, all the more so since his injury, but at heart he wasn't a harsh person. *I* might have behaved rather more sourly if I'd had to nurse a smashed wrist for four years! So I thought that Henchy intended to use this grumpiness to justify tough words with the keeper of the observatory.

Henchy's wrist didn't always hurt him. Sometimes the broken bones lay uncomplaining in their sling. Then the weather would alter, and they would ache. What constraints the injury placed on Henchy in all sorts of minor ways! He constantly had to watch his step so that he didn't bump the sling. These days he always tended to walk slightly offside and crablike so as to present his sound left arm to the world and to any obstacles in it. He slept on his back, with a ribbon tethering his left arm to the bed frame. He relied on our maid, Margarita, to change the cotton padding in his sling. Nor could he exercise his left hand too strenuously in dagger-play for fear of jogging the bones of his right.

He remained stoical – and stubborn.

Queen Isgalt had suggested diplomatically that Henchy might be better advised to ask chirurgeons to amputate his right arm at the elbow. Then at least he would be able to move about vigorously. To walk unhesitatingly, to roll over in bed, to stab and parry with a blade. The injury was magical; it would never heal unless Henchy personally killed the person who had inflicted it. This was impossible, since *I* had already killed the perpetrator, Bishop Zorn.

Henchy disagreed with such advice. 'I think my wrist's gradually getting better,' he would say. 'We aren't a hundred per cent certain a magical injury won't heal in time, even if the inflicter's dead.'

Once, in my hearing, King Karol was blunter. 'You're useless as a fighter in that state, Henchy. We might as well have lost you in the battle.' Isgalt soothed this outburst of ungenerous grumbling by her consort.

The truth was that Henchy was far from useless. As squire to the slain Bishop Slon he had inherited a number of responsibilities, which no one else at the palace was eager to take on. Somebody had to administer the Samo-stan, with its various suboffices. Amongst other things Henchy became Chairman of Governors of the Gymnasium, and also Visitor to the Observatory.

Hence our call on the astrologer, on that early autumn evening.

Perhaps the visit became necessary because Henchy had neglected the observatory? Did he feel awkward there? Did he feel that he didn't carry the same weight of personal clout as Bishop Slon had? Did he suspect that astrology was a bit beyond his scope? Thus he had allowed the astrologer to become eccentric and unreliable, until murmurs reached the ears of Queen Isgalt herself . . .

When Henchy asked me to accompany him I assumed this was for moral backing and, if need be, the threat of violent discipline. (Not that I had become a swaggering desperado, despite my enlarged acquaintance with Seveno night life!) How wrong I was.

The botanic gardens were on our route. At this season its maples, sumachs, and pagoda trees flushed fiery red and vivid orange; the female sumachs raised their fruit spikes like fuzzy crimson candles. I didn't care for this part of the gardens in autumn and I was glad that we were traversing at dusk when the colours were dimmed. Wildly flaming hues made me imagine the whole of Bellogard ablaze, on that last day – after the final battle with Chorny.

Why should town and kingdom necessarily be consumed by fire? Why not by the death of dust? Why should the very fabric not simply disintegrate; every city building, every farm and field in the country becoming a mere cobweb which the wind would whip away? Here in Bellogard, city of light, why such antipathy on my part to bright fire?

Well, I'd become something of a night-owl. And the grey aesthetics of Meshko, our imprisoned artist, had affected me.

By now Meshko had filled several hitherto-empty books out of the palace Bibliotek. His illustrations generally tended towards grisaille style: shades of grey. Since those once-blank volumes were magical, might this artistic tampering have produced a subtle cultural shift in the population, myself included?

The more likely explanation was the many hours which I'd spent poring over Meshko's charcoal portraits of Sara, my lost love, my dark foe, my dream, my desire. Sara's own absence and absence of colour intertwined achingly, tantalizingly in me.

I was glad when Henchy and I quit that dusk-flame foliage to mount, amidst heather, the path leading up Bresh Hill. A few clouds in the sky reminded me of grisaille streaks. Already a couple of planets were incandescing faintly.

Crowning the hill was a white marble dome with a glass cupola on top and supporting half-domes at the sides. The effect wasn't unlike an obese breast with a plump nipple.

We entered a door set in an archway. The main dome would have been impenetrably dark without the cupola which was admitting the last light of day. Most of the meagre light was blocked, even so, by the scaffold and the observation platform towering over us.

'Watcher!' Henchy shouted. 'Mr Matyash! *Gospodin!*' As Henchy uttered the polite form of address in the magic language I detected ironic disdain in his voice – and doubt too?

A door squeaked open, spilling lamplight from the side room where the astrologer slept during daylight hours. Mr Matyash was a burly, hairy giant, wrapped in a silken gown decorated with comets and half-moons. A grizzled beard enveloped cheeks and jaw and flopped down his breastbone. He gripped a lantern in a meaty, hirsute paw. Squeezed into one eye socket was a green-tinted monocle. An affectation – or a tool of his trade?

'So it's you, Mr Henchy? Who's the shrimp?'

Definitely I was no shrimp, except when weighed in the balance with this whale.

'May I present the queen's squire, Pedino. We want a word with you, Matyash. We hear you're in secret communication with the illuminati in Chorny. You've been revealing details of the skies over Bellogard.'

'Is the sky a secret?' roared Matyash. 'Of course not! The heavens can best be interpreted from two separate and distinct locations, Mr Henchy. Thus one can perceive the parallax of the celestial bodies. A watcher who only watches from one spot is watching with one eye closed.' The astrologer waved a hand aloft. 'Just look at this pathetic, rickety structure! No investment here! No magical guidance from Bishop Slon. Nor from you, Henchy. I must make and mend.'

'This doesn't excuse collusion with our enemies! I may

have been remiss – but remiss in not bridling your activities.'

'We men of science know no frontiers, Henchy. We're all inhabitants of the same world, whether our hearts are black or white.'

'Science indeed. What does your science tell you about *magical* space?'

'Quite a lot, as it happens. If you two gentlemen would care to mount my scaffold, I shall endeavour to explain.'

'Take care that this doesn't become your actual scaffold, Watcher.'

'Huh. Hang me up here, and my weight would likely pull it down. That's how wobbly it is. Isn't it remarkable, when a war's going badly, how repression should become the order of the day . . .'

'Mind your tongue!'

'. . . rather than illumination, which might liberate and open new avenues?'

'Such as a highway to Chorny?'

'Pah! I'm as patriotic as the next fellow. I'm loyal to our country and our people. But there's a higher type of patriotism: the patriotism of existence, allegiance to life and the universe.'

'How can you be loyal to a universe?' I exclaimed. 'The universe isn't loyal to you. That's as silly as saying you're loyal to water, or air. Our world is sustained by the royal war. That's the engine which powers all the life we know. That's the rationale; the cause. You should be casting horoscopes to guide mundane life.'

'Ah, so now the lad teaches the man.'

I felt irked. 'Somebody with a full soul tells someone with a tiny bit of soul the truth.'

'Huh. The arrogance of those with soul, so-called! The oppression they cause!'

'Don't be stupid,' said Henchy. 'Those with soul sustain the existence of everyone else.'

'And what, I wonder,' growled the giant, 'if there was a revolution? What if the common people both here and in Chorny rose up and killed or checked all their masters and mistresses?'

'That couldn't happen,' Henchy said. '*If* it did, the world would collapse upon itself. Is revolution what you're plotting together with Chorny's intellectuals? I'm interested in your lines of communication, Matyash. Do the robbers in the Lettish marshes smuggle your star maps over the border? Do those maps perhaps code for conspiracies to overthrow both kingdoms?'

'That's . . . ridiculous.' The giant's voice faltered. He had developed so much contempt for Samostan and palace, so much contempt for squires and nobles that he almost told us his plottings outright, almost taunted us with them – and expected us not to realize.

'You claim that you're loyal to life,' I said to him, 'but you act like someone who's sick of it.' I did my best to sound menacing, as if I was supported by a squad of guards; whereas there were only two of us confronting him, and one of us a cripple.

It seemed evident that Matyash was no *spy*, as such. A spy would have behaved less blatantly. However, his astrological work masked a political motive – which he might argue was a scientific motive. Were his horoscopes entirely honest? Had he been subverting the citizens of Bellogard by means of the stars?

I had kept my ears open in the bars of Seveno district. Recently I had overheard various inexplicable outbursts and innuendoes, which I had duly reported back to the palace. These now made better sense in the context of a dawning subversive movement. Not much of one! A movement of nocturnal drunks and diddle-brains. Bello-gard had always seemed a contented, complacent city. To my mind a political movement of commoners – a 'commonist' party – should stand a better chance of success in dark, harsh Chorny. Maybe I had been listening in the wrong bars; or bars were not the best places to listen.

Henchy plainly had more information than I had – and maybe what really interested him was a possible worm within *Chorny's* apple. Plus a way to make use of this worm.

'Are you coming up to view the stars and worlds?' nagged Matyash. 'The heavens are brightening. I shall point out how they indicate the nature of space.'

Henchy shook his head. 'You might feel tempted to demonstrate the instability of this structure – by helping us to tumble off and break our necks. Thus exemplifying your political philosophy. You would fail. We can protect ourselves magically against commoners.' (Not necessarily! We could easily suffer mundane wounds.) 'This folly would lead to your death as surely as a fly is squashed.' (Brave words!) 'I'm more interested in discussing how you can be allowed to continue in your post – for the sake of scientific enlightenment – while at the same time assisting the kingdom. I want you to fulfil certain reasonable conditions, Mr Matyash. Reasonable, as opposed to treasonable . . .'

Henchy may have lost the use of his fighting arm; but he had sharpened his wits to demonstrate his continuing usefulness to king and queen. I felt leery about the way this interview was proceeding, and wished Henchy had been more straightforward about the reasons for it.

As Henchy proceeded to outline conditions, the pal-ace's plan became all too clear. In the not-so-distant future a certain white pawn-squire was going to be advanced into Chorny territory. The said pawn must be furnished with underground contacts in Chorny, who would shelter him. He would present himself to those subversives as a messenger from Matyash, equipped with coded astrological charts which would serve as introduction and credentials.

And who would the lucky pawn-squire be? Who had been trained in the nocturnal habits of Seveno district? Who had been polished for life in the black city of Chorny? A life which might not last very long? I'll give you one guess.

'I can see a couple of things wrong with this plan,' I said to Henchy. We were descending Bresh Hill, with the constellations twinkling overhead.

The first deficiency was that the plan was just a copy of what Chorny had done when they infiltrated Squire Sara into Bellogard (except that Sara had needed no contacts to shelter her!). The second flaw was that Sara's eidolon hadn't even appeared on the chequerboard at the time. Her face was still unknown to us.

Only Queen Isgalt and I knew about Sara. In the nick of time I stopped myself blurting my secret out to Henchy.

'My face will hardly be unknown,' I said.

'That's no problem. By night, with a modicum of disguise, you'll be safe enough. It's about time we launched an attack! What security is there in passive defence? With Prince Feryava already injured, even a pawn could take him. But *not* if we all stay at home. Oh it's high time. Sir Brant will explain the details.'

'So this is Brant's plan?'

'In consultation with the queen, who cares deeply for your safety. What's your other objection?'

'Nothing, nothing.'

* * *

Obviously I ought to reassess Queen Isgalt's generosity in letting me keep Meshko's sketch-book with its enticing portraits of Sara, squire of Chorny.

The word 'keep' hardly conveys the intensity of my attachment to that sketch-book. I had treasured it. I had *possessed* it. Four years had slipped by since I fell in love with Sara, since she fled from Bellogard, yet I still often opened the book and gazed at her image, fixated.

On my return to the palace that night I did so once again.

My present room, high up in the pages' tower, was furnished in rococo style. Table, chairs, and a huge bed were carved and gilded. Ornamental plaster fruits and flowers clung about the door and window-frames, about the covings round the fireplace, and circuited the ceiling. Ornate paraffin sconces backed by cherub-framed mirrors lit the room by night.

Taking the sketch-book from a locked cupboard, I carried it to the table and opened it. Sara's fine features confronted me: slim nose, high cheeks, dark liquid eyes, pertly sentimental mouth, framed by a crinkly black cascade of hair. How I admired the soft hollow of her throat and the ivory of her shoulders – so smooth yet capable of so much hardness, as when she had advanced to attack me . . .

Here was inducement indeed to quit the security of Bellogard, willingly to risk my neck by sneaking into the enemy city.

As so often before, my lips hovered over the page and I kissed the air. I avoided touching the paper lest I moisten and smear the charcoal.

An onlooker might have regarded me as a fool. I even saw myself as foolish. Yet what a sweet folly this was. Until now my tryst with her image had only amounted to a romantic folly; one in which I had indulged myself achingly, and which had become something I needed nearly as much as a drunkard craves his drink. Now the demands of reality were intruding. In Chorny I might actually meet Sara in some dark street. Must I ignore her? If she recognized me, would she betray me?

Meshko's portraits were very faithful. As of four years ago. In the interim I had doted on image, rather than original. When next I saw Sara in the flesh, might I find her strange – because she would be mobile, and real? Might I recoil at some trivial – yet devastating – disparity?

An image possesses no wilful, impatient, personal motives of its own. What's more, an image contains no ordinariness. An image is detached from the stream of daily life, exalted. The portrait of one's self which exists in other people's minds may well excite those people intensely. An admirer might exclaim to a queen, 'How very thrilling to be you!' However, the queen might reply: 'Believe me, it isn't thrilling at all. It's very ordinary to be me.' One might admire, or lust after, a woman's long and graceful legs. To her, most of the time, those are simply sexless, familiar limbs she uses for walking about on. Her hindquarters are just something she sits down on. Her eyes are points of view, jelly organs she hopes not to get grit in on a windy day. Her teeth are for chewing food. Her arms are for lifting things. Sara's own ordinariness – to herself – might well be that fatal disparity.

I had made love to a number of other women down Groody Lane during the past four years. In the darkness I had found myself imagining that those women were Sara – and this had made me wonder whether I had ever genuinely made love to Sara herself! Or only, even while I embraced her, to a kind of erotic eidolon which I superimposed upon her. Margarita had long since stopped visiting my bed in the palace. For some reason I had never questioned why. Nor had I made any further attempt to entice Margarita, other than to pose for Meshko. I assumed that in some fashion I had outgrown the maid who had initiated me. It now occurred to me that the queen might have warned Margarita off me. Isgalt wanted me to yearn for Sara.

After a while yearning becomes an end in itself, perhaps preferable to the attainment of the dream. Sara hadn't magicked me at all. I had magicked myself, enchanted myself with her. I'd decided to fall in love, and I'd done so. Awareness of this fact made not a whit of difference to the disturbing power of that love.

I lowered my lips and this time I kissed the actual page.

And paper moved against my lips, twitching and rippling.

I jerked my head back.

Sara's portrait undulated. It might have been lying at the bottom of a stream. Did her lips really move? Did her eyes blink? Did she breathe?

I felt such a strong sense of her presence. A sense of indignation, mingled with excited curiosity. Of pleasure mixed with pain. Of angry delight; and sweet shock. Suddenly the side of my head ached violently – where I had clubbed Sara with my poniard hilt.

Hastily I closed the sketch-book. All such sensations vanished. Meshko must have brushed a trace of magic paint on to this picture – the same paint that Sara had supplied for espionage. Had he brushed some on to all the other portraits in the book? How often, during the past few years, had Sara sensed my presence? Almost, my touch. My parting, *stunning* touch!

In that strange moment of contact I had not sensed hatred. I had sensed a thrill of love; yet at the same time my blow continued to pain her magically – and the only possible cure would be for her to kill me. This realization put my dotings of the past four years into a different perspective. In another respect nothing was altered; only reinforced.

Was there any way to heal a magic hurt other than by killing the inflicter of it? When the hurt in question wasn't severe, when it didn't involve torn flesh or broken bones?

Nobody before had ever wished to heal an enemy's magic wound.

I decided to ask Bishop Veck's opinion, circumspectly.

Next day I sought the bishop out; and found him in the Bibliotek. Hunched in a dusty leather chair, he was scanning the even dustier surface of a desk through a powerful reading-glass, which he held steady by bridging his hands.

Correction: on the desk lay the most minuscule of books, held open by tweezers. Veck grunted in frustration.

I whispered so as not to blow the book away. 'Excuse me?'

Veck placed the reading-glass carefully atop the book, as one might entrap a flea beneath a glass dish.

'I've been thinking about Henchy's broken wrist, Bishop. He imagines it's getting better slowly. Is there no way to speed the healing?'

'He *imagines*. The little wound in my own cheek has never improved. Nor will it, till the world ends.'

'Will you heal up when the world ends, sir? In time for the next cycle of existence?'

'Not the *personal* me, Pedino. Otherwise I should remember a previous cycle of existence. As to the ideal me . . . maybe.'

'What if the person who wounded you was still alive and wanted to undo the wound?'

'Sir Oscaro is dead years since.'

'Yes, but what if?'

Veck knit his brow. 'Ah, now I see what's bothering you, Pedino! Henchy was injured by Bishop Zorn. You killed Zorn. If you had checked him instead and dragged him to Henchy for Henchy to kill . . . Ha! You couldn't have known that Henchy was hurt. Nor could you have effectively checked Zorn. You did the only possible thing; and did it well. Don't trouble your conscience, lad.'

I chose my words carefully. 'If the "ideal" you heals, surely that healing must occur *somewhere*? In the space between cycles, in the gap between worlds? Maybe there's some way to reach that space and time by magical travel before the world ends?'

'You've been harking to our astrologer's notion of other universes.'

'No, sir, I haven't. Henchy and I called on Mr Matyash yesterday. That was in connection with subversion.'

Veck nodded. 'Sir Brant will want you to pay more visits to the astrologer, so that you can plausibly pass for an associate of the fellow. No doubt Matyash will bend your ear with his theories of coexisting universes. I see no evidence, myself. Proof of *successive* universes, ah yes. That's another matter.' Veck tapped the glass atop the microscopic book, and chuckled wryly. 'Not that I can discern very much detail of those!'

'What exactly are these "coexisting" universes?'

'You had best ask Matyash. But briefly: he thinks he reads signs in the stars indicative of other regions of space where different natural laws apply. Different from those which apply to our own world. Other rules govern existence in those regions. According to him.'

'I *shall* ask him.'

'If Matyash discovers a universe next door to ours where Henchy's injury and mine can be healed – plus a way to reach that region – do tell me! I should be fascinated.' Veck's voice was heavy with sarcasm. 'The man's rather mad. He only has a tiny scrap of soul, and lacks magic. So he burns with resentment. He concocts imaginary worlds where our own magic wouldn't work; where he might be our equal. Such jealous pique unbalances his thinking. Personally I doubt the wisdom of using him as an entrée into Chorny.'

'You doubt?'

'Not very vigorously. It's worth a try.'

Troubled, I left the bishop to his indecipherable, microscopic book.

I addressed Sir Brant. 'Bishop Veck seems to doubt the sanity of this plan.'

We were in the Ex-Chequer Chamber. Isgalt sat on her ivory throne, her blue eyes regarding me wistfully. Yellow ringleted hair spilled from a chaplet of opals. By contrast she wore a brass breastplate, long honey-coloured tweed skirt, and beige suede boots: a functional, 'touch-me-not' costume.

In the companion throne lolled King Karol, portly and ruddy, puffing at his pipe and chuckling over his latest magic bubble.

High and haughty, Prince Ruk observed proceedings with hands clasped behind his back. He was elegantly suited in cloth of silver, with silver spats upon his ankles.

Sir Brant – burly, bluff, sandy-headed – was armoured in lightweight brassarts, cuirass, tasset, and sabatons. His legs were bare: hairy tree-trunks. He wore the same sword with which he had once run through his own squire in order to promote the queen.

'Veck doesn't actually *oppose* the scheme,' Brant said. 'It's a bold one; and I shall be guarding you, lad, on the journey. I shall carry you magically most of the way to

Chorny. Then I'll lurk in the countryside. I'll leap askew unpredictably every now and then. No one will pin me down. I'll dye my hair black. Prince Ruk will stay on alert here, ready to leap directly to Chorny – just so long as no one gets in his way.'

'Suppose Prince Ruk were to position himself closer to the border?' Isgalt suggested.

'What, leave the palace and Your Majesties unguarded?' Ruk shook his head firmly. 'I can guard you from a distance, that's true. If a single Chorny pawn were to interpose, immediate return would be blocked.'

'Look!' cried the king. Chortling, he rotated his glass bubble. Inside was an insect-clouded marsh curving upward to the equator of the bubble, where there was dry land. Marooned in the fly-infested watery waste were homunculi of Queen Babula and King Mastilo, tiny eidolons. The Chorny monarchs struggled to wade to the sanctuary of the equator, slapping furiously at the biting pests.

'Most amusing,' said Isgalt. 'Do the real Babula and Mastilo feel the slightest irritation?'

'No,' admitted King Karol. 'It's a pleasant conceit to imagine that they might possibly *dream* about this! Don't you think?'

Ruk cleared his throat. 'Could we continue with the business in hand? I say we should ignore Feryava as a target. The Chorny astrologer with whom Matyash intrigues is controlled from the Khram, the Chorny equivalent of our Samostan. Bishop Lovats presides over the Khram. From what I've heard about him, Lovats may be highly tantalized by some of Matyash's mad theories. A messenger purporting to come from Matyash has a good chance of getting close enough to the bishop to strike. Let's not forget how adept our lad is at catching black bishops *en passant*. Eh, Pedino? Or at least you can distract Lovats sufficiently while Brant and I overwhelm him.'

'In the battle four years ago,' I pointed out, 'Chorny attacked our Samostan first of all. Attacking the Khram is a copycat move.'

'It's only logical, in view of the astrology aspect.'

Abruptly King Karol turned his magic bubble upside-down. The whole swamp slid round, tumbling enemy king and queen, soaking and bedraggling them.

Soon I was visiting Matyash at the observatory, of an evening, and pestering him about his theories of those other universes next to ours. After a while it dawned on him (or, in his case, 'dusked') that I was more than just an over-privileged nuisance. I was genuinely and vitally interested in his notions; not that he guessed the real reason.

So here we both were, engaged in a typical night-watch atop that precarious platform underneath the glass dome . . .

He directed his astrolabe at the constellation of the Pig.

'Mark my words, Shrimp, other rules apply to parts of the cosmos beyond our immediate ken. That's written in the shapes the stars make. When you travel magically' – he felt obliged to spit exasperatedly over the edge – 'you pass through a zone that impinges on the metaspatial zones of those other regions.'

'Must you call me "Shrimp"?'

'I certainly don't intend to call you "Sir Squire"!'

'My name's Pedino. Now what does "metaspatial" mean? Is that a magical space which encloses mundane space, though mundane space seems far bigger? Is it the *seed* of mundane space, the foundation?'

Matyash gave a grudging grunt of approval. 'You're getting there, Shrimp.'

'So, Mr Matyash, whenever we jump magically we touch upon those other zones. But because we're adapted to the rules of our own world we always bounce back into our own domain.'

'I'd say so.'

'If our world happened to be destroyed while we were neither here nor there, might we cross into another world?'

'If you could thrust yourself with sufficient conviction! If you could ignore all the rules you've ever lived by. If you could turn all your beliefs inside out in a revolutionary spirit. Fat chance of that, I'd say. Now look you: those seven stars up there form a perfect septagon . . .'

'No they don't.'

'*If* you imagine them rotated about a line through the axis of the Quint. Metaspatially this indicates that there are seven prime dimensions in addition to the five we're already familiar with, namely, length, breadth, height, time, and your own brand of magic. I imagine these represent seven other sets of magic rules. I've devised no definite names for these, since I've little idea of their nature. For temporary convenience we could label them: *strangeness*, *colour*, *charm*, *flavour*, *mood*, *tone*, and *urine*.'

'Why urine?'

'It pisses me off that I can't discover more about them.'

I was working on the idea that if Sara and I could somehow move together magically in the right sort of way then we might hit some zone where the rule no longer held true that she should remain hurt in the head for ever. Otherwise this was all fairly ethereal stuff to me. Afterwards I was glad to head down into Seveno district for a few drinks.

Thus I discovered that Boris Slad, my sister's husband, had got himself a costly mistress and also was embezzling money to pay her gambling debts.

You may recall how proud my parents were for Drina to marry into the Slad family, and how upset Drina had been at the thought that I might shamefully stain the alliance through nocturnal misconduct in Seveno. (Drina changed her tune after I killed Bishop Zorn.)

The wedding had taken place two years previous; and splendidly so, at the Samostan, since Slad Senior was footing the bill. I had escorted the bride-to-be in my best palace uniform, brass buttons polished till they shone like suns. Drina seemed radiantly and childishly happy, while my parents were pleased as punch. I was in two minds about the value of this match, for which I felt responsible; as I've said.

Drina and Boris took up marital abode in a self-contained flat on the third floor of the Slad house overlooking Vertovy Gardens. To all appearances Boris buckled down dutifully in his father's counting house of which he was now, two years later, in nominal charge as junior partner.

I hadn't been to the *Grand Salon de Chance* in, oh, ages. Quite frankly the place made me feel uneasy; and for a long time I was hard put to work out exactly why.

On account of the Physiognomist? Hardly. It didn't matter a hoot if he knew who I was. Anyway, he was the soul of discretion.

Because of the presence of Bellogard's high society? How so, when *I* hobnobbed with the queen herself?

I'd paid dutiful visits to the other, less salubrious casinos in the vicinity. These dens specialized in rowdy games of hazard. I persuaded myself that it amused me to kibitz – this was all I ever did – yet in those establishments I also felt awkward, though the sensation was less intense.

It had taken me a good while to understand precisely why the *Salon* bothered me. The reason was: *chance* itself. That particular venue represented the acme, the quintessence of chance: chance raised to an art, and a style. In my guts I felt that there was something unnatural about games of chance – something discordant and awry. Games of chance were utterly at variance with my own view of the world and my sense of my own magic. To me, the world consisted of dynamic choices, not random events.

However, after a glass of wine or three I decided to revisit the *Grand Salon*. In disguise.

A word about the art of disguise, which I was attempting to master in preparation for Chorny . . .

It's possible to fool the eidolons in a number of ways. Long ago Queen Dama had carried out experiments with the assistance of squires. She found that those spectral images – on which both Chorny and Bellogard alike could spy by magic – presented an idealized average of their subjects. You could dye your hair, and the eidolon would ignore this change. (My own hair was already as black as a Chornyman's.) You could dress up in rags. For several weeks the eidolon would continue to show what you wore habitually, ceremonially. If you persevered in wearing rags the garb of your eidolon would in time grow tatty to match. A magical injury would show up immediately, being essential and intrinsic. Likewise if you shaved your moustache off. If you started to grow a beard your status was ambiguous for a week or so. During that time the eidolon would stay clean-shaven. Make-up would be ignored unless worn constantly.

By quick, deft application of powder and grey charcoal

I'd learned how to make my features seem narrower and longer – less open – and my eyes more deep-set. Margarita advised and assisted. She had shown me how to pencil round my eyes and mouth wrinkles which put ten years on my age. I'd let my neat moustache sprout bushily. One day I hacked it back to a tight black line along my upper lip. Duly fooled, my eidolon lost its whiskers. I applied black wax to the remaining bristles; anyone meeting me in the flesh perceived a genuine moustache. I also practised altering my hair-style with a few scoops of the comb, switching the parting from left to right.

Trivialities! They still added up, till I looked more like a half-brother of my eidolon than its identical twin.

When I left the inn on Gostion Street I ducked down an alley. I donned my make-up and changed my hair. I wanted to test my disguise on the Physiognomist at the *Grand Salon*, though I didn't really expect to fool him of all people.

I also felt an impulse to take part in a roulette game; which of course the Physiognomist wouldn't permit, on account of my magic. Yet maybe, maybe he mightn't recognize me?

I wasn't interested in gambling in the *salle privée*, pitting magic against stacked odds. How silly to request the management to open up and staff the upstairs chamber just so that I could stake a few crowns. The *salle privée* was like the royal box at the comic opera: permanently reserved out of deference, rarely if ever tenanted.

Nor did I wish to use magic downstairs in the *salle blanche*. I wanted to gamble ordinarily like anyone else, pitting hunches against chance. I wanted to experience the sovereignty of chance. I would take the advice of Matyash.

Arriving at the *Grand Salon*, I purchased an entry ticket from the commissariat and strolled through into

102

the *salle blanche*. No Physiognomist intercepted me. The white hall wasn't unduly crowded yet nowhere could I spy that cadaverous, dapper figure. Had *he* taken to disguising himself? I buttonholed a valet.

'I was hoping to speak to the Physiognomist.'

'Alas, young sir! He has taken to his bed, with a gripe. No doubt he'll be well by tomorrow. Meanwhile the croupiers are eagle-eyed.'

'I'm sure they are.'

Up till now I could pretend that I had every intention of playing roulette, knowing full well that I wouldn't be allowed. All of a sudden haphazard circumstance virtually obliged me to do so. Already I felt that I was in the thrall of chance.

I studied one particular roulette table for half an hour to brush up my memories of the betting combinations. Then I purchased ten crowns' worth of chips; no one prevented me.

I began to bet modestly – merely on red – and very modestly to win. Emboldened, I switched my bets to blocks of numbers. I alternated between the high *passe* numbers and the low *manque* ones. Enjoying further modest success, I now dared place simultaneous bets *en pleine* on a single number, in tandem with *passe* or *manque*. I chose the number twelve, since that number hadn't come up in a long while. I lost, and doubled my bet. I lost again, and redoubled. Each time the wheel spun I averted my eyes and recited the alphabet backwards silently to stop my mind fixing on numbers, and my magic interfering with the ball.

On the very next spin the ball tumbled into the twelve slot.

'*Douze, rouge, pair, et manque,*' the croupier chanted brusquely in the gambling language. He raked a pile of chips my way: fifty-two and a half crowns' worth, to be precise. If only I'd staked more money on that damn twelve – say four crowns, instead of one and a half – I could have cleaned up handsomely. Oh, a hundred and twenty crowns! I was beginning to appreciate the intoxications of chance.

I tried to imagine a world governed by chance, instead of by definite directions of magic. In such a world one's magical powers might vary capriciously. Their nature might alter, so that one moment you were pawn, next king, and after that nobody. You might find yourself acting arbitrarily, at random.

The Prophetess was watching me: she who supposedly advised on betting systems and arranged discreet amours for gentlemen. That night her plump body was swathed in billows of white tulle; and she wore the usual domino mask. Lowering her opera-glasses, she ambled closer.

'Normally,' she murmured, 'gamblers don't look away from the wheel as it spins. They try to will their number to come up.'

'Since the result's a matter of sheer luck, why waste one's energy?'

'Now you should bet on three, or thirty-three.'

'Why?'

'You won with twelve. The factors of twelve are one, two, and three. Twelve already includes the numbers one and two. That leaves three. Twice three is thirty-three. Don't run away with the idea that roulette is all luck! Mysterious patterns operate.'

Did she, I wondered, receive a percentage from the house for encouraging winners to persevere?

Her silky muslins sought to envelop me in a cloud. She purred, 'We don't witness disorder here, do we? On the contrary, we observe order. We discover a rigid framework of rules, combinations, and conventions! The very shape of the game imposes a structure upon luck and chaos. Consequently there's a tendency for subtle patterns to occur. Not obvious ones, but arcane ones. Why don't you join me on the sofa after your next win?' She withdrew her white, perfumed, powdery cloud.

I observed play for another few spins, then placed a three-crown chip on number thirty-three. I lost, though I recouped a crown on even numbers.

I staked six crowns on thirty-three.

And lost.

It was then that I noticed my brother-in-law Boris Slad enter the *salle blanche*. He was accompanied by an extremely beautiful young woman: dusky, sultry, sexy. Boris hastened to the sofa and whispered urgently to the Prophetess. She frowned, shook her head. Boris redoubled his pleas. This time she relented. She signalled subtly to the supervisor. The supervisor, and a ruefully smiling Boris, converged at the grille of the 'bank'. Boris scribbled on a chit of paper and received a stack of chips.

'*Trente-trois, noir, impair, et passe,*' announced my croupier.

Thirty-three had come up! Distracted by seeing Boris, I'd neglected to place a bet for the last few spins. What a fool I was.

The factors of thirty-three were eleven and three. Three was already included. That left eleven. What the hell *was* the system? I bet on eleven minus three: on eight.

I lost, and doubled my stake.

'*Huit, noir, pair, et manque.*'

I'd won!

Boris assisted his young lady to sit, further along. He slipped into the adjoining seat and stacked all his chips before her.

Boris looked at me. I gave no sign of knowing him. Puzzlement crossed his face. Frowning, he occupied himself with his inamorata. Whenever she lost his money she giggled frivolously. Whenever she won (which wasn't so often) she panted orgasmically – but in a trivial, phoney way. Boris ordered champagne from a valet.

I pocketed my winnings, rose, and went to sit by my plump adviser on the sofa.

'You prospered,' she said. 'Were you using my system?'

'Incorrectly, no doubt. Nevertheless, please accept a token of gratitude.' I pressed a twenty-crown chip into her palm, whence it slid swiftly into a purse.

'You require more of me, I think?'

'Yes. That fellow over there; name of B. Slad. Banker's son . . .'

She was ever so reluctant to breach a confidence. She even tried to hand back my gift. In the end we compromised: I made certain suggestions, and she either nodded or shrugged. Thus I discovered that the young lady was Boris's mistress, whom the Prophetess had introduced to him, and that Boris had run up substantial debts. I returned to the roulette table, but didn't sit.

The young woman had soon used up all Boris's chips, and demanded more. He demurred; she looked as peeved as a child forbidden a chocolate. They exchanged momentarily angry words. His anger was cut short by his own pleading infatuation. A kind of sensual pang, an animal thrill seemed to shoot through her nerves for no precise reason. She clutched Boris's arm and stared into his eyes.

I dumped the remainder of my chips in front of her.

'A loan,' I said. 'Till you recoup.'

'Oh yes,' she breathed, darting me a glad glance. Only a glance; already I was of no further interest to her.

Boris scowled furiously. He had been on the point of teasing her away from the table, away from the *Salon*.

I said, 'I want a word with you.'

He followed me, leaving his lady friend intent on roulette.

'I can't repay you,' he growled. 'You'd better under-stand *that*! And don't imagine you can snatch her away from me so simply.'

'I have no desire to, Brother-in-law.'

'Brother . . . Why, you *are* Pedino! My, how you've changed. You must have been sick.'

'And I imagine that Drina might feel sick if she could see this scene.'

'Do you? Let me tell you this: when a man's bed is cold he seeks ardour elsewhere.'

I understood immediately. Here was another result of my own unwitting emotional oppression of my sister. I had thought I was free of some of that burden when Boris wed Drina. He married her on account of me; because I was a squire at the royal palace. She married him to escape from the need to be her own woman. But even so – surely Drina might have bloomed thereafter? Instead, apparently, I still lay between them in bed like a chilly bolster separating them even as I united them.

Oh repetitions. How long could a victim continue to punish her victimizer? In Drina's case the answer seemed to be: for ever. Until the world ended.

Was there some hidden blessing in the world coming to an end? Namely, that all wrong moves in life would then be eradicated, swept away so that a whole new existence could commence?

A blessing for whom?

'I see,' I said.

'I shan't give Maxime up,' Boris said. 'You'd be a fool to sneak on me to Drina. You would only hurt her.'

'I agree. If you want some heat, though, surely there are houses down Groody Lane? Your behaviour seems rash. How would your father regard these mounting debts?'

'What *debts*?'

107

'Isn't it obvious? Your friend Maxime gambles so improvidently. It's plain to see.'

'What does it matter if I pledge all my father's assets?' Boris retorted. 'Nothing that *I* do counts for anything. What you lot in the palace get up to may sweep us away at any time. Let me amuse myself!'

'Is the banker's son becoming a revolutionary? Does revolution take the shape of bankruptcy, courtesy of the *Grand Salon*?'

'Revolutionaries? Huh! They're right about one thing: this regime is coming to an end. I can afford to run up debts.'

'What do you know about revolutionaries, Boris?'

'You mentioned those, not I. You raised the subject.'

True.

I brooded.

So we were coming to the end of an era of history? The long struggle between Bellogard and Chorny was entering a final phase? And all citizens were growing vaguely aware of this in their underminds . . . Thus agitators and malcontents emerged, weakening the kingdom in petty ways, sapping confidence further.

Was Sir Brant's bold scheme actually a last desperate fling?

Disaster might arrive with shocking suddenness; but premonitions preceded it.

'I can assure you that *I'm* no threat to Their Majesties, Pedino! If I regard myself as anything, it is as a nihilist. I believe in nil; in nothing.'

'That doesn't sound very . . .'

'Very *what*? Are you genuinely concerned with Drina's welfare?' he challenged me. 'Or are you just snooping for the palace? Seeing how the puppets dance?'

I said nothing to this cruelly accurate cut. My conscience pricked me once again. I left him to his own self-destruction. And the destruction of my sister's happiness.

Perhaps the greater destruction – of everything that existed – would occur before Drina or my parents ever found out about Boris's 'nihilism', and broke their hearts.

A few days later a bomb exploded in Bellogard. The Spomenik Monument was badly damaged.

Nobody was injured, and the target hardly seemed vital to the well-being of the kingdom, although it was in the centre of town. To my mind the fact that the monument wasn't totally demolished hinted at amateurism rather than an act of Chorny sabotage. Whoever placed the infernal device had been too virginal at violence to position it to best effect, and had scampered off quickly.

The explosion caused a disproportionate fit of jitters among the citizenry, culminating a couple of days later in an unprecedented demonstration in Terga Square.

Crudely printed posters had appeared mysteriously all over town to herald this protest. I observed it at first hand. Most of the cafés in Terga Square had taken in their chairs and tables, and fastened their shutters. I stood outside one which had stayed open.

The majority of demonstrators were labourers and artisans. Apprentices and errand-boys were obviously present for the fun of it. I also saw a surprising number of mothers with toddlers or babes in arms. These were shouting, 'Safety for our kids!' and 'A future for the wee ones!'

Soon people were shouting, 'We want the queen! Where's the queen? Why doesn't she come? Doesn't she care? Why should we care about her? Why should we care about princes? And bishops and knights? Who needs them? We want a republic!'

Were they challenging palace guards to come and disperse them so that some child or impetuous apprentice

109

should lie bleeding in the square, providing a martyr? But no such thing happened. As yet.

I couldn't spot who was orchestrating this outcry. The ringleaders stayed hidden in the crowd.

Who had advised the proprietors of most of the smart cafés to shut up shop that morning? Had they decided this of their own accord? Were they in their own way a silent part of this protest?

Next thing I knew, the demonstrators were crying out as though Spomenik had been a great champion of the common people; as though the damage to his statue was an insult tolerated by the palace.

Spomenik had been a composer of comic operettas. Admittedly those operettas featured commoners such as bird-netters or chimney-sweeps with pretensions to nobility or magic (misunderstood). This was why they were comic. Otto Spomenik happened to bear a name which was also a word in the magic language. Thus a monument had been erected to him rather than to any other light musician.

At the café where I loitered, the waiters had stopped gliding about amidst the outdoor tables and were clustered together in a knot. Disgruntled patrons waved in vain to attract their attention. The manager himself emerged, wearing white waistcoat and velvet tuxedo, to remonstrate with his staff.

His arrival on the scene might well have been a signal. Youths surged from the crowd towards the café. They snatched drinks from tables, stole gâteaus from plates. They insulted young ladies. They knocked hats off heads. The manager grabbed hold of one offender. The other youths immediately began overturning tables, while all the customers – and myself – retreated indoors for sanctuary. The manager broke away and followed us. A lout picked up a chair and threw it at the café window, shattering glass all over the display of strudel and baklava, melba and walnut cake.

At this point a party of royal guards, all leather and brass, did at last arrive. As they advanced on the café-wreckers with their batons those youths took to their heels. The bulk of the protest also melted away. Soon the square was clear, and café patrons could escape, stepping over wreckage in apprehension and astonishment.

Overnight, more crude posters appeared, referring to the 'Battle of Terga Square' which was nonsensical since there had been no such 'battle'.

I accompanied Henchy to the observatory to beard Matyash. Our astrologer denied all responsibility. 'There's more discontent than you realize,' he told us.

'Someone's stirring the pot,' insisted Henchy. 'Someone's printing those posters.'

'Not I! Please note how I'm collaborating with the Shrimp. If you ask my opinion, we're in a pre-revolutionary stage.'

'What sort of jargon is that?'

The giant ambled to a shelf piled high with star charts and horoscopes. He tugged loose a pamphlet.

'Have you seen this, then?'

Title: *The Capital: a Manifesto*.

I turned the twenty or so pages which were smudgily printed in ugly type. The 'capital' in question was Bello-gard, and the text purported to be a rigorous critical analysis of 'historical inevitability'. It would seem that rule by king and queen based upon magical values was inherently doomed. Salvation lay in a 'diktat of the commons' . . .

'Personally,' said Matyash, 'I think this is stupid compared with a metaphysical solution to our dilemma achieved through science. What's more, it preaches revolution in a single kingdom: ours. The anonymous author

111

assumes that this will "inevitably" cause a subsequent revolution in Chorny. It would have made more sense to call for a common revolution in both kingdoms simultaneously. But what do the common folk of Bellogard know about life in Chorny? Ignorant they are, ignorant! Hence the need for a scientific initiative.'

'Aiming,' enquired Henchy coldly, 'at a common revolution?'

'Aiming at astrological co-operation to ward off the doom of the world.' Matyash took the pamphlet back, as though we had no right to be looking at it. 'Incidentally, the author of *The Capital* predicts that as the court of Bellogard grows more desperate, so it will start to govern repressively. Soon guards will patrol the streets. There'll be arrests and executions. The palace dungeons will fill up. There'll be corpses gibbeted on the battlements to cow the populace. This repression will signal – and provoke – the dawn of angry revolution.'

'Hence that bomb?' said Henchy. 'And the ridiculous riot in Terga Square? All in an effort to provoke the palace. I suppose now there'll be more such provocations?'

'How should I know?' rejoined Matyash.

How indeed?

We held a war council in the Chequer Chamber, chaired by Sir Brant. I already knew the name of my contact in Chorny – a music teacher named Skripka – and I had his address. Matyash had furnished credentials, and by now I knew enough astrology to pass myself off as his trusted messenger. So we decided to wait no longer. We would launch the infiltration of Chorny two days hence.

Next we discussed the 'internal security' situation; and here Bishop Veck insisted on taking charge. The queen counselled moderation but Veck argued strenuously for severe new laws. Veck wanted travel restrictions imposed on countryfolk entering the capital and on townsfolk leaving it. He wanted internal passports issued. He wanted the streets patrolled. He insisted on recruiting more royal guards. He wanted our newspaper, *Noveeny*, strictly supervised and censored. Just as per *The Capital*, so the unknown author couldn't have been entirely an idiot.

Henchy demurred, but Henchy was only a pawn-squire. The idea of law and order appealed to Prince Ruk. Isgalt consented reluctantly.

I had no pressing need to visit Matyash again. However, on the morning when Sir Brant and I were due to depart, doubtless due to excitement and anxiety I woke up at four A.M. I decided to dash over to Bresh Hill for one last talk to the astrologer before he sank into bed for the day.

The sky was beginning to grey with impending dawn when I reached the observatory. Within, was black dark. I called out in vain, then lit the candle stub I'd brought.

Matyash lay on the floor in a pool of blood.

He'd been stabbed repeatedly, maybe by several assailants. His body was still slightly warm to the touch. I immediately drew my poniard for protection (though as it turned out the observatory was deserted).

Lighting a spare lantern, I climbed the scaffold but found no clue. Descending again, I inspected Matyash's private chamber; his charts and records all seemed undisturbed. I sat on his bed and thought hard.

Had he been assassinated as a new act of provocation? Irrespective of any private games which Matyash had been playing, he was the official astrologer, after all.

Or had he been murdered because of those games?

Because he knew the author of *The Capital* but disagreed with the thesis of revolution in one kingdom?

Or – this was the most disconcerting thought – had Matyash been killed on the orders of Bishop Veck, new head of 'security'?

I remembered Henchy's veiled threats to Matyash.

Suppose I needed to lurk in Chorny for a long time? Suppose Matyash changed his mind about co-operating? Suppose he decided to denounce me to his Chorny contacts – in the service of a common revolution? His death would protect our invasion plan.

I would be highly unlikely to learn of his murder, since I was due to depart within hours . . . I would be journeying magically, outstripping any common-or-garden traveller. In any case the news wouldn't reach Chorny at all quickly now that *Noveeny* was censored.

I resented this death. If Matyash's friends in Chorny did find out, how would they regard me – who had left only a few hours after he was butchered?

I walked through to the main dome again. How ungainly and undignified Matyash looked now that he was dead, like a felled hairy ox.

I decided not to accuse anyone, or say anything at all. Let some other visitor discover the stabbed corpse.

Towards noon we combatants gathered in the Ex-Chequer Chamber. I was in my disguise, was wearing off-duty clothes, and carrying a scrip containing gold, dagger, and astrology documents.

Sir Brant, with his hair newly dyed jet-black, was dressed in rustic finery like a prosperous farmer. He had wrapped his sword in oilcloth, and a bulging satchel held rations, as well as gold to purchase more from farmsteads in the Chorny hinterland.

Prince Ruk, well armoured, stood ready to guard our

journey with straight-line magic (so long as no enemy power interposed). Bishop Veck was absent, busy with security. To bring diagonal magic to bear would have needed at least two slantwise leaps.

The queen was there to see us off; also King Karol. The king puffed nutmeggy gusts from his pipe, as if nervous at the imminent withdrawal of knightly, and possible princely, protection from his royal person. Karol had gathered the two remaining able-bodied squires, Josip and Beno, close to him; at one stage he leaned over to clasp his young wife's hand.

Flunkies trundled out a step-ladder on wheels so that I could mount Sir Brant in dignified style. (Brant had no choice but to carry me pick-a-back on the magic stages of our journey, otherwise he would far outpace me.) Queen Isgalt addressed some encouraging words. Without further ado I climbed up and scrambled on to the knight's back.

'Easy off, lad! You're fair throttling me.'

'Sorry, sir.' I resettled myself on his hips.

'I won't drop you!'

I didn't imagine that he would. The muscles of Brant's arms and shoulders felt more like rock than flesh. *I* had muscles, but mine could be squeezed and shifted. Nothing short of an axe blow could dent Sir Brant's compacted musculature, so it seemed.

On the day four years earlier when Isgalt had become queen, I remembered Brant struggling to hold Squire Pyeshka erect after spitting him on his sword. Now I understood that Brant had not been faltering because of the effort of the task but on account of emotion.

He bellowed magic words.

We shifted sideways dizzyingly through a crackling blue emptiness. Momentarily we halted at somewhere which was nowhere. Due to some skill which I could never grasp – though I grasped Brant tightly enough! – we pivoted upon nothing, and rushed in a new direction . . .

Then we were standing in a woodland glade. Elms towered high: heaps of green cumulus. Fallen limbs, victims of past storms, littered the mossy forest floor. Fleeing squirrels leapt from bough to bough. A rook clattered away from the heights, cawing.

'You all right, lad?'

'I think so, sir.'

'Plain Brant will do fine, while we're campaigning together. You jump down till I get my wind back.'

I slid from his back, to perch on a broken branch.

'Ever been here before, lad?'

'Is this part of Shooma Forest?'

'No, it's Lisitsa Wood. I jumped a long leg to the south, then a short leg east. We'll carry on that way. Third leap will take us over the marshes into enemy territory. After that we'll turn west by south. One last jump, and you'll be a day's walk north-west of Chorny city.'

'Er, Brant, out in the midst of nowhere – when you pause between legs – do you ever, well, do you ever sense a borderland of *other* magics?'

'Other magics? Hrumph. You *have* been listening to Mr Matyash.'

To Matyash . . . who was murdered. I felt sure from Brant's tone that he knew nothing about that deed.

'Do you, Brant?'

'Funny you should ask. I'll tell you a true story, lad. It happened long ago, on my second ever jump.'

So commenced the following tale, which Brant continued at each successive stopping point . . .

    A Knight's Tale
    (abridged, for the sake of decency)

'I'm one of the old Originals, as you know, lad. So when the world started up, I was already a knight with a memory of knightly things. I hadn't exactly put those things into practice as yet. The very first time I jumped, I knew what I was supposed to do – but it was all fresh and new to me.

'After that first jump, I felt ever so sure of myself. I was younger then; I was cocky in more ways than one.

'Back in those days I had a maid called Lisa, whom I referred to as "my little Lisitsa". She was foxy, eh?'

'Lisitsa' was the name for 'fox' in the magic language. I mounted Sir Brant and we leapt again . . . We arrived on an open moor, to the startlement of a covey of partridges.

'Second time out, I invited my little Lisitsa along for the ride, the same way as you're riding me today. Ordinarily, as I'm sure we both know, it's a fellow who rides upon a lady – as surely as a cavalier mounts his steed! 'Cept that a fellow generally faces his lady while he tittups upon her; though not always, I'll admit.

'I thought I'd excite Lisitsa by letting her ride me through the magic spaces. What enterprising chit of a commoner would refuse the offer of a magic trip?

'I also had an overwhelming urge *to have Lisitsa*, there at the place where we pause and pivot. Would it be possible to take one's pleasure there, without the pull of the world crushing us together? Not that I quarrel with my bulk bearing down on a gal. Keeps her in place, eh? But I was curious to experiment. I wanted to see if I could prolong the pause – then put the long leg over her short one, if you get my drift.'

We jumped through the blue, tingly space – pausing for the merest moment – to a hot, sedgy, midge-buzzing fenland. We were on the fringe of the Lettish marshes near the border. Brant lowered me ankle-deep into black peaty water.

'So I suggested to Lisitsa that we should jump stark-naked from my room in the palace. Didn't want armour and gowns impeding my thrust, eh? Told her *that* was all part of the magic, when you were carrying a passenger. Skin contact, absolutely essential.

'She was game. So we both stripped. She climbed on my bed. I backed up. She clung to my neck, and I wrapped her legs round my waist. When we reached the half-way mark I intended to slide her lovely little body right round to the front of me. I might add that my shaft was already sticking out proud, eager to be saddled.'

Was this true? Or was Brant spinning a cock-and-filly tale to occupy my attention, in case *I* lost my nerve in the magic emptiness?

I'd done a spot of magic jumping, myself, when Veck and Ruk were training me. However, a pawn jumps quickly, only a little distance, straight from here to there. He doesn't tarry in the spaces between. Nor, after my initial training, had I done any more jumping simply for the joy of it. One didn't jump idly, without urgent reasons of war. This tradition had been drummed into me. Obviously Brant had behaved differently in his youth.

Ordinary travel could prove preferable for other reasons. On the night when I killed Bishop Zorn, if I had jumped magically from Sara's room in Groody Lane instead of running through the streets to Terga Square, the bishop might have sensed a magical collision and avoided me. Or stabbed me.

I had some trouble regaining my mount. The marsh water and soggy peat sucked at my boots, gluing me, making it wellnigh impossible to leap up on to Brant's back. After my third attempt, Brant hoisted me bodily and slung me astride his waist; I regained my seating.

We leapt again through magic space . . . arriving this time on the bank of a brook. Brown water rushed through

118

heather down a hot little glen. A bird of prey drifted lazily overhead.

'So, with Lisitsa aboard, I leapt to that place where I *ought* to make a half-hop the other way. Instead I paused, paused, paused. I slid her around me, Lisa still clinging tightly to my neck. I slipped my tongue betwixt her lips and my sceptre up between those other private lips of hers. At first we were both floating as light as that glede-kite up there.

'At first. Then my feet started trying to slide sideways. It was as if I was balancing on a glassy slope which was slowly getting steeper.

'I was determined, though. I was aroused.

'Lisitsa had her eyes shut, the way women do. But not me.

'Way beyond her darling little head I caught a misty glimpse of . . . Well, it looked like a whopping big snake. Not any tiddly grass-snake or viper such as you might find in this glen here. This was something *enormous*, muscular and long. Rippling and strong.

'Between you and me, lad – man to man – I reckon that serpent was a projected image of what *I* was up to! Me with my fleshy shaft, eh? But that's what I saw.

'Just then my shaft erupted deliciously, not to put too fine a point on it. Lisa was pushed upwards.' (Oh, this had to be a tall tale.) 'She lost her grip. Me too. By now I was skidding sideways. I had no choice but to jump.

'Jump I did. And I was standing erect and starkers half-way up Mount Planina. All on my ownsome! Lisitsa wasn't there.

'I quickly jumped back towards the palace. I was hoping against hope that I'd spy her floating in space when I paused mid-way. Somehow I'd manage to collar her and haul her home.

'No such luck. She was *nowhere*. I tell you, lad, I felt terribly cut up about this.'

Brant wiped a tear from his eye. He was genuinely moved. This was no tall tale after all. It was the crazy truth.

Now I knew who had established the tradition that we did not jump for idle fun.

'For months I feared if I jumped again I'd meet her ghost in the empty spaces. As she only had a fragment of a soul, I suppose she could only have become a fraction of a ghost. A ghostly hand, a ghostly foot. A ghost of a tit, or lips. Reproaching me for my careless lust.

'Two years after, word arrived at Bellogard of a skeleton found in Lisitsa Wood. The bare bones were high atop an elm; and it wasn't at all obvious how anyone could have climbed there even when alive. There were no rotten rags on the bones, or scraps of skin or tendon, or even hair on the head. Crows could have accounted for edible carrion, but not for clothes or hair. There was only the skeleton, the pattern of a body – the oddity of this was the reason why news travelled.

'I knew those bones were my Lisitsa's. Without magic, she'd died and decayed in magic space. Her bare bones had fallen out into that wood. Because of the pet name I'd given her, do you see? That name anchored her magically to that bit of our world. So that's where she skidded to, decomposing, nothing to sustain her or guide her.' Brant wiped a tear from his other eye. 'Mount up, me lad. It's the last leap for us.'

We ended up in a woodland of giant oaks. A solitary rift in the leaf canopy showed top-heavy anvil clouds, fast darkening. Brooding heat and gloomy stillness threatened an imminent outburst of lightning, a concert of thunderclaps. I hopped down. We were standing beside a rutted roadway.

'Yon storm should blow over,' said Brant. 'I smell nothing magical about it. Let's picnic.'

We sat against a great trunk and ate cold chicken which Brant had brought. We washed it down with beer and brandy. The air grew stickier and thicker. Thunder crashed deafeningly. Flashes illuminated the forest. Wind whipped wildly through the upper foliage. Water sluiced upon the green umbrella, ripping holes in it, dripping downwards, rinsing the air clean and cool.

Brant stood up; I followed suit.

'You'd best be off, lad. Once you're in Chorny, if you cry havoc I'll leap to your side. Nothing gets in the way of a knight whose dander's up. Mind you take care of yourself, now.'

He hugged me then shoved me gently in the right direction.

As Brant had predicted, by the time I cleared the forest the weather was fair. The road took me out of the trees, then down through sheep-cropped vales to the dark, barge-bearing river Vada. There, the rural road joined a highway leading south. This highway soon entered a small town with the big name of Kalkoz Gorodok.

What shall I say about the enemy population? Darker skin and black hair predominated; otherwise they looked much like our own population. Their speech presented no problems. It was the magic, not the common language which varied.

I found a jewellery and pawnbroking shop where I disposed of one of my thick gold rings in exchange for a handful of zolat coins of the realm. Brant and I were carrying our gold in the form of rings. It's always plausible to pawn or sell a wedding-ring.

Supplied with cash, I visited a bar–restaurant where I ordered hot beet soup with ham bones. Nobody accused me of being a stranger. Obviously I had an accent, though not an outlandish one. Within a few days I ought to conform to Chorny tones of voice.

I walked on southward along the highway amidst fields of wheat stubble, sometimes alongside the broad, winding Vada. Peasant carts, pulled by stocky nags or donkeys, were using the road. Occasionally a speedier rider cantered past. Once a small detachment of cavalry pranced by – my heart skipped, but the soldiers paid me no attention.

Evening was already drawing in. I toyed with the idea of finding a bed in some rural hamlet. Goose-down pillows, perhaps! It would be wiser to curl up in the corner of a pasture; and not unpleasant. The storm had swept away the previous oppressive heat. Warm tranquillity reigned. I visualized myself lying like a happy dog in a nest of grass, listening to crickets and nightcrakes and to an owl hooting somewhere in a nearby coppice, watching the southern stars slowly revolve overhead.

Evening notwithstanding, the road remained busy; so I pressed on. As night fell I found myself in the town of Garodskoy – where I was amazed to encounter a new means of transportation.

Peasants with baskets of cheeses or cages of chickens were flocking like moths towards a long platform of black marble lit by bright lanterns hanging from an ebon canopy, which was supported on columns of wrought iron.

A gravel track stretched away into the darkness. Iron rails bolted to baulks of timber were bedded in the gravel. Upon these rails there stood a row of long, open-sided carriages linked to one another by iron couplings. The carriages were lamp-lit. At the head of the row I saw an iron chariot with two tall chimneys. One chimney puffed grey smoke; steam hissed from the other.

Painted in silver letters along that chariot were the words: ROYAL CHORNY RAILWAYS. Below: THE QUEEN BABULA. Two powerful lanterns, located like eyes, focused beams of light ahead upon the track.

I made enquiries and found that for the cost of a mere half-zolat I could buy a ticket to ride all the rest of the way to Chorny. I would arrive at the capital within thirty minutes – just as the city was getting into the full swing of night.

Generally, a farmer's day extends from dawn till dusk. If country dwellers wanted to do business in the capital, obviously they had to suit themselves to the nocturnalism of Chorny city. So a 'railway' had been built to speed market-suppliers to the city and back home again. They needn't remain awake all night as well as all day.

I bought a ticket. Boarding one of the carriages, I squeezed on to a bench amidst burly peasant women wearing headscarves; and their hens, their trussed piglets, their strings of dried mushrooms. Soon steam squealed louder than any porker, the carriage jerked violently, and away we rattled through the night.

Half an hour later I was staring out at the gas-lit streets of Chorny; we were soon entering Vauxhall Station.

Vauxhall Station was a great, wrought-iron hall brightly lit by burning gas. Half a dozen sets of iron rails culminated here at half a dozen marble platforms. I spotted two more 'trains' of carriages with engines named THE BISHOP LOVATS and THE PRINCE KRAY (after a nobleman killed long ago in the war). At a third platform open-top goods wagons stood engineless; porters were unloading mesh sacks of potatoes on to a succession of horse-drawn carts.

Beyond the 'ticket-barrier' travellers thronged around refreshment kiosks buying soup, hot sausages, and drinks which I later learned were mead brewed from buckwheat or alfalfa. Black-clad militia were patrolling in pairs, but I was soon deep in a crowd. I could congratulate myself on arriving inconspicuously in the very heart of Chorny.

I went through an archway into Ploshad Square – one of many names I was to learn subsequently. Open-air cafés reminded me of Terga Square back home. This Chorny equivalent possessed none of the same piped-icing elegance. Ploshad Square was huger. Buildings were monolithic and flat-faced. Long black banners hung like shrouds or roosting bats, with royal features etched in silver reflecting the light of many powerful gas-lamps.

Newly arrived peasants were flocking along Peryulok Prospect towards a bazaar. Southward, lit by incandescent globes slung on overhead wires, Glavny Boulevard swept towards the palace by way of Perehod Square and Most Bridge.

I bought a copy of the *Gazeta*, and asked the vendor the easiest route to the address which I'd been given, on Zabludilsy Lane. This person regarded me suspiciously but advised that I head down Glavny almost to Perehod Square, then cut through Prakhoda Arcade on to Ulitsa Avenue and enquire again.

This I did. I arrived in a busy warren of alleys and wynds between Ulitsa and the river. Further pleas for advice brought me to the lane I sought: serpentine, solely lit by light spilling from uncurtained apartment windows. No curtains were closed anywhere; I saw people cooking, washing, working.

How abominable to decree a whole city of people to live by night, and never to enjoy the day! To compel all children to go to night-school! (I'd seen kids hurrying by with their satchels.) *And* to keep windows uncurtained by night! Any Bellogardian would have echoed my reaction. Besides, night was the time when naughty Seveno district came into its own. How could this be so, if everyone was busy working? The prospect of sin by day somehow seemed less satisfying.

If I seem pedantic about places, names, and directions, that's because I would need to familiarize myself swiftly to survive, and do so by darkness and artificial light. As I was to learn, it wasn't exactly forbidden to wander abroad by day through the city, but you would draw attention to yourself. The militia would want to know why.

Few tenements were named or numbered, but finally I located number 17, Zabludilsy. I pushed open the heavy front door, then . . . did not enter. Inside, the tenement was pitch-black. At least outside there was some light from windows.

Here was yet another way in which Chorny controlled its citizens; which explained the news-vendor's suspicions. Ordinarily people would only go to places they already knew well. I couldn't conceive of a Chorny child roaming freely around town, the way I had roamed around much of Bellogard at a tender age. If you don't roam as a child, how will you get into the habit as an adult?

I had a box of lucifers and some candles in my scrip. I lit one; pushed the door again. The hall of the tenement was surprisingly clean. I'd expected to find piles of rubbish lying about. On the principle of 'what the eye doesn't see', what impetus to tidiness was there?

Come to think of it, the alleys had seemed neater than any back lanes in Bellogard. If you can't see your course too clearly, it's only good sense to keep the way uncluttered!

I heard piano music from above. A nocturne, no doubt. Climbing to the next floor by candle-light, I banged on the door from which the music came.

The piano fell silent. The door opened, spilling bright

lamplight. A tall thin man scrutinized me through silver-rimmed spectacles. He wore a black suit with open wing-collar and loosened bow tie. What long slim fingers he had! But his knuckles were as hairy as an ape's.

'What is it?'

Opening my scrip, I showed the edge of a star chart. 'Matyash sent me.'

'Inside, quickly.'

Skripka had to leave in a few minutes to teach piano and violin at Shkola Gymnasium. He examined my star-coded credentials, then quickly set out a lavish buffet of salami, sardines, salad, pickles, bread, mineral water, and a bottle of peppery white spirit – perhaps I might be starving and dying of thirst? He sped me on a hasty tour of his apartment, pointing out every lamp and explaining any idiosyncracies, obviously another essential of hospitality in this murky city. Then he bade me farewell.

I ate. Afterwards I wandered around the apartment, thankful that I hadn't arrived outside Skripka's door half an hour later to find no one at home.

The amount of books on the shelves amazed me. This place was a veritable bibliotek, except that none of the volumes were blank. Many were musical scores. Others were works of musicology, philosophy . . . and fiction. What a large number of long, heavy 'novels' there were. I flipped through a few. They all seemed to concern the daily lives of farmers or fabricators, fishermen or foresters; commoners all. Judging by the paragraphs I scanned, all these novels were highly optimistic in tone, full of constructive and aspiring sentiments.

I'd been awake for hours on end – ever since discovering Matyash's body in another country. I needed to rest. Leaving all lamps lit, I lay on a couch . . . and awoke to find Skripka looming over me. He had taught all night, and returned.

Faint grey light was seeping through the windows, dimming the lamps. Skripka closed heavy black drapes throughout to banish this invading dawn-light. Then he replenished the buffet. We talked for two whole hours, then he insisted that we must put out the lamps and sleep till the sun went down again.

I had learned a good deal from him. (He had learned less from me.) Zabludilsy Lane was near the bottom of Kholm Hill; and Kholm Hill housed the Planetera, the astrology observatory. The river Vada, south-flowing up to this point, turned sharply westward beyond Kholm Hill, between it and the Abrif Cliffs. The east and north flanks of the hill were given over to the Sahdi Gardens. Those sloped down to encompass the Khram, where Bishop Lovats lived.

I had asked Skripka why there were so many 'novels' about commoners.

'Ordinary people, like me, read a lot,' Skripka explained. 'We like to read about ourselves – as everyday heroes. The palace encourages this. They hope that everyone will struggle as hard as can be to make the kingdom strong and prosperous. Actually, here's the Achilles' heel of our ruling class. One night our people will realize that they don't need the dictatorship of the court. The regime will wither away spontaneously.'

'But . . .' I started to object. I shut up, and instead I enquired about the Chorny equivalent of our Seveno district, which was where I imagined I would need to hang out. Perhaps Chorny's Seveno operated by day?

I had to explain Seveno to Skripka. He stared at me, nonplussed.

'Casinos? There's no such thing. Not in any public building . . . ! Houses of prostitution, where men buy women's bodies for an hour's use? There's nothing of the sort in Chorny. Not openly! That's a fact . . . *Danger* in dark streets? What danger? What cutpurses? That would be crime, and crime's forbidden. The militia would stamp out crime in a single night.'

I felt mildly embarrassed. 'I hope I'm not giving you the impression that Bellogard is a totally rowdy, lustful, feckless town!'

'Sounds to me as though it is.'

'Those are just . . . aspects, which add spice to life. Some amusement and excitement.'

'Which you *defend*? What a peculiar messenger for Matyash to send.'

I improvised hastily. 'One adopts protective coloration to pass oneself off in Bellogard.'

'No need for that in Chorny! Everything's black and white. Black of our city, white of our lamps. *Our* city, I hasten to add. The people's city, not the royal court's. King Mastilo and Queen Babula are hardly very moral in private, I fear. The king's reputed to be secretly sadistic, and the queen indulges in many covert lusts.'

'They sound a fine pair to impose strait-laced ethics and darkness on everybody else!'

'Nonsense. Bishop Lovats guides the soul of this city.'

'Lovats? Ah, tell me about him! Then please tell me about the other nobles. And oh yes, the squires. Especially the squires. Their behaviour, their habits.'

For the second time within twenty-four hours I slept soundly. There was something protective and comforting about slumbering the daylight away, as though I were a sick child being cared for, so that nothing could harm me.

That evening Skripka took me to the Planetera to meet the astrologer, Mr Augusti.

128

We set off as dusk was thickening. Presently we were following a gas-lit path up Kholm Hill through the north end of the Sahdi Gardens. Silvery foliage shone in the artificial lighting, and the air was heavy with the nocturnal scent of nicotiana. Away to the north-east Skripka pointed out the floodlit rectangular bulk of the Khram. The black marble of the bishop's residence presented a glossy mirror to the powerful beams of gaslight focused upon it.

The Khram was where Sara might well be. Skripka had told me the names and ranks of the three surviving Chorny squires. Queen Babula's personal squire was called Slooga. Prince Feryava's pawn-squire was named Jigger. Sara was officially squire to Bishop Lovats.

Might she sense my presence, through a sudden stab of migraine? If she suspected, might she try to seek me out solo? I was her cure, if she killed me . . .

Squire Sara had only turned up at court in recent years, according to Skripka. Well, *that* was no mystery to me. Nominal rank notwithstanding, maybe she was assigned to somebody other than Lovats. It had not been *Lovats* who had swept down on Bellogard four years earlier in company with Feryava. It had been Bishop Zorn.

The dome of the Planetera was, naturally, in darkness. When we arrived at the summit of the hill, and before we entered the observatory, I could see right across the Vada to the palace. Far huger than the Khram, the royal palace likewise was monolithic, black, and floodlit.

Maybe Sara was there.

What folly. Here was I, the bishop-slayer on an urgent, violent mission . . . and uppermost in my mind was love for an enemy squire, a love which might only amount to a concocted obsession. Here was I, wondering whether I could show her an alternative to war between us . . . whilst conspiring to kill Sara's own bishop.

As I stared across the river, it seemed as though the whole scene of spangled darkness was merely an evil duplicate of Bellogard. If I could view palace and Khram and river and city by day, naked under sunlight, I would at once know how very different this city and its buildings and the local topography were. To see Chorny by day when the streets were empty was the one thing I dared not do.

'I wonder about you,' said Skripka. 'I wonder if Matyash really sent you.'

'The starmaps prove he did.'

'Yes, yes, I know. You're highly recommended.'

We entered, and he lit a handy lantern.

No tottering wooden scaffold met my gaze. An elegant wrought-iron tower reared up, enclosing a spiral staircase.

We climbed to a broad, railed observation platform, open to the night air. The top section of the dome consisted of curved glass panels. These had been cranked apart, unfolding the window segments like the petals of some night-blooming flower.

Mr Augusti sat ensconced amidst an elaborate machine. A padded chair was slung at a tilt beneath a giant, sky-pointing tube resembling the muzzle of a great bombard. Wheels, fly-wheels, and levers were to hand to manoeuvre the machinery. Little mirrors and lenses surrounded his head. Candle-light fell on notebooks, pen and ink. The astrologer's hands moved nimbly, instinctively, adjusting levers, shifting little discs and toggles. If the machine were a bombard, he might have been about to blast a ball of flaming pitch into the heavens, creating a new comet amongst the stars.

'Skripka here, Mr Augusti! We have a visitor.'

A head ducked out. A body followed: of a skinny, slight, angular figure. Augusti was a spider of a man. He scuttled, and froze in odd poses. His voice was high and squeaky.

He heard Skripka out impatiently. Seizing Matyash's star charts, he rushed to pore over them. I wandered to his apparatus to examine it.

'Don't touch!' he squawked, as soon as my hand strayed out. 'You'll upset the gears. You'll warp the azimuths.' Like a spider he seemed alert to menacing movements from any quarter. I imagined him leaping suddenly from the platform to dangle by a silken thread.

'Sorry.'

'Hush, fellow. I'm concentrating.'

We waited in silence for ten minutes till Augusti had the new information wrapped up and sucked dry. At last, he condescended to pay attention to us.

'Hmm! It's as I said, Skripka: different dimensions rub against each other. Different universes! The boundaries repel one another. This generates radiations resembling the output of phantom stars far away. By analysing the spectra of those ghost suns we should be able to deduce the rules which govern the juxtaposed cosmoses. Meanwhile the magic-mongers of both kingdoms cavort ignorantly, intent only on mayhem, death, and power.'

He gestured urgently, so I hurried to his side. He held up a thin pane of glass before the candle flame. I saw bars and stripes annotated with astrological symbols. Principally I spotted a serpent coiled around some kind of ladder. This reminded me about Brant's tale of Lisa.

'Is that serpent the key to the universe next door?' I asked.

'It may well be! Where is the lock to fit it into? If only I could communicate with scientists of another world! Incompatibility of our respective nature laws? Hang that! Surely it's no ultimate barrier to communication. But our

131

own world is doomed by war. How shall I have time to carry out this grand experiment?'

I studied the serpent carefully, memorizing the way it coiled and how many times. Its body was a patchwork of red and green paint blobs.

'Our own world mightn't end for dozens of years,' I said idly.

'Didn't Matyash explain anything? The planets already portend the end. Their courses are influenced by events in our earthly kingdoms. Stars are the clue to other universes; planets keep the score of historical events. Planets and moons are moving swiftly into conjunction.'

'Matyash probably took that as a sign of imminent revolution,' I said. Immediately I realized that I'd used the past tense. I would only draw attemtion to this if I corrected myself.

Better not mention bombs or riots. How would I know about such things unless I had travelled to Chorny at magical speed?

'There's a revolutionary pamphlet circulating in Bellogard, called *The Capital*,' I added.

'Is there indeed.' This wasn't a question.

Time to try a different tack. 'Does Bishop Lovats often visit you, sir? How does he regard the theory of coexisting universes?'

'Lovats has a very perceptive intellect, my lad. If he wasn't a blood-stained bishop he might be a great scientist.'

'Blood-stained?'

'Everyone of so-called soul who is in charge of the state is blood-stained, either actually or potentially.'

'You do find Lovats worth talking to? When he visits here? Or when you visit the Khram?'

Augusti shrugged his shoulders. 'Lovats both protects me, and menaces me. A visit from him is like a visit from a friendly tiger. How else would he have such influence over court and country?'

'Mr Matyash rather hoped that you would take me on as an assistant. To familiarize myself with Chorny science for a while.'

'Yes, yes; and I owe him a favour. Happens I could use a servant lad – one who doesn't get in my hair or pester me with stupid questions. Define "stupid"? Well, Bellogardian science lags far behind ours. You just hang on my words. Obey my instructions. Observe and infer. You may sleep in a cubby-hole down below there, if you clear it out.'

So I became – for a while – an astrologer's apprentice, placing me very conveniently for a strike at Bishop Lovats . . . who may have been instrumental in sending Sara to Bellogard, to whom I might owe my acquaintance with her.

Mr Augusti wasn't exactly good company. On the other hand he was far too involved in staring through lenses, and calculating the 'spectra' of spectre suns away at the edges of space, to bother quizzing me about my own background or motives.

Within a few days I felt that I had found a safe niche. I had worked hard, too. Begging my new master's permission, I ventured down into black, gas-lit Chorny city of a midnight to sightsee.

How odd, at dead of night, to explore crowded thoroughfares. How disconcerting, even frustrating. Daylight opens up perspectives. Sunshine lets you peer from a safe distance. You can see through archways, down long boulevards. Here no distances were safe. Far perspectives were drained of content, reduced to basic geometry. The world only filled up with precise detail in your immediate vicinity. This city yielded no colourful 'spectra' from which to extract enough information. The inhabitants knew what they were about; but I didn't know. I seemed to have developed a curious species of blindness, so that I could see but not recognize what I saw. I was walking in a taunting, elusive dream.

I strolled along the esplanade by the black waters of the Vada. I wandered through a busy, funereal fish bazaar. On sale were mounds of Stygian sturgeon, sombre salmon, umbral trout, sooty eels. Somehow the gaslights did not properly restore colour to the glistening bodies. After a while in Chorny your eyes no longer paid attention to rainbow hues, only to grey, white, and black.

I crossed Most Bridge to stare up at the blackly-reflective planes of the palace. I retraced my steps, and walked along Glavny towards Perehod Square.

People's clothing was mostly grey or black. White ghosts did not haunt these streets – but perhaps something worse? People who had died while still remaining alive. People who had become shadows; who had been born as shadows.

Dominating the north side of Perehod Square was the Magheela Tomb – equivalent to Bellogard's own Spomenik Monument, now vandalized. No infernal device could have done much to harm the monstrous solidity of the tomb. It likewise was a shrine to music, though of a different calibre entirely. The composer Mahgeela had created enormous music dramas and oratorios lasting four or five hours apiece, requiring hundred-strong orchestras and massed choirs.

Atop the tomb was a reviewing stand. On the first of October every year King Mastilo and Queen Babula would stand there to greet a torchlight procession of their people, who had been specially marshalled by the royal militia. Quite a contrast to King Karol's reclusive eccentricity, pantoufles, and magic bubble-blowing!

I found myself in the Prakhoda Arcade. Marble flooring. High wrought-iron columns. Gas mantles. The arcade wasn't unlike an elongated version of Vauxhall Station. There were huge tubs of ferns, and hanging baskets of silver starflowers. The goods on display in shop windows looked uninspiring.

I entered a café. Imitating the customer in front of me, I ordered a hundred grams of spirit and a caviar pancake; then found a vacant table. The pancake tasted of yeast, though not unpleasantly, and the red caviar was salty. The chilled spirit was faintly oily, and powerful.

A couple of youths dressed in dark grey overalls decided to share my table. They had ordered a half-litre bottle of spirit. One of the youths amiably raised his glass to me.

'Here's to the future! May it be black!'

I lifted my own glass. 'Here's to you. Health and wealth.'

'So where are you coming from, fellow?'

'Up north,' I answered vaguely. 'Why?'

'You call that a proper toast?'

'Go blind!' said his friend. 'Drop dead!'

'Go to sleep in Babula's bed!'

'No: wake up there!'

They hooted with laughter.

'How about this one? May your soul survive!'

I asked them quietly, 'Are you unhappy with the way your country's run?'

'What have we here, my brother? An agitator?'

'Or is it an informer, brother mine? A *provocateur*?'

'No, that sort would string us along a bit more subtly. I think this one's an idiot. A holy idiot. Here's to idiocy!'

'Does he see visions of a bright light in the sky?'

Hastily I excused myself.

* * *

135

Two nights later Bishop Lovats paid a surprise visit to the Planetera. I was up on the platform, oiling certain gears which Augusti claimed were not working as smoothly as they might. Augusti was down below, deducing spectral horoscopes by candle-light.

Footsteps, lanterns, voices. I looked down cautiously.

A figure wearing a black cassock: that was the bishop without a doubt. Accompanying him was someone slighter, black-suited, with a mass of long dark hair.

Sara. She was ten metres below me. I lay flat so as to peer without attracting attention.

Augusti was soon showing the bishop a sheaf of diagrams. Lovats studied these for a while.

'It seems to me, Augusti' – I overheard – 'that the world starts from a set of simple rules. Those are the fundamentals of existence; the constants. As soon as an *actual* world exfoliates from those rules – as a whole leafy tree from a seed – the plain rules become *masked*. The world no longer quite obeys them. Otherwise the world would never become full and rich. It would stay a mere skeleton of a world, lacking living flesh; a schematic, an outline . . .'

I couldn't make out Augusti's reply.

Lovats, again: 'I believe the universe is controlled by twin deities. Call them a God and a Devil. These deities play games using these basic rules; in the process they compel us to make war on each other. I see *no possible* means of communication with those deities. They are outside of our universe. I doubt if they're aware of our existence – or would care a hoot about us, if they were.

'What's more, Augusti, I fancy that those deities do not themselves *make* the simple rules. They inherit those. They, too, are prisoners of the rules – to a greater extent than us! How paradoxical, that we may be destroyed – and yet we are free – while they are immortal but in chains, condemned to play together throughout eternity, presiding over world after world. They are the real victims. Yet only in this way can a world such as ours evolve spontaneously . . .

'What's that? Of course two deities are required. Without the negative and positive – the constant pull and push – how could there be any growth of life or kingdoms?'

This time I did hear Augusti clearly. 'Required, is it? Yet they don't set the rules? I hardly see any need for deities!'

'Paradoxes abound. I'm inclined to say that those deities probably *express* the rules.'

'Express, is it? A moment ago you said that we're free. Do those deities move kings and queens into action, or do kings and queens move themselves?'

'Both! Neither!'

Sara moaned loudly and held her head.

'My dear,' Lovats exclaimed, steadying her.

'Apprentice!' Augusti squawked upwards. 'A glass of spirit for this squire!'

I squirmed out of sight.

'The pang will pass,' said Lovats. 'They always do. You have taken an apprentice, have you?'

'Did you hear me up there, boy?'

'Please don't screech in our ears,' said Lovats. 'One of us has a headache already.'

'I'm sorry, my Lord. The idiot seems deaf.'

I muffled my mouth and called, 'My hands are oily, sir. By the time I clean up and climb down . . . The spirit's in the usual cupboard.'

'Impertinence!'

'Your apprentice may have a point,' drawled the bishop. 'If you'll kindly tell me which cupboard?'

'I'll fetch a glass with pleasure, my Lord.' Augusti must have recollected – tardily! – my origin and nationality, since he called, less raucously, 'Stay where you are! Keep out of our way! Carry on oiling then polish all the brass.'

Silence for a while, punctuated by the chinking collision of glass and bottle.

Presently I heard Lovats say, 'I think we shall return to the Khram and pursue our discussion some other night.'

'No need,' Sara assured him. 'I'm quite all right now.' Oh her voice.

'In that case let us inspect your new apprentice, Mr Augusti.'

Again I was called. My heart thumped. I checked that my dagger was available; I prepared to cry magic to summon Sir Brant.

Summon him into this dim, unfamiliar building? Brant might be asleep when I summoned him. The countryside didn't follow city time. He would wake up and jump, feeling a bit fuddled . . . I might as well invite him into an ambush.

Dubiously I descended the spiral stairs. Staying in shadows, I halted some way from the trio.

The bishop's features were familiar to me from his eidolon. A pursed, down-turning mouth: expression of sour meditation. Long cavernous cheeks. Eyes that were watchful and alert. Wrinkle lines aplenty, suggestive of humour, wisdom – those traits weren't often on open show. His was a cautious, far from innocent face which spoke of a reserve of patient energy, flexibility, experience. He wore his grey hair close-cropped.

'Step forward, young man.'

I shuffled a few paces, hanging my head.

And Sara exclaimed, 'Surely he's . . . !'

I was on the brink, on the absolute verge of shouting to invoke Sir Brant – and Prince Ruk too, if he was in line. Blessedly, Sara bit her words back.

'What, my dear?'

138

'He's rather young.' Her voice shook.

'To be an apprentice? Whatever do you mean?'

'I can't think properly, Bishop. My head suddenly hurts me worse than ever.'

Had she actually recognized me? Did I only remind her of a certain Squire Pedino? If she recognized me, had she kept quiet because she genuinely cared about me? Or in order to avoid an immediate, chaotic fray – during the course of which the bishop, not she, might have killed me?

Nodding to Augusti, Lovats took Sara by the elbow and guided her towards the door.

Both their backs were turned on me. I might never see a better chance. I could probably kill Lovats unaided. I would be doubly a bishop-slayer, the boldest, most successful pawn-squire in the history of Bellogard.

Yet Sara had kept quiet.

They left.

Conceivably she had *not* pierced my disguise. What emotions had my resemblance to Pedino stirred? Revenge? Afflicted, forbidden affection? I spent the remainder of that working night in an agony of indecision, provoking Augusti's squeaky choler several times.

I was shaken violently out of sleep. Couldn't move. Couldn't utter a single word, magic or otherwise. A firm hand gagged my mouth. Other hands clamped my wrists and ankles. Sunlight glared through the tiny window of the cubby-hole where the curtain was ripped aside. Crowded! A pack of black militia. A dagger poised over my heart – held by Bishop Lovats.

Lovats bent to say, 'Any trouble, and you die immediately. Understand? We'll gag you properly. And bind you; and take you to the Khram.'

I let my mouth be gagged with a black scarf, and my

wrists be tied with cord. I was hauled to my feet. Lovats found my dagger which I had tucked beneath the mattress. He sniffed at the weapon, smiled, and slipped it inside his cassock.

Soon I was being force-marched in broad, dazzling daylight down through the otherwise deserted Sahdi Gardens. For the first time I took in the full vista of Chorny, at this hour a no man's land. The city wasn't beautiful, as Bellogard was. But at this moment the idea of Bellogard seemed specially inviting.

The chamber was panelled with sheets of glassy black obsidian. These were highly polished so that ghost images of myself and others appeared to be imprisoned inside the walls themselves. A single window was heavily draped. Twin oil-lamps cast deep, luminous mirror-pools in the obsidian which sought to drown our captive reflections.

I was forced into an oak chair. A militiaman looped a length of cord round my neck. He jerked the loop tight, blocking my breath. This was only to test the noose. He slackened the cord and positioned himself behind me. I felt a constant threatening pressure on my windpipe. My gag was removed, and the other militiamen drew back. Lovats planted himself before me, pointing a rapier at my heart. Behind him stood Sara.

She shook her head urgently as if to convey, 'Not me!'

Lovats must have read the look I darted her, since he smiled droopily.

'If you're wondering, it was *I* who guessed you were an imposter. Aided, I admit, by my squire's peculiar behaviour. When I questioned her, she confessed her suspicions about your identity. And a bit more, a bit more. This presents me with a pretty problem. In the normal course of events, after your interrogation you

140

would simply be held in check – permanently. Or else disposed of. It seems that either outcome might pain her; literally. Yet she's reluctant to kill you herself.'

I breathed out.

'Do *not* try to shout any magic words, will you? My man will garotte you at the very first such syllable. Feel free to speak ordinarily. In fact, become voluble. Explain your presence in fine detail. Unravel Bellogard's plan.'

How much had Sara told him? Had her shake of the head perhaps meant, 'Don't tell him that you spared my life! Don't tell him *all* about us!'?

Lovats pricked my chest with the tip of his rapier. I winced. Sara moaned faintly as if in sympathy.

'Sara suffers lightning headaches,' remarked Lovats. 'You must have injured her magically, mustn't you? Without spilling blood or cleaving flesh or breaking bones. How odd.'

'Should so many commoners overhear this conversation, Bishop?'

'Hmm, perhaps not. *I* shall hold your noose. Sara: you stay. Everyone else: wait in the corridor.'

The chamber soon cleared except for the three of us. Lovats stood at my shoulder; he had swapped his rapier for a dagger.

'With one hand I strangle you,' he said casually. 'With the other hand I stab you dead. Now, confess your follies to me as if to a father.'

'I may know a cure for your squire's headaches.' My voice quavered. 'Other than killing her,' I hastened to add.

'Is that the main reason why you smuggled yourself into Chorny?'

'One's motives are sometimes mixed.'

'I'm sure they are.'

141

'Our own Queen Dama used to dream of mutual survival through stalemate.'

'Never mind her. What's this cure of yours?'

'It involves our travelling into the Beyond together, shaking ourselves free from the rules of this world.'

'I see. Eloping from reality. Using *what* as a guide?'

'I think I know the answer to that, sir. We would use the sign of the serpent.' I described how a certain knight of my acquaintance had glimpsed an enormous serpent out in magic space. I mentioned how Mr Augusti had deduced the same image from his study of the spectra of ghost stars. 'If this sign of Augusti's were sketched in magic paint, and if this were used as a guide – as a focus, a compass – maybe we could reach the actual boundary zone between one universe and another. If we could, the law about magical injuries might be suspended. She would be cured.'

Sara was staring in amazement. 'We would travel there together?'

'You see, there's a resonance between us. Congruence; sympathetic vibration.'

'*If* the two of you could kindly postpone your courtship till a later occasion? I should like to know more about this "certain knight". Such as his exact whereabouts at this moment.'

'Honestly, I've no idea.'

'Honestly, indeed. I'll rephrase my question. He's lurking somewhere in our kingdom, right? You would hardly have travelled here without any back-up. From what you say you must recently have hitched a ride through magical space. Bellogard's mounting an attack; isn't that so?'

I said nothing.

'A single knight isn't sufficient. Prince Ruk or Bishop Veck must also be involved. Kindly tell me.' Lovats jerked the noose but slackened it before causing too much discomfort. 'You planted yourself in the Planetera, Squire. Presumably I'm the main target. Am I supposed to feel kindly disposed towards you?'

'Bishop Lovats isn't evil.' Sara spoke pleadingly, as if it was I who held a dagger to the *bishop's* throat.

'If somebody's backing me up,' I said, 'and if I tell, you would want me to lure them. How could I ever do that?'

Lovats sighed. 'There's no advantage, whoever wins. One gets so very tired at times! The endless struggle, the knowledge of doom. One yearns for the final day. Are you feeling sick of existence, Squire?' The blade touched my throat.

'It might be possible for a few of us to escape magically into some other universe.'

'I do believe you're trying to seduce me from my solemn duties. Enough of this prevarication! Answer me.'

I had no chance to answer, or not answer. The door crashed open. Surrounded by black militia, a wiry, wily, bitter figure hobbled into the chamber, a crutch tucked under his armpit. I recognized Prince Feryava.

'Well captured, Bishop! Well captured, indeed.'

The prince's eyes were black coals but they also burned feverishly. A slim drooping black moustache framed his mouth.

'You mustn't keep him to yourself, Bishop! King Mastilo will enjoy interrogating this whelp. I shall escort him to the palace.'

'How did you know about this so soon, Feryava?'

'We don't have personal secrets, do we, noble Bishop? We *are* on the same side, aren't we?'

'Aye, that we are – by destiny! I suppose a militiaman tipped you off. I wonder which one?' Lovats patted me upon the shoulder. 'You'll have to go with the prince, young man.'

'No!' cried Sara.

'No?' Feryava echoed sarcastically. 'Did I hear a squire of Chorny speak? Has your stay in Bellogard corrupted you?'

Lovats said to Sara, 'Obedience. Loyalty. *Patience*.' He stressed the last word. 'The final battle may be imminent. All may soon be over. Nothing much will happen till nightfall. We wouldn't wish to disturb Their Majesties' rest, eh, Feryava?'

'True.'

'You had best use the time to question Mr Augusti, Sara. Wake him up. Don't let him *snake* out of answering. See that he paints a true picture for us.'

'Oh yes. I will.'

Dared I hope?

I was gagged again and led out. Several curtained carriages waited outside the Khram, their horses sneezing and snickering in the unfamiliar sunlight.

Twenty minutes later I was hustled out of a carriage into the deep, shady well of a palace courtyard. Torches were lit, and I was shoved through a stone doorway. Worn, narrow steps, forty or fifty of them, led steeply downward.

Into the bowels of an enormous vaulted dungeon.

I didn't like what I saw. Two obese, hairy-chested gaolers snored on straw pallets. A brazier glowed, with a branding-iron resting in the charcoals. A set of stocks was riveted to one roughstone wall – at least three metres from the ground so that any prisoner locked in that contrivance would have to hang upside-down by the ankles. Worse, his feet would be fixed horizontally. How long could he keep his knees bent to ease the strain? Ten minutes? While his twisted ankles, gouged by rigid iron loops, took his whole weight. Ankles might snap. The

144

victim would hang by broken bones with his own bulk dragging dreadfully.

There were other vile devices. A rack. Hoists and pulleys. An iron maiden. Thumbscrews.

This was *Chorny*? The city of gaslight and science and the railway? I felt utterly sick. Faint with fear. Feryava hadn't come downstairs. The militia roused the gaolers, who chained my wrists behind my back, and added a leather gag. Bare-chested, dressed in open leather waistcoats, with leather skirts like butchery aprons cloaking their great thighs, the brutes stank of body odour.

One gaoler nodded hopefully at those stocks upon the wall. The other grunted questioningly.

'No,' said a militiaman. 'Not quite yet. Stick him in a cell.'

Tiny cells occupied one wall. I was crammed into one of these filthy little cages. In the adjacent cubicle of bars lay a ragged human scarecrow. Maybe asleep, maybe dead. The rest of the cells were empty.

'Welcome to my pleasure chamber!'

Thus King Mastilo greeted me. The king's stout body was stuffed into a black uniform which did not quite manage to hide all his bulges. Red sash and sunburst and braid proclaimed him to be Generalissimo, or Grand Commander, or even High Admiral for all I knew. His legs tapered into incongruously dainty ankle-boots against which he tapped a furled whip.

('Is the wretch in the next cell your tailor by any chance, Majesty?') No, I didn't say anything of the sort. I had hardly shut my eyes all day. I was dizzy with terror and exhaustion.

Freshly fed and puffed by bellows, the brazier glowed hotly. Flaming torches had been lit. Sharp, precise militiamen stood to attention, reminding me of slim black hunting hounds. The gaolers shuffled about, grinning smugly and inanely.

Queen Babula had accompanied the king into the dungeon. Black silk clung voluptuously to the generous curves of a somewhat overblown, overripe body. Exposed flesh was powdered to a peachy bloom. Red hair was piled high with a black lace snood netting it, baring a sleek strong neck. Scarlet rouge painted a cupid's kiss smaller than her actual sulky lips. She held a bottle of scent or of drugs to her nose. Her dark eyes sparkled, dilated by what she inhaled. Purple kohl drew bruises of indulgence and depravity around them. She wore a dagger in a loose jewelled sheath.

The king rubbed kid-gloved hands together. 'First we shall provide a modest demonstration for our new guest. Gaoler! Haul out our *favourite* captive.'

The other man – so gaunt and raggy and crumpled – had hardly moved up until now. As soon as a gaoler unlocked his cell, the prisoner wailed and clung to the bars with demonic strength. The other gaoler had to assist at unpeeling the desperate man's fingers.

The man keened ever more shrilly as he was dragged to the rack. Once he was roped to it by wrists and ankles he fell silent, knowing his doom.

Gloating, Mastilo positioned himself close to the poor man's face. The gaolers started to turn handles.

Soon terrible screams and wild gasping groans were being wrenched from the fellow as he was stretched unbearably. I could hardly bring myself to look – only an occasional, horrified glance. King and torturers almost blocked my view.

Queen Babula sniffed her bottle more vigorously. Was that to dull her senses – or to enliven them?

'And now,' cried Mastilo, 'let's brand his privates with the iron, and really hear him sing!'

This was done.

The excruciated wretch sang his way into insensibility. I vomited emptily. Gagged, I almost choked on what bile there was.

The rack was slackened, the ropes loosened. The man was dragged back to his cell. He lay moaning like a creaky door.

How had he clung to those bars with any strength whatever, if he was a frequent victim of such torture? When horror is extreme, perhaps a man can run on broken legs!

'Now it's your turn, Squire. What shall it be? The iron boot, with splints hammered in? The pulley, and dislocated arms? Or will you tell us Bellogard's plan?'

'Please, Your Majesty, I'm a prisoner of war.'

Mastilo sniggered.

I was dragged to the rack and tied to it. The handles were turned sufficiently to pull me taut. The king held a poniard to my heart as my gags were removed. My throat was raw from the bile. At Mastilo's signal the rack-ropes were pulled even tighter. How long could I hold out while I was being strained out of shape, bones unsocketed, sinews stretching like elastic till they tore?

I'm not ashamed to say that I began to babble out our plan of attack, before any actual agony could deform me. The ropes relaxed a little.

Soon after, Bishop Lovats came hastening down into the dungeon. Sara followed, carrying something small. The bishop's gaze flicked over the scene; he laughed barkingly, derisively.

At me, in my terrible predicament?

Wrenching my head up, I caught a fleeting glimpse of the previous torture victim. He was standing quietly by the bars of his cage, watching the rack and me in frank fascination.

A hateful understanding dawned. The favourite victim was a hireling! He was an actor who only pretended to suffer grievous torments – agonies which were never actually inflicted! King Mastilo was as big a buffoon as our own King Karol. The one enjoyed blowing magic bubbles. The other revelled in mock torture scenes, sadistic masquerades.

I did groan then.

Babula mopped my brow with a frilly handkerchief reeking of patchouli. She stroked my cheek.

'Aha, sweet little pigeon, you have guessed! But *that* alters nothing.'

Another arrival in the dungeon: a bearded knight wearing black chain-mail. Sir Loshad, no less. Behind, came two armed squires who must be Slooga and Jigger. All the forces of Chorny had gathered except for Feryava who must have difficulty negotiating stairs with his injured leg.

Babula called for order.

'All persons without magic: clear off!' (Militiamen and gaolers hastily departed.) 'The pigeon has sung, my dears! Sir Brant of Bellogard lurks in our woods, eager to gallop down on us. Prince Ruk hopes to leap all the way from Bellogard itself, so long as nobody gets in his way – and *nobody will*.

'Jigger: upstairs to the armoury! Bring sabres – then be off with you to Feryava's side. *Here* will be the field of penultimate battle. You and Feryava will cover the exit.' An obedient Jigger rushed away.

'As soon as we've destroyed Brant and Ruk, we'll set out for Bellogard. You, Lovats, carrying Sara. Loshad with Slooga. And me. Feryava and Jigger can stay to guard the king.

'We shall easily destroy Bishop Veck and that quarterqueen of theirs. Sara and Slooga can cope with the

Bellogard squires. We shall check and mate silly King Karol gloriously, with true panache. *Shamat!*'

Jigger returned with a clutch of sabres and was briefed. The assembled warriors (save for Sara) tested the blades, causing them to spark and flicker with the blue energy of magic. Jigger hurried back upstairs.

Babula said to the king, 'Would you kindly step aside out of harm's way into one of these cells of yours?'

'But, but, but!' blustered Mastilo.

'No buts.'

Tamely King Mastilo shut himself inside a vacant cell.

The queen waved a sabre in one hand, a dagger in the other. With the dagger point she pricked my bound hand stingingly.

'Sing again, Pedino the pigeon! Sing the magic attack call!'

I didn't sing.

'Come now, don't be coy!'

'My love,' the king called from behind bars, 'all the instruments of pain genuinely work. Please let's use them this once. This is a war emergency. It's the first time we've caught a bravo from Bellogard. He won't sing till you agonize him. Please let's use the thumbscrew! Hee, hee.'

The queen walked over to remonstrate; Lovats and Sara drifted closer to my side.

Sara stooped over me casually. 'You must cry the attack,' she whispered. She showed me what she held in her left hand. (A dagger was in her right.) It was a small picture, painted on glass, of a serpent coiling around a ladder. She had copied Augusti's spectral astrological discovery.

'Lovats and I will save you,' she murmured, 'and ourselves too, if anyone can be saved. So do it.' She drew away.

149

Mastilo was still trying to convince his wife that screws should be applied to my thumbnails. I didn't wait to see whether he would succeed. Sucking in breath, focusing my power, I bellowed, *'Opasnost po Zhivot!'* My bound hands prickled with electric magic.

Crying magic too, the queen and Sir Loshad immediately deployed.

Some fifteen seconds later, Sir Brant appeared from nowhere, bleary-eyed but waving his broadsword. A hint of mail showed beneath his rustic garb.

Brant didn't stand much of a chance. He was still summing up dungeon and pain-machines and personnel when Babula challenged him. This was a mere feint. While Brant defended himself against Babula, Sir Loshad hacked his neck from behind. Blood spouted. (With her blade Sara slit the ropes tying my ankles.)

Prince Ruk arrived magically a few moments later, wearing half-armour. He immediately attacked Sir Loshad who was still dispatching the staggering, blood-gushing Brant. Ruk disarmed Loshad with one powerful blow. Loshad's sabre clattered away. Squire Slooga leapt in the way, twirling another sabre at Ruk's face. Ruk hacked this weapon aside, savaging Slooga's forearm. Babula bustled bravely in and spitted Ruk's sword-arm. Ruk turned, still swinging his sword. Babula tried for his chest but the point of her sabre glanced aside. She retreated, weaving slashes in the air. Slooga, though injured, grabbed up a length of chain in his left hand, swung this, and by sheer luck caught Ruk around the neck, halting him in his tracks.

The air crackled with blue fire. Loshad had recovered his sabre. He shouted a war-cry which distacted Ruk who was still being throttled by the chain. Babula darted in and chopped Ruk across the wrist. (While Sara cut my left hand free.) Ruk was doomed now. His sword fell uselessly. With his sound hand he plucked a dagger from its sheath. Uttering a magic curse he hurled this dagger – the queen threw herself aside. The blade impacted instead in Lovats' belly, doubling the bishop over. Babula pranced at the disarmed Ruk and slashed through his throat. Ruk collapsed, to join dead Sir Brant on the flagstones. (Sara cut my last bond. She held my hand in place, and I made no effort to move.)

Lovats straightened up, keeping careful hold of the dagger. His face sweated pain as he trod slowly to the head of the rack. (Meanwhile Babula was ensuring that Ruk was dead.)

'It's a mortal wound . . . Leap a little way with me, my children. I uncheck you, Pedino. Both of you, help me.'

I scrambled up from the rack. Sara had tucked her dagger in her belt, and the painting inside her black chemise. She and I held tight to Lovats.

'On a magic count of three we'll jump a pawn-span together, just as far as the Sahdi Gardens – '

'But you're diagonal – '

'Jump *en passant*, idiot!'

'What's going on?' cried Babula.

'*Ahdyeen. Dvah – ,*' counted Lovats and Sara.

'*Yehdan. Dvah,*' I counted.

'*Tri,*' we chorused. We each spoke journey-magic. And moved.

We landed on a lawn in those silvery, gas-lit, scented gardens. Strollers on a nearby path took to their heels, perhaps to inform the militia. Lovats sagged against me, gasping. We helped him to lie down.

'Wonder . . . if Babula and Loshad . . . will still attack Bellogard? They've lost me and Sara . . . Slooga's hurt

. . . Might carry Jigger along with them instead . . . leave gammy-legged Feryava to guard the king . . .

'Quarter-queen, in Bellogard, and Bishop Veck . . . couple of able-bodied pawns . . . King Karol, mustn't forget King Karol . . .'

'Don't talk,' begged Sara.

'First they'll kill Veck . . . he's the real danger. With him out of the way they can easily take Queen Isgalt . . . then it'll be "*shamat!*" for old King Karol . . . and the world will end . . .'

Lovats writhed briefly before he spoke again.

'It'll take Loshad a few jumps to reach Bellogard . . . rendezvous with Babula . . . Isgalt'll be keeping an eye on her eidolons if she has any sense . . . she'll know Brant and Ruk are dead, she'll know I'm dying . . . "*shamat!*" for me, "*shamat!*" for everyone . . .'

He began to ramble; with an effort he concentrated.

'Leave me now . . . lurk in the city for an hour or two . . . when the world starts to fade or crack, leap out. Oh the *shamat* of the world.'

'How can we leave him?' asked Sara. 'Should we pull the dagger out?'

'Of course not,' I said.

Blood bubbled on Lovats' lips. Or a froth of saliva – hard to tell which in the darkness.

'Leave!' he barked. 'I command you.'

I suppose it was harder for Sara to walk away from Bishop Lovats. Until recently I'd only known Lovats as an enemy I was pledged to kill; Sara had known the bishop as a colleague and friend.

When we abandoned him in the gardens I did feel a pang of guilt. I may have been transferring an unacknowledgable burden of guilt at the way I had led Sir Brant into an ambush of death. Not entirely, though. I

152

regretted not having the chance to know Lovats better. I had much to regret.

I had something to rejoice in also, did I not? Namely, Sara's presence by my side? Just then, this did not compensate quite as much as it should have done. I felt emotionally numb. The world, the whole world, was about to end. The awful fire was coming; or the death of dust. With Bellogard defeated, with King Karol checked and mated by Babula, the war would be over. Both our kingdoms must decay, evaporate.

And yet Queen Babula was launching that final attack. And we of Bellogard had provoked it. By what daemons we were all driven!

Except, in this last hour, for Sara and me.

Cascade of crinkly black hair, delicate dark-eyed features . . .

We had reached Ulitsa Avenue by way of the back wynds – and who was Sara really, inside herself?

She was someone such as I had guessed her to be long ago – *known* her to be, when we were lovers – or she would not have saved me, as I had saved her.

She was a person whose life had been shaped by a daemon of destiny, but who then rebelled. Alas, no rebellion could ever overthrow the system – that was where our revolutionaries were in error – since the fabric of reality itself depended on the system. The physical world was only a projection of the magical war, which had always powered it.

We halted to take stock. Housewives, errand-boys, workmen in cloth caps hurried by. I gazed at Sara's face in the gaslight of the thoroughfare.

'Who are you, Sara? And who am I? Maybe now we can start to find the answer to both those questions!'

She wrinkled her nose in what I took for a panicked

moment to be a sneer of disgust. Then she moaned, and touched the side of her head.

'I ache . . .'

Her head, where I had clubbed her unconscious. She was driven by her daemon; she would have killed me otherwise.

She sighed. 'Pain'll pass.'

My own flesh stung where I had been pricked.

'Pain'll pass for ever, soon, Sara.'

'One way or another.'

'There's a café in Prakhoda Arcade,' I began.

She laughed. 'It would be really stupid to get drunk, and miss the end of the world.'

'Hmm, I didn't do too well the last time I drank there.'

'We should wait in the open. That way we can watch the sky, the roofs, the stars. We can be warned.'

We walked along to Perehod Square, crossroads of the city, and sat on a marble bench. Sara's migraine had faded away. We watched carts, carriages, and *fiacres* pass. We watched nameless Chornyfolk who all thought of themselves as individuals, even though each possessed only a tiny fraction of soul. A militiaman stared at us, so we held hands. We looked at the Mahgeela Tomb, dominating the north side of the square. Sara hummed a patriotic anthem from one of the composer's oratorios; I responded by whistling something frivolous of Spomenik's. An hour passed. Elderly folk sat on other benches; one ancient man fed crusts to pigeons. Two middle-aged lovers kissed. Mothers rested with toddlers. Women in dark serge swept the pavements with brooms.

A pair of militiamen approached. Sara's black chemise was open half-way to her breasts. One of the obsidian buttons was missing from her black uniform jacket. I was dressed in my off-duty Bellogard duds – jerkin, trousers, and shirt – which were dirtied and rumpled by a night in the cell and a spell on the rack.

The militiamen halted before us.

'You've both been here a long time.'

'On royal duty, Officers,' said Sara. '*Ahstav' meenya!* Go away.'

This particular phrase in the magical language of Chorny must have been familiar to the militia; an agreed palace code. The men nodded, moved on.

'Poor buggers,' she muttered.

'Them?'

'Yes, them. All of them.'

The sky was clear that night, and the civic gas-lighting only dimmed, but did not eclipse the stars. Thunder grumbled far away. The air trembled.

Glavny Boulevard was a valley between buildings, dammed by Vauxhall Station. Lightning flickered far beyond that dam, high in the heavens. Black cloud boiled into view from the north, eating the constellations. The ominous cloud-front rolled swiftly towards us.

'It's starting, Pedino!' We both stood up.

She produced the painting of the serpent. Together we held the painted pane towards the tomb so that reflected floodlighting shone through the glass, through that red and green serpent coiling about a ladder, jaws agape. We clung tightly to each other as though a storm wind was about to sweep us from the pavement.

Half the sky was hidden; or had ceased to exist. A curtain as wide as the world was rushing ever closer.

'Now, Sara?'

'No; watch Vauxhall Station. When something happens to that, we'll jump.'

We were both trembling. The city was trembling. Of a sudden Chorny was built not of stone and marble and ebony, but of sculpted black jelly.

One moment the floodlit façade of the station a couple of kilometres away was as monumental as ever. The next moment the station became . . . a ghost of itself. An image, not substance. A construction of dust; which vanished. Darkness gobbled Glavny.

'Now!'

We spoke magic, we leapt . . .

We didn't let ourselves return from the space-beyond-space. We knew there was nowhere to return to, only oblivion. I tried to put from my mind as nonsense everything I had ever known about our kingdoms, about kings, queens, knights, and bishops. About forward magic, crosswise magic, magic of the diagonal kind. These had no more meaning, no more relevance. I sought – without knowing what I sought – for othermagic. For strangemagic. I didn't try to image what strangemagic might be – how could I? I tried to *submit* to it.

Even whilst leaping we leapt again. We held the symbol of the serpent out before us.

From ultimate distance the serpent's huge head rushed towards us!

Its body stretched back to for ever, long and strong. The skin was a flexible mosaic, blotched green and red. Jaws yawned open, fangs wide apart. Tiny beads of eyes stared fixedly. Its gullet was red, black-dark deeper down. The mouth was a cave – we were only little birds or pipistrelles.

Down into itself the serpent sucked us . . . we were rushing, falling, sliding downhill through darkness absolute . . . towards a spark of light which suddenly swelled, dilated.

We lay sprawled in the filthy gutter of a sandy street. Fish-heads and maize husks rotted in a trickling stream that stank of urine. A scrawny cat spat, fur erect, and fled. Flies swarmed. Blinding sun beat down on endless rude shacks made from board and rusty metal sheets. Smoke drifted from eccentric chimney pipes. Grey scavenger birds spiralled overhead on wide, serrated wings.

As we scrambled up, skinny brown children shrieked and pitched pebbles at us. A fat woman in ballooning skirts and tatty blouse yelled resoundingly from a doorway. Perched on her head was a bowler hat.

Voices took up the cry: 'Snake-drop! Snake-drop!' Within moments a whole crowd of ill-clad men, women, and kids had boiled out of shanty doors, spilled from side-alleys.

They scowled, jostled, argued, grabbed one another, broke loose. Some ran up the sandy street; a few ran down past us. Others scaled the sides of shacks to scan the vicinity. Half a dozen people rushed directly at us.

Sara drew her dagger – I had none. Her blade held them at bay.

Or did it? Their actions made no sense. Did they want to rob us, strip us? Or what?

I heard a loud 'twanging' noise. As one person, all the beggar-people swung their heads towards the source. The tin roof of a sturdier dwelling built of mud-bricks was shining brilliantly. Sunlight rebounded upwards in a column of light. Within the light stood a tall ladder. It rose almost vertically without any support. The topmost rungs were foggy, vague, like a drawing half-erased.

First arrivals were already scaling the side of that adobe house, kicking toe-holds, clawing for finger-grips. Screaming, elbowing, shouldering, tripping, a mob thrust past us. Very soon a scrimmage milled against the wall. The strongest, the nimblest made progress upwards.

A tall burly man, atop the tin roof, hurled himself towards the ladder and climbed furiously. A lithe raggy woman was second. Next, an urchin of a boy. More people reached the roof and scrambled towards the ladder.

The first climber reached those top rungs. He too grew vague . . . he disappeared.

Followed by the young woman.

The urchin, too.

By now three more people were climbing furiously. One surged up the backside of the ladder, heedless of feet upon his fingers. The roof was starting to sag under the weight of bodies.

T-wang! The ladder vanished. Also the column of light. Three climbers fell out of mid-air on to their fellows below. Abruptly the roof gave way; the front wall collapsed as well. From amidst a cloud of dust came wailing and cries of pain.

Another ragged boy raced up to us and stuck his tongue out.

'You mista! You mista! Tha' wa' yer ladder, if you'd had a' sense. Now you'se a' neighbour, hey?' He grinned; a few teeth were missing. I could understand his slovenly talk after a fashion.

As the disappointed contenders extricated themselves from the wreckage, cursing and nursing minor injuries, some stumbled away disconsolately with no further interest in anything. Others eyed us, and headed in our direction.

The boy danced a circle round us, singing:

> Miss yer ladder
> Makes yer madder
> Than any adder!

I placed my hand over Sara's, upon the dagger hilt. I spoke magic: '*Opasnost po Zhivot!*'

No blue fire flickered round the blade.

'Let's leap, Sara. I don't like the look of this.'

'Yes.'

We spoke our journey-magic. Nothing happened.
Nothing at all.

'We seem to have succeeded,' I said to her. 'We're in
another world with other laws. What sort of laws? What
sort of world?'

The disgruntled slum dwellers idled towards us, cut
and bruised, their rags more tattered than ever by the
tussle.

Sara spoke quickly. 'I can guess a couple of the rules!
Kids play a game in Chorny – with dice on a board. It's
called *snakes and ladders*. Snakes swallow you and dump
you in the shit, far from your goal. Ladders let you climb
a long way to somewhere better. This is a world of snakes
and ladders. I'll bet you we've just slid into the worst of
slums, furthest from anywhere we ever want to be. And
I'll bet you that normal travel won't get us anywhere with
any certainty!'

'Shall we ask our new hosts?' (Who continued to
advance, with no great haste.) 'Or shall we run for it?'

Many other spectators were arriving, attracted by all
the commotion, or by the recent sighting in the distance
of the magic ladder.

It was rather too late to run anywhere.

PART THREE
Strangemagic, Kingmagic

The boy's name was Albertini. He seemed to have adopted us as his good luck, which was good luck for us since Albertini knew slum life inside out.

'Never short'n me name!' he warned us. Albertini (not 'Teeny') looked seven years old, but was actually twice that age. Some disease of the glands had retarded his growth, making him a likely loser in the scramble for magic ladders. The few times when he found himself close to a ladder and tried to scamper over other people's backs he had been plucked loose and hurled aside hurtfully, not least to his pride.

'A'm gonna 'scape someday,' he vowed.

'Us too,' said Sara. 'Not just some day. Next week! Tomorrow! I hate it here.'

We were sharing Albertini's new billet: a large hole scooped in the side of a chalky pimple of a hill ten minutes' trot from where we'd been dumped by the snake. Sections of rusty corrugated iron propped on struts reinforced the crumbly ceiling. Sacking hung over the entrance.

This den used to belong to the agile urchin who had succeeded in scaling the ladder. Albertini had promptly occupied this choice dwelling, with some assistance from us.

'No use tryin' fer the big fella's place – or the wench's. Too many other grabbers,' Albertini explained. We had arrived neck and neck with another savage orphan, who also witnessed the departure of the previous owner to some happier part of the world. We'd established squatters' rights by virtue of muscle, a few flourishes of

163

Sara's knife, and belligerent screams from Albertini. Slum etiquette dictated that we now owned this shelter. This hole in the hill was a big improvement on the boy's previous circumstances, namely dossing in the open.

A slum wasn't necessarily full of vicious people who were always perpetually at odds; merely of men, women, and children who were numbly desperate, whose daily life was one of degradation salted with wild, selfish, unlikely hope. An etiquette did exist. If need be, rules of behaviour were enforced by a 'people's court' and brutal beatings. Area by area there was even civic organization in such matters as maintaining the water supply, carting excrement away, and guarding communal goats that grazed the weeds. As citizens of this new realm we must soon take our turn at labour or else be beaten up and expelled into another sector.

These slum dwellers grew maize and vegetables, kept chickens, pigs, and goats, and farmed fish in dirty ponds. Other foods appeared by magic every now and then in the form of little hills of scraps and stale left-overs. Second-hand goods, too: used building materials, worn-out clothes, whatever. Snakes regurgitated these tawdry supplies by night, presumably having extracted them from more prosperous, salubrious parts of the world. Thus the slum subsisted, always hungry, always dreary, ragged, and dirty.

At first Sara and I were cautious how much we told Albertini of our previous magic lives. When he realized that we were holding back he flew into a bitter rage. I decided that offending our diminutive ally wasn't the wisest policy.

Amazing what a compact presence Albertini had. He wasn't a little boy; he was a wild gnome, a skinny bundle of passions, dreams, ambitions. He was cunning, bitter, honourable, intelligent, ignorant.

Had he knowledge of sex? Even with himself? Was he potent? He showed scant interest in Sara's body when we lay together in the chalk cave at night, with a candle stub for our lamp and sacks for bedding. Admittedly Sara didn't expose too much of herself. Maybe sex hadn't yet crossed Albertini's mind. It certainly crossed mine (which is why I mention the matter). Sara and I hadn't made love for four years. The present surroundings hardly seemed propitious, but when I lay in the sack I ached.

To backtrack, our confessions quickly sweetened the boy. Albertini's immediate assumption was that Bellogard and Chorny must be remote cities somewhere else in his own world, desirable residences which might be reached by magic ladder. It took a while to convince him that a place could exist which wasn't ruled by magic snakes and ladders – especially when I admitted that it no longer *did* exist. Was this a subterfuge of ours? He huffed and puffed. Weight of detail persuaded him.

He accepted our account of the crackling blue void as what you would experience when mounting the topmost rungs of a ladder; should you be so lucky.

From tales – some hearsay, some first-hand – of people snatched by snakes and dumped in this slum to live as paupers, Albertini had a foggy idea of the better parts of the world. Did he embroider romantically, luxuriantly, upon this sketch in his mind? I guessed this might be Albertini's fatal flaw (in addition to his glandular stature). He made the 'outside' seem too wonderful, too distant. A dream. Which meant that in his heart of hearts he didn't genuinely believe in eventual success. Thus he would fail.

The boy's scepticism at aspects of my description of Bellogard modified my opinion. How easy it would have been to incorporate Bellogard fantastically into personal mythology. Albertini refused this option. Instead he pierced through to what he claimed was the most salient item of all: Sara's picture of the serpent which had summoned an actual snake to swallow us.

She still had the glass with her; it hadn't broken in transit.

Albertini grew excited. 'Yer scrape the magic paint off. Colour by colour. Yer wet it again. Yer paint a ladder!'

She explained, 'You can't *do* that with paint.'

Myself, I spotted a more fundamental obstacle. 'Why should that magic still work? Our other magic won't work here.'

'Ha! Yer other magic b'longed to yer Chorny an' Bellogard. Snakes b'long 'ere.'

'Even if we could summon a snake,' said Sara, 'what's the point?'

'A'll tell yer. Ladders of'n 'appen near snake-drops, soon after. Saw that yerself. Gives the dumped sods a chance; not as they're of'n in much of a state to take 'vantage.'

So far as Albertini could tell, only one person in a thousand ever climbed a ladder or was swallowed by a snake. However, once this had happened to a person they were likely to encounter more snakes and ladders.

'Most folks live ord'nary, see? Sweet lives, shit lives. Stuck in 'em.'

I was puzzled. 'Why don't people walk away from shitty lives to somewhere better?'

'Can't cross squares, stupid.'

'Squares?' asked Sara. 'Same as on a chequerboard?'

'Dunno nuthin' 'bout boards. In't boards as stop us. It's cracks. Great plungin' cracks as wide as from 'ere to the reservoir divin' down f'rever. Only way to 'nother square's by snake or ladder.'

'So this world's divided up into huge separate squares of land? Square countries?'

'Hasta be, Sara! Seen the nearest crack, meself.

Wouldn't much fancy fallin' in. Listen a me: yer call a snake . . .'

'And it dumps us somewhere else in this neighbourhood where we don't even own a hole in the ground.'

'Naw, Puddino. Yer hold yer magic glass backwards or upside down. Mebbe snake has to b'have like a ladder? Whisk us away? If not, yer'll see a ladder next.'

We decided to give this a try the very next night. Sara was no more anxious than I was to commence our civic duties of scavenging, shit-shifting, and goat-herding. The slum was vast, but – as I say – petty bosses ran each zone and we could expect a visit before long.

Sara and I perched on top of our chalk hill watching a splendid crimson sunset, the only gorgeous thing hereabouts. Smoke rose from cooking fires. The air was hot and foetid. Buzzards and vultures circled. Albertini was elsewhere, on the scrounge.

She and I held hands.

And she told me about herself; many things which I'd never known.

The Squire's Tale

'I was an orphan, though I wasn't raised in quite the same way as Albertini! In Chorny the state looked after orphans, and it often took kids of cruel or indifferent parents into custody. I was told that my own parents – a metallurgist at the Royal Mint and his wife – both died in a flu epidemic when I was three months old; I had no memories of them. I was brought up amidst five hundred brothers and sisters in the state orphanage operated by the Khram, supervised by Bishop Lovats.'

'Five hundred brothers and sisters!' I thought how I had screwed up the life of my one and only sister.

'We were a cadre of comrades. Bishop Lovats was our

commander; and our father too. He was the only father we knew. I was thirteen years old when the magic rose in me, to my considerable surprise. It was an even bigger surprise when Lovats revealed to me in private that he was *actually* my father.'

'What?'

'Flesh of his flesh: that was me.'

'Was the man at the Royal Mint an invention?'

'Oh no, he existed. The bishop had arranged the marriage – and the royal appointment. Lovats had already coined me in my mother's womb, had Lovats. He stamped his die upon her virgin womb-flesh in an episode of passion and magic and scientific astrology. Joy entered into the event – he swore – but calculation too. You see, Lovats wanted to create a magic child of full soul. He wanted to see if we can determine our own destinies magically. If we can endow another human being deliberately with *special* magic.'

'He succeeded royally! I'm so sorry, Sara.'

'Sorry that he succeeded?'

'Sorry that he died, you goose! Sorry that I came to Chorny meaning to murder him.'

'Hmm. After he told me, I wondered whether any of the *other* orphans were also flesh of his flesh. Maybe so! Since they never showed magic talent, he never acknowledged them. Or maybe I had half-sisters or brothers in the city, whose parents hadn't died of flu . . . His goal was to breed a "strange-piece". Someone who could act in a different way from a pawn or a bishop, or a knight or a prince. A magical piece never seen before. Well, I was only a squire. I didn't possess a medley of talents, though he persisted in trying to tease these out of me.'

'Your mother couldn't have been magical herself?'

'Hardly! There's only space in any kingdom for twelve

people with full soul, isn't there? My mother had to be a commoner – endowed with a decent slice of soul.'

'Were there no female squires before you? Ones who died in the war? Lovats would have preferred to experiment with a magic woman, wouldn't he?'

'There weren't any. As for Queen Babula, well . . . ! Whore that she was with handsome young soldiers, the notion of a bishop in her bed would have offended her sense of propriety. I'll rephrase that: a bishop would have been her equal, almost. Her casual lovers were just dildos, not personalities.'

'Whore . . .' I hadn't meant to repeat that word. When I met her, Sara had been a whore on Groody Lane. To change the subject I asked, 'What's a dildo?'

'You don't know?'

'No. Should I?'

She giggled. 'A dildo is an artificial erect penis, made of wood or stiff rubber or throbbing clockwork machinery. An impotent man might wear one. Or a woman who loved another woman. A man might want a woman to use one to penetrate *him*. That's how Mastilo got his rocks off with his queen. King Mastilo liked to pretend to inflict pain. Submission to a dildo was the other side of that coin. It amused Babula to have her monarch crying out beneath her. That didn't entirely *satisfy* her. Hence the young soldiers. Babula would quit the king's bed and summon a private. A whore,' Sara added, 'needs to know such things.'

'Um,' I said.

'How to satisfy men – often in odd ways. A whore is an actress.'

'Were you an actress when we made love in Bellogard?'

'At first. Not the second time. Don't look so solemn, Pedino! Such things as dildos and men's oddities matter less to women. The machinery of love matters less.

169

Feelings matter, that's what. The antics amuse us. I used to talk to the other ladies on Groody Lane.'

'So nothing you did in Groody Lane counts. You're telling me this in case I'm jealous?' (Was there a whine in my voice?)

'I'm telling you so that you don't feel the need to compete – or over-exert yourself fancifully. If so, you would be competing with the dead. Not *very* much did happen in Groody Lane, you know! I was only looking for big catches. By the way, what became of Meshko?'

'Queen Isgalt had him locked up permanently, along with his painting set.'

'She did? Or did *you* have him locked up? Don't answer that!' Sara put her arm around me. 'At this moment a kiss would make me rather happy.'

I kissed her, deeply. She kissed me likewise.

A wolf-whistle rudely disturbed us. Albertini was scrambling up the chalk slope, clutching a bucket. Night was falling, but even in the poor light I could see that the bucket had a fair-sized hole in the bottom.

'Whatever's that for?' I asked him 'A tin hat?'

'Carries stuff, don' it? Lotsa *stuff*. What we'll pick up beyond yer ladder!'

Sara said, 'You believe we'll come back here, don't you? We'll only have time to grab a bucketful of . . . fresh oysters and a bottle of champagne; and a snake will swallow us.' Evidently she suspected what I had suspected. 'Well, we *shan't* come back. Throw your bucket away, Albertini. It might weigh you down. It might stop you climbing fast enough. Or is that bucket your anchor – to ensure that you fail, because you're secretly scared of succeeding?'

Albertini glared. He stamped petulantly. He swung the bucket. I thought he was going to clobber Sara with it but he sent the bucket flying away over the hill, to land with a clang and a clatter.

* * *

Midnight or thereabouts. A gibbous moon glowed bale-fully. The patterns of the stars were strange. The slum was silent.

Sara and I held the painted pane towards the moon, upside-down.

'Come, Snake! Come!' she cried.

We concentrated fiercely. I tried to arrange those alien stars in my mind into the spangles of a serpent's hide, the points of its fangs, the beads of its eyes.

Nothing happened for a while. Then I heard a sighing which became a hissing. Albertini performed a stifled dance of excitement, raising one leg high then the other in the style of a urinating dog. Perhaps he was limbering up for the climb.

A shadow hid stars. A shape loomed in the sky. A head rushed down towards our little hill. A mouth gaped – and spewed a torrent of all sorts of 'stuff'. Rotten apples, artichokes, dead fish, bundles of rags, turkey carcasses, calves' heads, sheets of cardboard: these tumbled, bounced, avalanched down the chalky slope to form a second hill alongside.

'We's rich!' Albertini dodged and snatched. He snared half a cucumber. Sara snatched this from him and threw it away.

The heavy rain subsided. The snake's mouth yawned over us emptily. Then the creature rushed away, vanished.

'Wait! Wait!' cried Sara. At the snake? Oh no, at Albertini. She was clutching his rag of a collar. He was trying to tear free to launch himself upon the adjoining hillock of rotten riches.

As though the moon had settled upon the earth, bright light bathed us. Glowing slopes and side-rails of a ladder sprang up from the tip of our hill.

Sara picked Albertini up bodily and jammed him on to

171

the ladder. 'Up! Up!' She followed, punching and jabbing at his heels. I climbed immediately behind.

'My dears, nobody – but nobody – has yet attained the final square, the happy isle of paradise. If any social climber ever. arrives there, why, that's the end of the world for the also-rans! All the squares will roll over and shake their denizens loose into the abyss. *Finis!* Save, no doubt, for the lucky winner who will enjoy bliss for evermore. Hence the incentive. Fortunately I hear that the last square is absolutely ringed by hungry snakes.'

The speaker was a corpulent, scented merchant, a purveyor of gourmet foods from whose shop Albertini had tried to filch a cheese to feed us. The merchant might have been fat but he was fast. He had seized Albertini. Sara had intervened and introduced us. Upshot: the merchant, Mendrix by name, had escorted the three of us to a restaurant which he owned, where he stood us a slap-up meal in a private room in exchange for our stories.

The room was beautifully panelled with many kinds of mock marble, jigsawed marquetry-style. Tangled up in Mendrix's acute questions I soon foolishly alluded to our magic glass. Sara kicked me on the shin under cover of the tablecloth. More questions followed. She had no choice but to show the glass to Mendrix, though she kept tight hold of it.

Mendrix excused himself. On his return, before he closed the door, I spotted a couple of hulking kitchen staff loitering outside. It was soon evident that Mendrix wished to buy the glass from me. ('Handsomely! Ample recompense!')

Albertini's face turned sallow, almost green. Had he too noticed those doughty 'bouncers', who could easily shake the glass from our grasp? No, his stomach was rebelling. He had stuffed himself with quails' eggs in

172

spiced cream, venison steak topped with cranberries, asparagus, avocado loaded with lobster in mayonnaise. The boy slid from his chair, reeled to a corner of the room, and vomited convulsively. He stood stamping (though not in the vomit), furious with himself, angrier at losing the food than at his poor table manners.

'Not to worry, loves. Boston!' Mendrix called loudly. One of the hulks burst into the room.

Mendrix gestured at the corner. 'Alas, the cat has been sick. Do please clear up.'

Boston fetched brush and pan, bucket and mop, and obliged; retreated outside again.

Mendrix beamed at Albertini. '*Do* rejoin us. Try some buttered spinach. Blander! Must fill up those cracks, mustn't we?' He only wrinkled his nostrils somewhat as the boy reclaimed his seat.

We were in the heart of a large and prosperous city. The second-floor window of the room looked out on a fine thoroughfare. Buildings were of clean white brick, pink stone, glazed tiles. Street attire was elegant: flounced skirts, bolero jackets, brocade hats with feathers for the ladies, well-tailored tweed suits, silk shirts, and cravats for the men. Our ladder had taken us a long way up in the social scale. Unfortunately we had no apparel to match; we resembled the contents of dustbins.

'Who would want to leave here?' asked Sara, nodding at the window and the world outside. 'Can there be a better place?'

'There can indeed,' replied Mendrix. 'A demesne of fine estates, stately homes, and faery castles. Utter aristocratic elegance! Sheer sensual freedom. Frivolous quests for that last brief ladder which flees like a rainbow from the seeker, impossible to attain, *totally* impossible, my sweets! I find *this* place somewhat bourgeois for my taste. Now, about the magic glass . . .'

Albertini jerked a thumb at Sara and me. 'Only works for them two. Can't run off yerself an' use it.'

'Who knows, maybe it only works for the delightful Sara?' Mendrix patted her on the knee. 'And for whoever accompanies her.' An acute observation . . .

Conscious of his error, Albertini growled in annoyance.

'When we reach the demesne,' Mendrix continued, 'we should of course smash the glass, don't you think? Do take another caviar vol-au-vent!'

'Smash it?' I asked.

'Oh yes. The demesne is only one step short of the happy isle. We wouldn't wish some fool to purloin the glass and actually reach the isle! What, wreck everything?'

Sara said, 'Why do you want to *buy* the glass, if we're all going to climb together?'

Mendrix shrugged amiably. 'Who knows what weight a ladder will bear? Someone may be left behind. They'll need resources. I would *hate* anyone to feel hard done by. To have to thieve cheeses.'

'Yon slobs outside might want a go if *they* find out,' said Albertini.

'Oh my boys know their proper place.'

'Look, yer okay 'ere. Well stacked. Minute yer got there, snake might snatch yer. Whee! Be in wor old stinkin' slum.'

'A calculated risk, I'd say. I never attracted the attention of snakes before.'

'Mix wiv magic, an' yer will.'

'Maybe we should keep the glass for a while . . . as a precaution. Try some halva, Sara. It's too palate-teasing.'

Just then, we heard a hubbub rising from the street. Albertini scuttled to the window. We followed.

People were hastening this way and that. Cries, alarm, excitement! A great snake was swooping slowly down between the rooftops. Descending low, it snatched at a fleeing couple, sucked them into its mouth.

'Poor dears,' sighed Mendrix. 'For their sake let's hope it's only a *short* snake.'

The snake had departed. Down below people were staring expectantly hither and yon.

A flash of light! A ladder rearing from the street! Before anyone could reach the spot, that shining route upward vanished.

'Ga! Tha' wuz quick!'

'The closer you are to paradise, the slimmer your chance,' Mendrix commented.

'Yer'll need a jumbo one.'

'Which I shall have. Shan't I?'

'I'm going to have to stick my knife in him,' muttered Sara. Mendrix was by the open door, whispering to his burly employees.

'Lotsa blubber. Could cushion 'im.'

'I don't *want* to do that.'

'Want to do what, my dear?' asked Mendrix, returning.

'Eat any more, thank you.'

'Good. We shall now undertake a short journey.'

'To yer home. Grab yer strong-box?'

'Dear boy, *I* am my own strong-box.' Mendrix patted his girth. 'When a snake might snatch a person from the street, only an idiot would fail to carry at least some of his wealth in portable gems. No, we shall visit the Predmest Gardens. Lots of wide open space. Do let me have the glass for safe-keeping.' He slapped himself. 'Well padded against shocks, eh?' He burrowed in an inner pocket, took out a small leather bag, unpopped a metal clasp. His plump fingers drew out a large diamond of the first water; two, three.

'For you, boy.' Albertini snatched the sparkler.

'Yours, Pedino.' When I frowned, Mendrix gave my jewel to the boy.

'And yours, my precious.'

Sara shook her head. 'I'm not selling.' The third jewel also ended up in Albertini's clutches.

Mendrix stuck out his empty hand. 'For security's sake. Come, come! Those lumps of ice have been accepted in all good faith on your behalf by tiny Teeny here.'

'Whadya mean!' Insensate, Albertini threw himself at Mendrix, impacting on his upper slopes, clawing, gouging, kicking.

Mendrix staggered, ripped the boy loose, and tried to hurl him at – and through – the window. Albertini clung round the man's arm like several infuriated tomcats. A moment later Sara was at Mendrix's throat, holding her blade close against his windpipe.

'Freeze! Don't call out!'

Albertini scrambled acrobatically up to Mendrix's shoulders. He swiftly recovered his wits.

'Gimme knife, Sara. Me hold.'

Sara passed the knife just as Boston and companion erupted through the door to investigate the commotion. Mendrix emitted a gurgling bleat. 'Staaay awaaay!' Both beefy bouncers obeyed, gaping at the knife-wielding monkey riding their master.

'Merely a minor impasse,' mumbled Mendrix.

'Quiet!' Sara went to the window, threw it open. 'Over here, lard-tub.' She produced the painted pane, beckoned me urgently. Together we held the glass up at the sky.

'Come, Snake! Come, ladder! Come to me!'

'Ooooh,' moaned Mendrix in excitement, frustration, apprehension.

To the amazement of pedestrians a second snake homed in on the thoroughfare – and disgorged a gorgeously costumed fellow, upon his butt. He wore a short *diamanté* cape and fluted lace ruff, velvet breeches tucked into bucket-top boots. No doubt he was some princeling or baronet from the demesne. His broad-brim hat with sweeping plumes had fallen off. Clapping this back on his head, the dandy scrambled up, cursing and raving as the snake sped away.

Our window-ledge was bathed in light. A ladder rose up towards the rooftop. Sara gestured me out, and on to the ladder. I managed the transfer with only one dire moment of vertigo. She followed me.

I glanced back, to see Albertini emerge and climb, knife clamped between his teeth. Seconds later, Mendrix was wallowing half-way out of the window. He gripped a glowing spoke. He hauled.

The three of us found ourselves in a palisaded park. Fallow deer scampered in flight. A stag snorted, pawed, dipped the shovels of its antlers before turning bobtail.

Mendrix hadn't followed us through. He must still be sprawled across that window-ledge – unless he had tumbled into the street.

Well-spaced oak trees shadowed the pasture. A hall of sandstone, broad leaded windows, and many curiously spiralling black chimneys fronted the green across a gravel drive. Letters of carved stone as tall as a man stood up all around the cornice, spelling out this motto: NOBILITY IS A GRACEFUL ORNAMENT.

Three lean black hounds on a triple leash tugged a man in livery along. Several horse-drawn carriages stood attended by swanky grooms. A lady and gentleman paraded under parasols, arm in arm.

I said to Sara, 'You must have othermagic! You couldn't use it while you were in Chorny, that's all. It had no place there. But now . . .'

She flashed a grin. 'I'll tell you one thing I certainly *don't* have, and haven't had ever since we landed in the dump.'

'Headaches? You're cured?'

'I believe so.'

'Ahh.'

'We bin noticed.'

A stately figure of a fellow was approaching at leisurely pace through the trees, surrounded by a feather-brained entourage of maids and pages, to whom he indicated us with an ormolu cane. He was clad much like the unfortunate whom the snake had dumped, though this grandee was older and silvery-haired.

'Holy Kerist! We's in clover. Well, a'll be a king.' Albertini capered.

'Hoy there! Raggy parsons, I say!'

Our two parties converged.

With a wink to me, Sara curtsied to the eminence. 'Please excuse our trespass, sir! May we present ourselves? Here is Sir Pedino of Bellogard. I'm the Lady Sara of Chorny.'

'Indeed? Delighted. At least you're well-spoken. Where might those places be? Somewhere in the lower strata, I presume. No matter. Fate may snatch anyone upward, or lay them low. I expect this is your son?'

Albertini produced the three diamonds. 'Me, a'm their purse.'

'What a mature sounding lad, if uncouth! What amusing gemstones.'

Albertini made two jewels disappear and thrust the third at the noble. 'Gift, sir, Lord. Yer give us a roof, few nights, huh?'

'Goodness me.' As if inadvertently the noble's hand strayed to claim the offering. 'Doubtless a space may be found in our stables.'

'Stables, nuthin'.'

We were scrutinized.

'Hmm. A hot barth, liberal application of toilet water, one's hair dressed properly, a decent gown loaned . . . one might be presentable. Lovely, even! A fair ornament to our frolics. You too, Sir What's-your-name.'

'Pedino.'

178

'Me an' all!' Albertini juggled the two remaining diamonds.

'You are the merest child.'

Albertini puffed himself up. 'Me, a'm a dwarf, Lord, sir.'

The entourage giggled, till Albertini darted a ferocious glare. 'Watch it. A take no guff.'

'I *see* . . . a jester. Oh very well.'

Several hours later, pink from our baths, perfumed, primped, and reapparelled, we attended a soirée in the ballroom.

Sara was a sensuous dream in a low-cut evening gown, flounced and furbelowed, her hair piled high. I cut a dash in a frock-coat with aggressive lapels and high, padded collar. My high-waisted tight white pantaloons made my legs seem like naked white marble. Albertini writhed uncomfortably in a miniature spangled black satin suit and buckled winkle-pickers borrowed from the nursery.

Our silver-haired host, the Honourable Marcus, was paying exaggerated court to Sara. The ballroom was thronged with elegance but the Hon. Marcus wouldn't let Sara leave his side, insisting on dance after dance to the music of the string quartet. Sara looked none too delighted at his suggestive endearments. Whenever I tried to cut in, the Hon. Marcus frowned thunderously.

'Me shoes pinch,' Albertini grumbled. 'Me clothes is stranglin' me. These phoney folk! Posh, smart talk. Two-faced toads.'

A plump, *décolletée* lady with black beauty spots on cheek and breast advanced fluttering an ivory fan. She frankly eyed my blatant thighs.

'The mysterious stranger! How absolutely special.'

'Let's get out of here, young Albert.'

'Where to, boss?'

'To the happy isle, the final square.' I had our painted

pane in an inside pocket; along with Sara's knife. She had nowhere to store anything, unless squeezed between her breasts or gartered to her thigh, where the blade would have been slow to retrieve.

I thrust through the crowd, Albertini at my heels. I slapped the Hon. Marcus brusquely on the shoulder, with an '*Excuse* me!' and caught Sara by the wrist. 'Let's step outside for a breather.'

'I say, sir!'

I let Marcus glimpse the knife.

'In yer tripes?' Albertini poked him by way of demonstration.

The three of us fled through French windows out on to a lawn. The gibbous moon loomed amidst curious constellations. Music and astonished chatter pursued us.

'They'll turn nasty,' warned Sara. 'Grooms. Dogs.'

I held up the glass. 'Call.'

She hesitated. 'It'll mean the end of their world. The end of all these squares . . . the slum, Mendrix's city.'

'Is that our fault? We don't belong, Sara.'

'Too right,' agreed Albertini.

'We have to move on. To the happy isle; maybe beyond to another world. Please call.'

'Why don't *you*?' She didn't wish to take responsibility.

'All right.' I held the glass to the moon. 'Come to me, Snake! Come to me, ladder!'

No snake veered down from the heavens. No sparkling ladder sprang up. Voices were calling out behind us. A hound gave tongue.

'Oh here, I'll do it.' She gripped the glass and called.

A snake came, and plucked at our hunters.

A ladder rose; we climbed.

A yellow beach curved along a turquoise bay. A far line of froth hinted at a reef. Palm trees drowsed. Some bird of paradise – emerald and scarlet – flapped from perch to perch. Albertini heeled off his narrow shoes and squirmed his toes deliciously in the sand. He ripped his suit open.

'Don' s'pose Lord Muck'd like this much!'

'Nor Mendrix,' said Sara. 'Quite uncivilized!'

'Suits *me* fine.'

'It looks promising.'

'For how long?' I asked.

I was starting to overheat in my clinging frock-coat and skin-tight pantaloons. Sara was luckier; her skirts made an airy tent for her legs.

My question was soon answered. The ground heaved ominously. Nuts showered down, fronds flapped. The entire island tilted with a groan, as if trying to turn turtle in the ocean. As the land rose, so the sea ran away from the shore.

The bay emptied out as we braced ourselves for balance. Sandy shelves were exposed, bedraggled weed, corals, and thousands of flamboyant fish. Big fish flexed and flopped; little ones bounced like fleas.

The island relapsed. Prior to a second effort to heave itself over? As the land sank the sea started to rush back – in a long, curling wave that looked higher than any tree on shore.

'Wha' a damn cheat! Five minutes, tha's yer lot. Call a snake, Sara! Get us outa 'ere!'

A ladder obviously couldn't help us out of this fix. Where could a ladder take us to? We'd won through to the last square of all. The other squares would already be turning topsy-turvy, shedding their inhabitants the way a tree sheds leaves . . .

'Hold hands!' Sara brandished the glass in her left hand.

The roaring wave was almost upon us when the snake arrived. The serpent head swooped down ahead of the wall of water. We were sucked up.

We rushed through a tunnel of darkness till the snake

vomited us out – into crackling blue emptiness. The snake immediately withdrew, abandoning us in the middle of nowhere. There was nothing visible in any direction. Nevertheless Sara and I both shouted journey-magic. Our former magic seemed effective. We sped onward.

But where to? We flew without a goal. I visualized beloved Bellogard. I tried to conjure the city of light. Alas, Bellogard no longer existed, so this was a waste of time.

'Where to?' Albertini squealed.

'*You* tell us!'

'Me? A'd pay any munny!' To indicate his willingness the boy jerked a hand free . . .

'Hold *on*!'

. . . and displayed one of our remaining diamonds. As a bribe to the blue.

'Any munny!'

'So would I!' cried Sara.

We appeared to change direction.

'Go to jail,' said the nondescript man who wore a blue uniform. He clashed bars shut before our bewildered eyes, and turned a large key.

'Hey! Wha' 'appened? Where are we?'

'You'll have your next turn this evening,' said the man in blue.

'Wha' turn?'

'You know the rules. Either you throw a double or you pay a fine, and you're back on the streets.'

'Double wha'?'

'Beats me what a kid's doing in here. But here you are.' With a shrug, our jailer departed.

Cells on two levels surrounded a tiled, iron-balconied hall which was lit by incandescent wires in glass tubes. This prison at least bore no resemblance to that ghastly dungeon in Chorny. Wasn't our turnkey *surprised* that three people had appeared out of nowhere in a vacant cell? Apparently not. He seemed a dullard.

Fortunately the very next cell was occupied by a gabby fellow. All soon became clear; relatively.

This whole world was ruled by money and by the acquisition of property, of 'real estate'. Life here was a constant round of purchasing houses, buying whole streets, charging rent, mortgaging streets to buy more streets – and to pay the exorbitant rents demanded by owners of other streets. All administration was in the hands of a labyrinthine bank where thousands of clerks worked. Maybe these drudges were the fortunate members of the community since bank employees were exempt – though also debarred from the rewards – in the everlasting battle for financial supremacy. In theory one single smart operator would one day become the 'monopolist' who owned the whole world, bank included. That day seemed far distant.

According to our informant every speculator was legally obliged to use his bank 'scrip' to play the game of property once a day. To this end, the bank paid a 'salary' to all speculators. But besides buying property a speculator worked at an ordinary job. Otherwise how could manufacturing or food production of any of the other necessities have been possible? We felt a bit perplexed. Did the whole property-owning population move house on a daily basis? How utterly confusing.

'No, no,' said our neighbour. 'Those are *legalmagic* moves I'm talking about.' He was a tubby, spotty man who perspired a lot. His name was Charley.

'Legalmagic?' repeated Sara.

'Yeah, yeah. Didn't your mummy and daddy tell you anything? You wouldn't have landed in jail unless you were making moves. Where do you guys come from, the utter sticks? I mean, this stuff about kings and queens and snakes. Really! And your funny, oh-so-rich clothes! Are you trying to set me up? What's the idea?'

'Please be patient with us, Charley.'

'Okay, so you know nothing. You just fell from the moon. Right: eyeball the magic box.' Charley indicated a red box bolted to the rear wall of his cell. An identical box was fitted in our own cell. An opaque glass plate occupied the middle part. Below, was an opening large enough to take a person's hand, with a metal bar to grip. At the top there was a thin slot.

'What's "bankrupt"?' asked Albertini. 'Yer menshoned tha' word a few times.'

Charley groaned. 'You go *broke*. Can't pay your rents or fines or taxes. No luck comes your way. You've already mortgaged or sold everything; you've no more scrip left. A big penalty hits you. You rupture, boyo. You just burst apart. Explode. Splat, blat. You're spread all over the street, kaput. Seen it happen myself. Guess it's a quick way to go. Beats life imprisonment with nothing to occupy yourself. How much scrip you got?'

I searched my pockets, just in case. 'We don't seem to have any.'

'*No* scrip? Zero? Zilch?' Charley jumped clear of the intervening bars, theatrically. 'I'm taking cover. Unless your luck's fantastic at the next spin of the box I'll be wiping pieces off me.'

'Maybe we ought to apply for a bank job,' I called.

'Personally I'd rather explode,' he called back.

'We go' this.' Albertini held up a diamond.

'Hey . . .' Charley rapidly shed his scruples about us disintegrating all over him.

Soon enough, scrip changed hands through the bars. A grinning Albertini flourished grey, green, and pink paper bills marked BANK OF MONOPOLIS and valued 10, 20, 50.

'If yer go' munny, man, why yer in jail?'

'On account of I was *sent* here, half-pint. Why else?'

'Half-pint!' Two seconds later Albertini was clinging to the bars, chattering with rage. Cautiously Sara and I soothed and unpeeled the boy. We mollified Charley, too, who had ducked and scrambled clear.

'The magic box?' she reminded Charley.

Once a day, it transpired, every speculator must stick his hand in one of those boxes and grip the handle. This put him in magic contact with the bank. The glass plate would light up, displaying a pair of random numbers from one to ten. The total would dictate your next 'move'. This move might 'land' you on vacant property worth buying, or on owned property where you would have to pay rent. You might win a surprise reward: a dividend, a tax rebate, which would pop out of the little slot at the top of the box. That slot was also where you would insert your rent and any other payments. You were just as likely to be fined, or taxed, or sent to jail.

'When both numbers come up the same, you get a second turn. If you score a subsequent double, that's fine. Three doubles in a row sends you to jail, right?'

Besides being an actual building employing a staff of thousands the bank was also a sort of brain using its spiritless clerks as its thoughts and memories. Collectively it was magical, with absolute power. If the bank sent you to jail you were instantly transported behind bars from wherever you happened to be, and be damned to your ordinary workaday existence.

'Who built the bank?' asked Sara. 'Who founded it?'

Charley scratched his head. 'There's always been a bank. The basis of society is financial, don't you see? Flow of wealth. Ownership of the means. Economic law of motion. Can't have life without lucre. Can't have territory without title-deeds. Economy precedes existence.'

* * *

185

Rations of black bread and watery lentil soup were wheeled round by blue-clad warders, who were bank employees. When the empty bowls had been collected again, a bell rang.

Charley hastened to his red box and stuck his hand in.

'Double seven!' he crowed. 'I'm out. What are you guys *waiting* for?' He vanished from his cell.

'I guess we follow suit,' said Sara.

'What happens,' I asked, 'if we *don't* use the box?'

'Presumably we stay in jail. I can think of merrier places to be. We'd better stick our hands in together. We don't want to get split up.'

'A'm fer cheatin',' said Albertini. 'How 'bout we push our magic glass in the top slot? Might gimmick the bank.'

'Why not?' agreed Sara. 'Let's do it.'

I handed the pane back to her. It slid easily into the gap and disappeared. We all squashed together, each pushed a hand into the big aperture, and gripped part of the handle.

The box hummed. The glass panel lit with a running message: JOINT ACCOUNT OPENED . . . ACCOUNT NAME: PEDINOALBERTINISARA . . . SCORE: 5 + 5 = 10 . . . GET OUT OF JAIL FREE; MOVE TO MONOPOLIS CENTRAL STATION . . .

With no sense of transition we found ourselves in the thronged concourse of a railway station. We were still clutching the handle of an identical magic box; quickly we withdrew our hands.

Brighter and slicker by far than Vauxhall in Chorny, this station was brilliantly lit from overhead by white-hot wires in glass tubes. No wrought-iron work here; only soaring planes and curves of some smooth, shiny material tinted crocus-yellow and azure. The floor was of the same substance, coloured grey. Engines waiting at the platforms had no chimneys. Engines and carriages alike were streamlined cylinders with flush, curved windows.

Crowds were hastening to catch those trains, to depart. Most men wore suits, of pin-stripe or corduroy or denim. Women wore frocks, or twin sets, or suits just like the men's. My own tight, chest-high pantaloons and Sara's *décolletée* ball-gown attracted amused comments, but really everyone was in too much of a hurry to linger.

The box beeped urgently. STATION FOR SALE . . . COST: 200 . . . DO YOU WISH TO BUY?

'What does it think we are? The Royal Chorny Railway Company?'

'Lemme buy, Sara! Charley paid couple 'underd.'

'We'll have nothing left.'

'Look a' all these folk! We charge 'em rent. Charley said so. An' wor'll have a home.'

'A home in a station?'

'A'm seein' food 'n' drink. Seats to sleep on.'

Albertini fed our BANK OF MONOPOLIS bills into the top slot. In return a stiff glossy square popped out. Albertini frowned and handed this to me.

TITLE-DEED. Lines of instructions and figures followed this heading; on the backside, dire warnings about mortgages. I read the deed aloud slowly then gave it back to Albertini.

The glass continued to glow. DOUBLE THROW . . . SPIN AGAIN . . . 7 + 3 = 10 . . . MONEY CHEST! BANK PAYS YOU DIVIDEND OF: 200 . . .

Two crisp red money-bills emerged. Albertini leapt up and down.

Alas, we weren't to receive any rent from the thousands of commuters using our station. The true situation was drummed into Albertini by the third traveller he accosted, clinging to their jacket, waving our title-deed, clamouring for cash.

Rent was only transferred to our account when the bank spun numbers which theoretically landed another speculator on Monopolis Central Station. The speculator wouldn't turn up in person; the only magical, instant journeys were those to jail, and out of jail again. Since the bank spun numbers randomly there was no guarantee that anyone would land on our property. Yet considering the huge number of speculators the law of averages suggested that we should soon be racking up invisible earnings . . .

Another rude awakening was our discovery that bank scrip couldn't be used to pay for the daily necessities. When we tried to buy some food in the station café, the cashier rebuffed our red 100 bill. 'Credit cards' were used for all such mundane transactions. These were oblongs of the stiff, glossy stuff called plastic which kept a magical tally of your consumer spending balanced against your ordinary income. The cashier showed us her own. We had no such cards, nor any source of routine income.

A skinny, amiable cleaning woman who was waiting for café and station to empty out for the night took pity. She said that at nine o'clock the next morning we should present ourselves at the job centre outside the station to register for employment. On our way from there to whatever work was allocated we could call in at any branch of the bank, show our job centre chit, and apply for a credit card.

'Can't we ge' a card wi' this?' Alternately smirking to propitiate the woman and scowling to deter her from any criminal ambition – a mad medley of facial tics – Albertini let her see our last remaining diamond.

Her eyes widened. 'Oh yes. Oh I should think so. If it's real, not paste. Take it straight to a bank tomorrow, that's my advice!'

''S real all right. Or tha' Charley wouldn't ha' bin so

eager. The bastard swopped junk scrip fer a jool! He swindled us.'

'We *did* buy this station with it,' Sara pointed out.

'He coulda told us 'bout real munny too. Wha' da they mean by callin' yer prop'ty "real estate" – if yer don' pay real munny fer it? Ga! S'pose it's realler than magic plastic munny!'

'What shall we do till nine o'clock, kind lady?'

The cleaning woman lowered her voice. 'Shouldn't really be doing this – against the law, but no one's looking. If you give me some scrip, say a hundred, I'll buy you some tea and sandwiches on my own card. You can spend the night in the waiting-room. I'll see as you ain't bothered.'

''Underd fer some bloody bread,' muttered the boy. ''Alf the cost of this whole effing station.'

'Beggars can't be choosers,' observed our benefactress. 'Who wants to own stations? The rent's so low. I'll bet you no more than five hundred people own this one.'

'Whadyamean? Fivc 'undred?'

'How do you suppose everyone can own property?'

'That's crazy,' said Sara. 'Hundreds of different people can buy the same property?'

'Thousands can – and do. Course, there's an upper limit to ownership. Bank ensures that.'

'What a mad set-up – when there's a whole parallel existence of real work, real life, and that credit money! Why do people play the bank's games?'

'You're weird,' the woman said. 'I'm not sure I ought to buy you any supper. Course it ain't crazy! If you don't play every day of your grown-up life, rain or shine, the bank explodes you. Same as going bankrupt.'

'Ker-ist!' Albertini fished out one of the hundreds and pressed it on the woman. 'A'd like chicken sand'ich, or mebbe goat.'

'*Goat?* We don't sell goat sandwiches here.'

We spent an uncomfortable night on benches in the waiting-room. In the morning we used our final hundred to bribe a porter who had just come on duty. He bought us breakfasts of greasy sausages, fried bread, and beans. We washed and brushed up, for free. We watched the early morning trains sigh to a halt and disgorge the same commuters who had left the evening before. By nine o'clock we were outside a branch of the Bank of Monopolis in Central Station Square, waiting for the glass doors to open.

The cleaning woman had neglected to mention that banks opened half an hour later than most other places; so we had ample time to watch the world go by. The square was surrounded by great glossy towers of metal and glass. Concrete thoroughfares which led from the square were likewise lined with towers. Plastic chariots with no visible source of power purred along rapidly on rubber wheels.

Once the branch opened we headed for a section of the counter marked 'Valuables & Securities'. We explained our predicament to a grey-clad, sad young lady. She put our diamond into a machine called a lapidometer which valued it. Before long a credit card was issued in our joint names. (There was some dispute about including a child, but our title-deed to Central Station proved to be sufficient precedent.)

Albertini clung to the edge of the counter. 'Er, miss?'

'How can I help you?' our clerk asked brightly. Unlike our diamond she lacked any real sparkle. She had asked exactly the same question in an identical tone five minutes earlier.

'Where's yer bank's headquarters?'

'That's on Arrow-go Avenue, sir.'

'How far's zat? Which way?'

'Ten minutes by taxi, sir. You can buy a map at any newsvendor.'

'Why did you ask her that?'

'Tha's where yer bosses gotta hang out, Sara. Them as make these nutty rules. As can explode folk. Saw a sign in there, said "Manager". Headquarters hasta have a head manager. We oughta go 'n' level with 'im.'

'I get the impression that the bank is its *own* manager. Why should any head manager want to see us?'

'Mebbe he's curious 'bout who made the rules 'riginally; an' how. Yer Bishops Veck an' Lovats were curious.'

'The bank manager mightn't be curious,' I said. 'He might send people to jail for curiosity.'

Sara gesticulated at the shining towers flanking the square. 'Aren't these buildings overwhelming! Dominating! Diminishing of a person. I think I'm feeling homesick. For Chorny, for Bellogard – for either town! Don't you pine, Pedino, my darling?'

'Yes; but both towns were destroyed.'

My darling. She had called me darling. Yet after four whole years we had still only kissed each other. Absurdly it seemed that we had skipped forgetfully over something like half a decade of love and of love-making, short-cutting the early amorous years entirely, and already we had our offspring with us. Albertini. As if by magic.

'Look, Sara,' I said, 'this Monopolis world doesn't strike me as very likely to get itself destroyed. Not soon. Maybe not ever! How could one person possibly become monopolist? And own the bank too? I mean to say, when thousands of people own the same places! This world's different from our world – and from Albertini's. Then, only a few principal magical personalities were involved in a struggle. But not here. Everyone's in on the game, apart from a few thousand bank employees. Nostalgia or no, I think we ought to consider living out our lives here.

I'm sure we could adapt. You probably have more chance of being knocked over by one of these chariots than of going bankrupt and exploding. Let's do nothing rash. We mightn't be wise to go aiming for the top, start taking on the bank.'

A sleek carriage slid to a halt by the kerb. Mounted on its roof a plaque announced: *Taxi-Cab*. The rear door sprang open of its own accord.

The driver leaned out of his window. 'You flagged me, lady. Where to?'

'To Arrow-go Avenue, fella.' Albertini swiftly scrambled in.

'You two coming?' the driver asked impatiently.

'Only to look,' I cautioned.

'Okay, Pud, wor'll only peep.'

Sara and I followed our 'son' into the back of the taxi and the door shut itself. A string serenade wafted in perfect synchrony from two musical boxes which I assumed the driver must wind up before each trip.

After a speedy journey past yet more towering offices and shops, hotels and restaurants and whatever, the driver deposited us in an avenue, one whole side of which was occupied by a single glass and metal behemoth twenty storeys tall. Repeated several times along its façade in tubular letters a storey high: *Central Bank of Monopolis*. Albertini's idea of marching inside and being ushered to the manager evaporated. Thanks be! Instead we bought a map and a daily newspaper and retired to a coffee bar opposite where we ordered slabs of chocolate gâteau and cups of *cappuccino*.

While Albertini was wolfing his cake Sara and I examined the map together. One side showed in tiny printing the thousands of actual streets of Monopolis. The other side had a circuit of eighty numbered squares commencing and ending at one marked GO! These were the ports of call which your daily numbers landed you on.

'Lez see!'

Sara explained the map to our illiterate son. She read off names of avenues, tax traps, penalties and rewards while he dabbed a chocolaty finger at a query mark with the legend 'Chance', at a light-tube labelled 'Electric Company'. I unfolded the *Monopolis Market Mirror*.

All news whatever seemed to be entirely concerned with the 'invisible' Monopolis, the Monopolis of property purchase and loss. The stories related who had bought what yesterday, who had gone to jail, who had won a lucky chance, in one instance who had exploded. Remarkably realistic engravings of properties and buyers – composed of tiny dots – illustrated the pages. Tucked half-way down a back column I found our own composite name listed as new joint purchasers of the Central Station.

The headline stories concerned the thirty or so biggest property owners. A study of their 'portfolios' suggested that I was right in my earlier surmise: no one individual could ever possibly own the whole shebang.

I pointed this out to Sara. 'Let's just enjoy ourselves today,' I recommended. 'Let's see the sights.'

Which is exactly what we did.

We visited spacious shops boasting moving stairways. Paying by credit card yet again, we bought Albertini some soft shoes and looser clothing. I obtained a cord suit, Sara a denim one. (Whereupon she reclaimed her knife.) Our previous outfits were bundled up. Later we passed a costumier's where we succeeded in selling the ball-gown, pantaloons and so forth for their oddity value, receiving some credit on our card.

We viewed the 'electricity' factory by the river, with its fat concave towers thirty storeys high venting lazy clouds of steam. We toured the Museum of Modern Architecture. We visited Monopolis Art Gallery which was wholly devoted to paintings of properties: houses, streets, stations, public edifices executed in a variety of styles gallery by gallery: 'Primitive', 'Impressionist', 'Abstract', 'Constructivist', 'Structuralist'.

We crossed a public park where privet had been topiaried into the shapes of houses, arrows, numbers, and question marks. In the middle of the park was a hedge-maze based on the streets of the city, but we passed up the option of getting lost in it. We lunched on steak and chips in a crowded café.

Afterwards we passed several auction rooms where properties were being bid for. These private sales were registered with the bank by 'phone', another kind of slot-box which took in title-deeds and spat them out again.

All the while we kept our ears open. Most conversations we overheard seemed to have some bearing on the subject-matter of the *Mirror*, being larded with names of properties, owners, and prices, spiced with supposition, scandal, and slander.

Everywhere – on walls and utility poles, in foyers and arcades, even on trees in the park – were magic red boxes. The commonest sight in Monopolis was of men and women of all ages and degree plunging their hands into these boxes, to depart in despondency or delight.

As evening drew near we rented rooms at the 'three-star' Palazzo Hotel. A single one for Albertini, a double for Sara and myself. Albertini would rather have crowded into the same room as us two but I put my foot emphatically down. I had to give the boy our credit card for safe-keeping, rather as a dog owner tosses a rag that smells of master into his hound's kennel before going on a long journey.

Once we had obtained our room keys (and had declined the services of a porter to carry our non-existent luggage)

I was in favour of an early dinner in the hotel restaurant, followed by bed. My feet were sore from all the tramping; a different part of me was aching with proximity to Sara. She thought we ought to use the magic box first. The hotel had several, housed in plastic booths.

The glass panel lit. We scored a double and were rewarded with 400 units of scrip. Our second turn landed us another station, which we bought. That turn also had been a double. Our apprehensions of jail were groundless: we landed on another reward, receiving 150 'from sale of stock'. I wondered how the bank could pretend we owned a herd of cattle, but no matter.

HOLD ON, the screen instructed. TRIPLE PLAYER RECEIVES TRIPLE TURNS.

'Ohboyohboy!' gurgled Albertini.

'We've hexed the bank, Sara!'

Property began to flow our way.

Later, with a fine meal in our bellies, the proud possessors of a bundle of scrip and a good few title-deeds, we retired upstairs. I scooted Albertini into his single room and shut the door firmly. In our own room, for the first time in four years and two worlds, Sara and I made love. Very satisfactorily. And slept, and made love, and slept.

The three of us were sitting at breakfast in the dining-room next morning scoffing scrambled eggs with devilled kidneys, when we received a visitor. He was a wiry, urgent fellow in a charcoal suit. Stuck in the hatband of his trilby, a printed card lettered *MMM*.

The intruder laid the morning's copy of the *Mirror* on the table-cloth, folded to a story about 'the unprecedented mystery triple-player, Pedinoalbertinisara' and our over-night acquisitions.

'I'm the *Mirror*'s social-diary reporter, folks. Name of Max Jonson.'

'How did you know we were staying here, Mr Jonson?' asked Sara.

'Credit card info, natch. You haven't too much. What are your plans? Are you three people, or one with three bodies? How do you pull that trick? Are you the fulfilment of the prophecy?'

'What prophecy, Mr Jonson?'

'That the world will end soon after the Three-in-One appears. The Antibanker. Never heard of the Antibanker? Who you kidding?'

I butted in. 'How do you mean, "we haven't too much"? Too much *what*?'

'Too much credit. Approx two weeks' worth, if you're aiming to stay here.'

Albertini hastily speared the remaining kidneys; his cheeks inflated like a squirrel's.

'Reckon you can break the bank in a fortnight? What're your plans? Who are you? Why d'you have one name between the three of you? Where did you get that fancy gown and the pantaloons and the kid's velvet suit?'

'How ever did you . . . ? Don't tell me,' sighed Sara. 'Credit info.'

'Ran checks. Hustled a few people out of bed. News warrant! Been here earlier, otherwise.'

'Our plans are to settle in Monopolis,' I said. 'We'll own a few select properties. Be good citizens.'

Sara raised an eyebrow at me.

Jonson raised a higher eyebrow. 'Own a *few*? Who you kidding, Mr Pedinoalbertinisara? Are you the Antibanker?' From out of his pocket Jonson pulled a flat plastic box with two eyes, one of which flashed in our faces, half-blinding us.

Images danced. Albertini started up, jabbing his fork at the reporter.

'Cool, kid, cool. Took your pics for tomorrow's paper.

Big honour, your pic in Triple-Em. "Are these the Antibanker?" Max Jonson's byline.'

We got rid of the reporter with difficulty, without telling him any tales of Bellogard or of magic snakes and ladders.

By the end of that week we had amassed quite a lot of property and scrip; rent and salary were accumulating. We had won rewards and fallen foul of no penalties whatever. Albertini, now master of the map – though he couldn't actually *read* it – was buying extra property at auction through a broker who visited to volunteer his firm's services.

The boy ignored my words of caution. Unsurprisingly so, since Sara encouraged him. She had no desire to settle in a Monopolis where we had to hide indoors. Our pictures had been published and our affairs were main headline news from one day to the next. Little crowds were forever collecting outside the Palazzo hoping to catch a glimpse of us. The hotel hired more commission-aires. If we left our rooms we were pestered politely by waiters and chambermaids. We took to ordering all our meals from room service, only opening the door after the porter had departed. We made our own beds. We raced downstairs to use one of the magic boxes and raced back up to our rooms again.

Really, life was becoming intolerable. Though the nights were neat. Mostly. A honeymoon, mostly. We spent the days reading the *Mirror* aloud, eating, drinking, peering cautiously out of the window, telling each other stories, arguing now and then. Albertini's stories were the liveliest. I tried to keep a low profile in arguments. At night Sara and I exhausted each other with love, so that we could go to sleep.

If the outside pressure kept up, how much more of this could we abide? Pressure only increased as our portfolio expanded. When our credit ran out, how would we get a job? The problem of ordinary funds melted away when a letter was slipped under our door, offering a large sum of non-scrip credit if we would license a book based on interviews with ourselves. Now the frustrating prospect loomed of being able to hide in our burrow for many weeks longer.

'We should accept,' said Sara. 'That'll buy us time. We'll become monopolist.'

'We'll own the effing world,' crowed Albertini.

'Provided our luck doesn't crash,' I said. It seemed to me we would be a lot happier if our fortunes did suffer a set-back and we reverted to being typical middling speculators. I was still nursing the idea of settling in Monopolis. The idea needed nursing; by now it was seriously ill.

'*Luck?*' asked Sara. 'What *luck?* This isn't luck, Pedino, it's magic. It's moneymagic, legalmagic. Our magic has changed, don't you see? Magic isn't something that we *do* any longer, with a sword or a painted pane. The whole magic fabric of the world responds to us. It arranges events for us. Shall I tell you why?'

'Please do.'

'I'd say this world is trying to get rid of us as quickly as possible. We're a splinter in its skin, a lump of grit in its eye. We're intruders, with othermagic. Albertini's world reacted similarly, don't you think? Remember, when we were at that soirée, how you said, "we don't belong"? Well, we didn't then, and we don't now. There's only one way a world can expel us. That's by making us *win* – thus finishing off the present cycle of struggle as soon as can be.'

'If this world wants rid of us, why can't it put us permanently in jail? Why can't it explode us?'

'Maybe killing us magically while we're in a world of foreign magic would violate some fundamental law, destroy some sort of symmetry. Maybe that would unbalance the logic of everything. The intrusion has to be purged by the smoothest route.'

'Yer didn't havta leave the slum,' Albertini pointed out. 'Yer coulda stayed put.'

'But once we *did* make a move, those ladders rushed us away to the happy isle in three quick climbs.'

'We cud still ge' killed, ord'nary. Tha' mob out there cud clobber us.'

This made sense to me. 'Perhaps that's what the bank wants. Speculators could tear us to pieces for lucky souvenirs, or out of jealousy or greed, or from terror of the mythical Antibanker. We should back-pedal if possible.'

'We are fast *becoming* the Antibanker!' cried Sara. 'Let's face it! Oh it makes me sick to contemplate destroying a whole world of people, even if their ways do seem weird. That's hardly their fault! Question of upbringing. We don't seem to have a choice. Only if we refuse to use the magic box could we be exploded legitimately, I suppose. Monopolis could carry on.'

'You aren't suggesting we *don't* use the box?'

'Moral dilemma, my darling?'

'*A'm* not bein' exploded,' announced Albertini. 'Nuts to tha'. Nuthin' doin'. So much fer yer dilemma.'

I tried not to look too relieved. I said placatingly, 'It's the cosmos that's guilty, Sara, not us. If conditions were different, life might not even be possible.'

'Spoken like a patriotic Bellogardian! My father hoped that science and the birth of newmagic might set us free. Might let us decide our destiny. Here we are. We're set free – after a fashion. What are we doing with our freedom? We're pawns collaborating in a property game.'

'More than mere pawns!'

'Ultimately, what are we?'

'Ultimately, does *another* magical world await us –

beyond this one? According to astrologer Matyash there are at least seven. Eight, if you count Bellogard-Chorny. Do we have to wreck them all?'

Sara hid her face in her hands and wept.

I thought that she wept for the worlds we might destroy *en passant*. I tried to comfort her, to reconcile her to this unenviable prospect. Presently she raised her head and stared at me. She seemed elsewhere, disconnected, like an eidolon.

'My father,' she said quietly. 'Bishop Lovats the perceptive, the beloved . . . Someone once asked whether Lovats would have preferred to "experiment" with a magic woman. Yes, he would. Of course. He did. Bishop Lovats experimented with Squire Sara. With his magic daughter. The magic father's seed in the magic daughter's womb might have conceived a granddaughter endowed with intensified magic . . . even though the twelve had already been born. The granddaughter might have possessed *wildmagic*. Therefore the father possessed the daughter. Not brutally or offensively. Oh no. Ever so gently. Several times, when the moon's horoscope favoured fruitfulness.

'No wildmagic grandchild was conceived. Or else it was conceived but blood washed it away. Because the twelve had already been born.'

She blinked and shook her head as though snapping out of a trance.

'What nonsense. What things one invents. Maybe I could believe that such a thing happened – because, if it *had*, then I would really have known my father! I've listened to too many of young Albert's stories.'

I felt stunned. Sara did not refer to this again. Nor did I.

Throughout the second week our portfolio expanded dramatically. We signed a contract for our book, earning enough credit to maintain us in imprisoned comfort at the Palazzo for months to come. Over the weekend in the hotel room we told our story to a trio of author-interviewers.

I suggested that we invent a pack of lies. Sara insisted that we tell the truth in the hope of alerting some luminary of the calibre of Lovats, Augusti, or even Matyash.

Personally I thought Sara was being disingenuous. How could we aim to become monopolist, thus triumphantly causing world-doom – and simultaneously subvert monopolist philosophy? Subvert, with what possible outcome? Would a monetary guru ride to our rescue, proposing an alternative magico-economic strategy? Would enlightened mobs storm the bank, defuse its magic, establish common ownership by everyone of everything? Would *that* not be a very Antibankerish act? To avoid a quarrel I kept quiet about my qualms.

Once we began to recount our adventures a kind of storymagic swept me into the swing of fulsome frankness. Our interviewers soaked up our story like sponges and departed to squeeze themselves into a book, which they estimated would take about a week to produce. They wouldn't commit themselves 'credibility-wise'.

Half-way through the third week one of the leading property magnates went bankrupt trying to pay rent to us. The bank had dealt him a run of bad luck. We took over his assets; we raised his mortgages.

Two days later, another of the 'top thirty' fell foul of us.

Worse! Dozens of small speculators were coming to grief by now, going bankrupt and exploding. We sat in our hotel room like a trio of bombardiers, blasting citizens of Monopolis to pieces financially and literally. This was the opposite of any orthodox siege; three invaders were laying siege to a whole city with the full connivance and say-so of its treasury and without needing to stir from their billet (apart from a quick dash to the magic box). Connivance on the part of the bank was amply demonstrated – and Sara's thesis proved – when Securicorpsmen, the police of the bank, threw a cordon round the Palazzo to keep anxious, hostile crowds at bay. We still did not land in jail or pay any taxes.

We saw death in the street below when poor speculators used the boxes on utility poles and went bang, messily. An avalanche began, a crash of portfolios proud and humble. Soon, throughout Monopolis, hundreds of new paupers were exploding.

The dawn of the fifth week. No book had appeared. Doubtless our authors and their publishers had exploded. A fair percentage of the potential readership had followed suit. A cohort of Securicorpsmen continued to surround the Palazzo; being bank personnel they were immune. The street was no longer crowded with distraught spectators. Few pedestrians hurried past, those who did looking haunted. The occasional carriage purred by. An exploded body lay strewn, uncollected. City services were collapsing. At night the lights would flicker and black out; the electricity factory must be undermanned. The water taps wouldn't always work. The air smelled of spiritual death; a scared silence fell over once-bustling Monopolis.

We all needed to be together if a crisis occurred, so Albertini moved in at last to share the double room, dragging his mattress with my reluctant assistance. It was some while since Sara and I had made love. How could we do so, when our embraces might be disrupted by the distant 'pop' of some hapless wretch disintegrating, all because of us?

One morning we opened the drapes to find the street deserted. No Securicorpsmen; nobody. Only some corpses in many small pieces.

We walked downstairs through an empty hotel. No one was about. In the lobby we found the scattered remains of (maybe) the receptionist. We said nothing; the sound of our voices would have seemed obscene.

One of the magic boxes was glowing and beeping in its booth. Silently we went and stuck our hands into it.

CONGRATULATIONS, MONOPOLIST! ADVANCE TO GO! GO TO GO! GO!

The plastic box began to soften and slump. It dripped coldly – no heat was involved. We snatched our hands away, and headed out into the vacant street, the first time in weeks that we had set foot outside the hotel. The cloudless morning sky was a familiar, crackling, vacuous blue. The city buildings were becoming vague in outline.

We owned Monopolis, and Monopolis – this particular incarnation – was dissolving back into the matrix from which all such cities of Monopolis arose.

We held hands. Quietly the world tiptoed away.

'. . . *check at intersection number 1,703 . . . bridging from starpoint 21 . . . impasse at points 2,171 through 2,191 . . . area around 2,000 is dead, abandon . . . connect at number 99 . . . this is General Shiro. . . .*'

This flow of orders from an invisible source was gradually drowned by drumming, the clash of metal, cries and screams, a bray of battle trumpets. A frightful clamour reverberated in a blank void. The din of war gave way to cheering, drunken laughter, ribald songs. This, too, faded.

Of a sudden tents appeared. Pavilions, flags on poles. We were standing in a town of tents. Slim, enticing women wandered arm in arm with tipsy warriors who were dressed in chain-mail shirts and leather skirts. Fat old women laboured over cooking fires. Brats scampered about. Babies bawled. Lambs bleated in pens. Chickens pecked the dirt. An ox was being roasted. An injured man lay on a straw pallet, leg wrapped in bloody bandages. A conjuror juggled balls that seemed to change colour in mid-air. A clown stalked by on stilts. Red-faced fellows ambled from a marquee, gripping pots of ale.

Were we in the midst of a war or a fair-ground? The encampment reeked of smoke, sour beer, blood, charred flesh, perfume, piss.

A squad of metal-clad spear bearers, led by an officer in silver mail, charged through the mêlée scattering chickens and knocking over panniers of rice. Skinny curs yapped and cringed. The soldiers pounded to a halt beside us. The officer pointed a finger at me.

'You, you're enlisted.'

'What?'

'Don't imagine you can slack just because the war's over! Now we tidy up this mess. We get the lines sorted out. That's quite as important. It'll take long enough. Grab your kit, and fall in.'

'My wife, my child.' I gestured at Sara and Albertini.

'They'll come too. Chattels and impedimenta *usually* accompany a soldier! Campaigning's a life's work, eh?'

'Who won this war?' asked Sara.

'How should I know? General Shiro himself doesn't know yet. Nobody knows till we straighten out the lines, exchange prisoners, clear the living dead away. Fall in!'

By that evening we understood the situation a bit more clearly courtesy of new comrades in arms.

For as long as anyone could remember, a long, slow war had been waged between the 'Whites' and the 'Blacks'. In the beginning there had only been a few isolated groups of White and Black forces scattered apparently at random across vast grassy steppes. Each unit was accompanied by its own tented village of wives, kids, washerwomen,

prostitutes, barmaids, cooks, prestidigitators, saltim-
bancos, chirurgeons, armourers, fiddlers, thieves, vaga-
bonds, invalids, minstrels, tailors, and a dozen other sorts
of hangers-on.

The aim of the war was to surround and defend as
much territory as possible. At each new stage in the
conflict a fresh encampment of Whites – then a fresh
encampment of Blacks – would spring magically into
existence at whichever point was designated first by
General Shiro, then by the enemy general, Kuro.

After a while camps would link up. Lines of White
camps would encircle a few Black camps. Black camps
would spring into being behind White lines, trying to
forge the 'double-eye' formation which was ruled to be
invulnerable. To prevent this, White would attempt to
cut across Black lines by bringing new camps into existence. Black would seek a path to survival by generating
more new camps. Some 'single-eye' groups of camps and
solitary camps would be surrounded and obliterated.
Other such camps would linger on, impotent and ignored,
inhabited by the living dead. Now and then a 'repeat
situation' occurred. Black would wipe out a White camp.
White would reinvade, wiping out the Black victor. Black
would counter-attack, wasting White. Presently the generals' attention would be diverted elsewhere.

My new comrades didn't seem unduly bothered that I
was ignorant of the rules of war. Ever since the war
began whole mobs of soldiers and camp-followers had
been materializing by magic, some well primed for their
role, others less so.

Once a camp had sprung up it wouldn't shift position
as long as the war continued (though it might be obliterated). Minstrels and strays wandered from one camp to
another, even across empty steppes, but army units stayed
put in their immediate home area. As a result of this the
earlier camps had long histories behind them. Tents had

been replaced by wooden huts, then by houses of adobe or stone. The troubadours told tales of thriving, quirky, individualistic 'cultures', quirkiest of all in cases where an ancient camp was isolated or on a frontier. The particular camp where we had arrived was a Johnny-come-lately.

Now, apparently, the war was over. Yet not *entirely* over. The two sides had been evenly matched in skill. Until the boundaries of Black and White territory were firmed up and rearranged neither knew which had won. Consequently a host of people must uproot themselves and set out on a massive trek, a minor aspect of which I was conscripted to help organize.

Damn fortunate 'our' camp wasn't one of the long-settled townships! Us soldiers might have needed to burn it to the ground to persuade everyone to clear out.

What chaos there was the next morning! What a fuss, what a pother. Only Albertini was in his element.

Our various squads of soldiery, some still nursing hangovers, got the show on the road after what seemed hours of cajoling and cutting guy-ropes and chasing chickens. Not that there *was* any road as such! The vanguard tramped a path through the head-high grass. The rest of the lengthy column followed this path.

My squad was assigned to the rearguard where heavy baggage, mothers burdened with babies (in uterus or out of it), the wounded and the aged gravitated. I was kitted out in a chain-mail shirt and leather skirt. I hadn't been able to lay my hands on one of those wickedly hooked spears, but Sergeant Hosh – who had inducted me – had supplied a razor-sharp sword which for preference I kept safely in its scabbard.

Sara stayed as close by me as she could. Albertini scampered to and fro. He soon teamed up with that clown on stilts. The clown proved disposed to act as a mobile watch-tower, keeping an eye out for any laggards or recalcitrants who tried to slip away, to return to the abandoned site which had been home to them for several years.

I asked spearman Jigo what happened *after* the lines had been tidied up and the war was decided.

'If we've fought impeccably, like champions,' he told me, 'the finishing stage is the way the world will remain for ever after. No point in any further moves!'

'Do you mean: if we win, the Blacks will still control their own territory?'

Jigo nodded.

'In that case what's the point of the war?'

'Why, to decide the shape of the map! To make sure that ours is the bigger share!'

'If it isn't, how will you feel?'

'Humiliated – for ever. Don't speak of it. This is an anxious time.'

We marched until late afternoon, when a halt was called by the banks of a stream. Tents were pitched. People sprawled or bathed. Fires were lit. Rice was boiled. Cooks cooked, entertainers entertained, whores whored, babies had their bottoms washed.

We marched for most of the following day. Around two o'clock the clown called down that he could see another White column, complete with civilians, following a course roughly parallel to ours off to the east. At three o'clock he sighted another line of soldiers and followers off to the right. At four o'clock word came back that we had arrived; we must close up and pitch a permanent camp.

The soldiers, whose hooked spears doubled conveniently as scythes, cleared a site and the tented town which we had quit two days earlier was reconstructed. When night fell our elevated clown reported that he could see other tented towns and bonfires to our left, to our right, and ahead of us. Behind us the grassland was deserted.

Sergeant Hosh stopped by. 'Private Pedino, you are demobilized.'

'I am, sir?'

'Mission accomplished! Last in, first out. At dawn General Shiro and General Kuro will meet formally to conclude the war. Ah peace, sweet peace – 'tis the sweeter after conflict.'

'I'm sure it is, sir.'

The clown invited the three of us to share his tent. His name was Koko – derived from the magic name for the 'repeat situation' I mentioned earlier. Ingeniously he wore that tent as a costume. His stilts were the poles. His baggy silken robe ballooned out to become the fabric, which he pegged to the ground. The tent was crowded with four of us inside but no one seemed to mind. Koko, still wearing a billowy undershirt and baggy bloomers, lit an oil-lamp for light. Albertini volunteered to fetch supper and ducked out. Ten minutes later our expert scrounger returned with someone's helmet tucked under his arm. This was filled with saffron rice and chunks of jugged hare. Albertini had also lifted a newly opened bottle of rice wine.

'Knew we'd needs bucket, didn't a?'

We tucked in with our fingers, and passed the bottle.

'Who *grows* the rice?' asked Sara. 'Who digs the metal to make weapons? Where are the farms and the mines?'

'Stuff turns up,' explained Albertini, before the clown could do so. Apparently he had checked this out. 'Bit like snake-drops a' the dump. Camps o' folk pop outa nowhere. Stuff too. World i'n't full up till the very end, ya see? Gotta be added on to all the time.'

'Ho ho. The end! Just so.' A perpetual grin was painted around Koko's mouth; tears were painted tumbling from his eyes. Hilarity and grief combined. His voice shook.

'Tomorrow's the fun day when everything stops dead. It will stop dead, you know! And I'll die laughing.'

'Jigo told me . . .'

'Those silly soldiers – they're the real clowns! I must be up high on my stilts at dawn to see. Forgive me if the tent collapses.'

'I feared as much,' I said.

'Oh, it won't fall down before then! Never you fear.'

'Pedino's talking about the end of the world,' said Sara, licking her fingers. 'We've seen it happen before.'

'Oh no you haven't.'

'Oh yes we 'ave,' chirped Albertini.

'Oh no you . . . Cross your heart?'

'An' 'ope to die. 'Cept we won't die, not if wor luck 'olds.'

'Er, joking apart, dear guests and sharers of my humble tent . . .'

Sara proceeded to explain about our travels.

'Ayee!' cried Koko when she had done. 'Would you believe it? That's an even bigger bleeding comedy than I ever guessed!'

'*We'll* be up at dawn too,' she vowed.

'Problem,' said Albertini. 'Wha' magic bails us outa 'ere? Why should it? Wha' we won this time? Nuthin'.'

'Our side may have won the war,' I said.

'Fat lotta diff'rence wor presence made.'

'I'd view things in a different light,' Sara said. 'This world's based on an imaginary grid pattern. Like a chequerboard, only with a lot more squares. Camps occupy these squares, right?'

Koko shook his head. 'It's the points where the lines meet that count.'

'Okay then. But the main ingredient, as I understand this war, is that *chance* plays no part. It's all a matter of skill and geometrical calculation. Hell, it's a real war too, just like at home. In Monopolis there were no actual battles. Same with your world, Albertini. But here there's war. We're getting closer to home. I feel it in my bones.'

'Home sweet home is a bloodthirsty war?'

'Home,' she said to me firmly, 'is what goes on in between military actions. It's the peace which punctuates the skirmishes of war. The ordinary lives.'

'Which depend on magic conflict for their very existence.'

'As you're forever saying!'

'I'm not. It's a fact of life. That doesn't mean I approve of it. Does the sun like being on fire? If it wasn't on fire, it would be dead. Maybe the sun is writhing in agony.'

'Balls,' she said. 'Astrological balls.'

'Sorry, Sara. When I get close to the end of a world, I feel on edge.'

Koko guffawed.

'Seriously, love, if we're near to home – if your instinct's right – then we're depending on your magic to take us there. Your othermagic. But . . .'

'We lost the magic glass in Monopolis. Exactly.'

'I was going to say: you still have your dagger.'

'Pardon,' interrupted Koko, 'how can you go home when your home was destroyed? You said it was swept off the board.'

'A new cycle must begin some time,' Sara answered him. 'Our own world has been getting ready to revive while we've been wandering through other worlds. That's why I feel close to Chorny and Bellogard. They're about to begin again. How does a dagger help?'

'Let's see it.'

She showed Koko.

'Ha! Haven't you realized that a dagger is also a *compass*? A *pointer*? Look: north, south, east, west. The point is north, the hilt is south. The quillons – the cross-piece – are east and west. A dagger points the true way –

usually into someone's heart. Why not to your heart's desire?'

'A compass! Yes, I *see*.'

'Will you take me with you?'

'I thought your big ambition was a ripe belly-laugh, come the end of the world,' I said.

'I'll gladly do without, if there's something better on offer. Is there?' The clown face peered intently at Sara, laughing and weeping.

'Four of us? We can try, Koko.'

'Pick-a-back style,' I said, 'that's how. Albertini will ride on your shoulders, love. Koko can mount my back the way I mounted Sir Brant. We'll hold hands, you and I, Sara. You'll point the poniard. And magic us away. We hope.'

Most of the camp dwellers were snoring soundly when the sun rose. Sergeant Hosh and some other soldiers were abroad, looking wearily anticipative. We ourselves presented a curious spectacle; perhaps we ought to have sneaked off into the grasslands.

Albertini was wreathed around Sara's neck. She stood pointing her dagger at the dawn sky as if to ward off attack from a randy eagle. I held her left hand. Koko leaned against my back, hunchbacked on splayed stilts, his knees clamped to my waist, his hands around my chest.

'Good morning!' Hosh hailed us. 'Are you all practising to become clowns? Or is it acrobats?'

'We're doing the disappearing trick,' said Koko. 'Takes a lot of concentration.'

'Sorry to bother you, I'm sure!'

'A pleasure to be bothered by you, Sergeant,' I assured Hosh. 'Do you know how long it will take the two generals to decide?'

211

'The lines are straightened out, so it's easy to count territory. Not too long.'

'Hope not,' said Koko. 'All this bending's going to give me backache. Not to mention my poor *knees*.'

'*You'll* have backache? How about us?'

Bemused, Sergeant Hosh walked away.

'Even if we have to stand here all morning we mustn't break ranks,' I insisted.

Half an hour had gone by. More people were up and about. Kids especially. They had mobbed us a few minutes ago, clamouring for a performance. Albertini had snarled savagely. I stood sullenly, hoping the brats wouldn't find some rotten eggs to toss. Now we had another problem.

'Wanna piss,' Albertini repeated. 'Only take halfa minute.'

'No! Try to hold out.'

Sara groaned. For one grim moment I thought her migraine had returned. 'If necessary,' she said tightly, 'if *absolutely* necessary wet your trousers, and me too.'

'A couldn't.'

'You will if you have to. We aren't losing you now.'

I did wish that Albertini hadn't drawn my attention to calls of nature. I rapidly traced part of my own discomfort to exactly the same symptom, a burgeoning bladder. Once I had noticed this it became hard to ignore. Oh magic, oh urination.

Hosh and his men came by again. Before they could accost us they snapped to attention in unison.

'Listen!' Sara exclaimed unnecessarily. 'Listen in your mind!'

The very same voice we had heard while we were arriving in this world: General Shiro's . . .

'*White surrounds one hundred and fifty-seven cross-points . . . Black surrounds one hundred and fifty-three . . . White wins! Rejoice!*'

A victory by four points. Hosh bowed to his men; they bowed low to him. They hurrahed. From all over a tide of cheers arose, raggedly at first, soon swelling into a single thunderous voice.

At that moment the risen sun grew abnormally bright. As bright as midday, brighter. The sun flooded the world with light. So intense was this light that it shone right through tents, right through people's bodies, dissolving fabric and flesh. Men and women and kids became living skeletons wearing a faint pink fog upon their bones.

The radiance blazed even brighter, and those bones were mere lines, intersections of lines with white mist clinging to them, as though bones were flesh enclosing other simpler bones inside. The terrible light strengthened; all I could see now were patterns of points where those lines had once met.

I realized that we were no longer there. 'There' was no longer there, either . . .

A full house of courtiers had crowded into the Chequer Chamber. The oh-so-familiar Chequer Chamber, overlooking oh-so-familiar Bellogard. With Lake Riboo in the distance. I felt shocked to the core, exhilarated, joyful – and maddened. Sure enough, as Sara had predicted, a new cycle had commenced. Palace, town, kingdom, and people had been re-created – in the mid-stream of things. Down in the town citizens were going about their business, living lives which hadn't existed five minutes before. Lives with which they were fully familiar. It was late afternoon.

Wait. Had those houses fronting the river looked *quite* like that formerly? Had the bridge across the Rehka stood in exactly that position? Maybe, maybe not. If the town was different, it was also the same.

The court was full of nobles because the magic war

with our ancient enemies had only just begun. No one had been killed yet.

So here were the two princes, Roque and Krasno the Magnificent. I knew their names well. Here were the two bishops, Vax and Meesa. Knights, Sir Jerebet and Sir Brian. Here was vigorous, clever Queen Adama.

Here was me.

King Pedino.

I was King of Bellogard. I kid you not. I'd only just realized. I'd suddenly known where I was; who I was. I was young King Pedino. I had been king for as many years as I could recall. First infant king, then boy king, then stripling king.

Except, of course, that I *hadn't* been anything of the sort! A few minutes earlier, in another world, I'd been watching the victorious White forces dissolve, while I supported a clown on my back.

King Pedino! Before anybody claps and cheers, please recall how feeble a king is compared to a knight. Or to a prince or a bishop. But especially compared to a queen. A king is a kind of glorified pawn equipped with a crown. A king is the prime target for the enemy. He has to be kept out of harm's way. He has to be guarded by the real powers of the realm. Protected by his nobles; but especially by his puissant queen.

Had dotty King Karol been more assertive and effective in his younger days? Before he took to blowing magic bubbles? I couldn't imagine so. Maybe my predecessor had attempted to assert himself, and failed. Maybe he never had a chance.

I was married to a mature, powerful queen. I'd been married to her for years. She was older and more experienced than me. As a toddler I'd been betrothed – to a twelve-year-old. As soon as I reached puberty I had wed my consort. It took no great genius to deduce that

214

Adama was a reincarnation of Queen Dama of yore; a reconstruction of her, a facsimile.

Likewise, in the previous existence, Bishop Vax had been Bishop Veck. Sandy Sir Brian had been Sir Brant. Elegant, snooty Prince Roque had been Prince Ruk. Bishop Meesa had been Bishop Slon. I was also aware, as an abstract fact, that in Chorny lustful Queen Boola and cruel King Martel reigned.

To date, there were six pawn-squires in Bellogard. Two more had yet to emerge from the general population, just as I had emerged. These six were named Dennis, Pyet, Ben, Peterlin, Irina – and Sara.

Sara. The same. She, too, was in the Chequer Chamber. I was sneaking cautious glances at her. She, at me.

Could it be that she had reverted to being a loyal daughter of Chorny? She might be marvelling at the lucky stroke – some act of cunning subversion or of magical possession! – which had planted her here at the heart of the Bellogard court. She might merely be wondering the same thing that I was wondering: namely, did we still *know* each other? There was no sign of Albertini or Koko, nor did I know anything as to their present whereabouts. I absolutely had to speak to Sara as soon as possible.

Adama clapped her hands. A tall, athletic, glamorous blonde of some thirty apparent years, she sported a dashing outfit with a hint of the huntress: red jacket over busty silk blouse, tan boots, plaid skirt, diamond coronet. I myself was clad in a purple-trimmed cream blazer with a royal coat of arms as badge, and cavalry-twill trousers, the costume of an amiable chump.

'We must hold a Jubilation!' proclaimed the queen. 'Let the royal banners be run up on all spires. Let bells be rung, and blaziers lit by night. Let the town enjoy two days of carnival. Wine shall spout from the fountains.

215

Organize a gala fête at the Samostan, will you, Bishop Meesa?'

'Why?' I interrupted.

'Why?' she echoed with affectionate contempt. 'Because today, my loving happy-go-lucky liege, we shall make the first significant move in the war.'

'Couldn't we put it off for a few weeks? Where's the urgency?'

She indicated the vacant white and black slabs of the chequerboard. 'In a short while I shall sing the summoning, then we shall see.'

'If there are no eidolons on view, Chorny hasn't made a move.'

'Ah! You're beginning to comprehend politics, my lordly salad-lamb! How refreshing, how encouraging.'

'Excuse me one moment.' I strode over to the group of pawn-squires, all smartly decked out in their brass-buttoned white livery.

'Sara. Do you remember Koko the Clown? Monopolis? Albertini?'

'Yes! Yes!'

'Do you remember snakes and ladders? Meshko and Groody Lane?'

'I do! Oh Pedino, do you think we saved Albertini? And Koko? Where can they be?'

'Capering through Bellogard, perhaps. Let's hope so.'

'I'm so glad, Pedino.'

'Me too, Sara.'

'My lordly lambkin!' cooed Adama. 'We don't allow His Majesty to consort with pretty young ladies who may give him a pox, now do we? *We* believe in perfect fidelity in marriage, as an example to the people.'

Sara flushed – at my humiliation as well as hers.

I faced the queen. 'I'm merely talking to her, madam. I hardly imagine this squire has a pox, unless it's a magic pox wished on her by jealousy or malice!'

Adama raised an amused eyebrow; perhaps she wasn't so amused within. Sara and I may have seemed rather intense, and in public too. But hell, was I supposed to shun her? Not to have anything to do with my magic love? What cruel comedy was this?

'*Malice?* Jealousy? You must surely be thinking of Queen Boola. Otherwise it's as though we two hardly know each other, my pretty Pedino.'

I knew Adama well enough; and didn't know her.

'Come, my kingling. We need to summon the black eidolons to see if any appear. Even if none do, we'd be well advised to advance a pawn-squire.'

'Aye!' agreed bluff Sir Brian. 'A knight can leap over a squire. No one else can do it, except for me and Jerebet. You're all blocked till squires make their move.'

'I suspect Squire Sara wishes to advance herself,' said the queen.

'Oh no,' said I. 'Not likely.'

'My lordnik, do please remember yourself.'

'I just did, Adama; I remembered myself.' I stepped out on to the empty chequerboard and faced the assembly. 'I have an important announcement, my lady, lords, and squires. The whole damn world only began a few minutes ago! Fully fledged! Complete with people, history, memories – like skeletons of antique monsters we find encased in rocks. So: remember *yourselves*, if you can.'

A buzz ran through the ranks.

'Oh dear!' cried Adama. 'Our poor king is exhibiting the hereditary misfortune, the malady of mind. So young too! I should postpone this council until tomorrow. I need to summon an apothecary.'

'I'll arrange it, madam.' Nodding, Sir Jerebet started to take his leave.

I held up my hand. 'Stop! Listen to me! I remember the *previous* war between Bellogard and Chorny. I lived through it. When that war ended, the world came to an end. I escaped through magic space. I travelled through worlds of foreign magic. I came back here only minutes ago. I suddenly became King Pedino. I was only a squire before. At that very same moment you all sprang back into existence, in time for the next cycle of the eternal war!'

Squire Irina giggled.

'This is most unfortunate.' Prince Roque directed a sympathetic glance at the queen.

'I wasn't alone in my travels! I journeyed with Squire Sara there. She also escaped.' I hesitated. '*She* escaped from Chorny.'

Anxiously Sara spoke up. 'It's true. Here's the magic dagger we used as our compass. I still have it.' This was an error. As Sara showed her blade it crackled with blue fire.

'Assassin!' hissed the queen. The two knights made a pincer move towards Sara.

'I'm no assassin!' Hastily Sara put the weapon away. Sir Brian and Sir Jerebet subsided for the moment.

'We also picked up two companions *en route*,' I said. 'Citizens of two other magic worlds. One is a clown called Koko. The other looks like a seven-year-old boy but he's really a lot older. Name of Albertini. They ought to be somewhere in the kingdom. I want a search proclaimed.'

Adama smiled fleetingly. 'Our king seeks a clown to amuse him, and a childish playmate. Note how the imaginary companion is mature, yet only seven years old. What a mirror of King Pedino's own moods.'

Bishop Vax cleared his throat. This was a younger version of Veck, his cheek unpatched, unblemished.

'Madam, I think we ought to listen to the king. It may be the case that the conflict between Bellogard and Chorny has been fought before – won many times, lost many times. Our bibliotek houses many puzzling volumes.

I recall raising this subject in the past. A past which may well be a phantom!' Thank goodness for Vax.

'Do you mean the empty books? Or the *miniature* ones?' I asked quickly, as a different kind of buzz ran through the room. A buzz of appalled acknowledgement.

To my amazed delight, Bishop Vax knelt before me. 'My liege, this may be the first occasion that information – genuine information – has passed over from a previous cycle of existence. If only you can verify what you say. Substantiate it.'

'Sara is verification. Also Koko and Albertini, when we can locate them.'

Vax stood up – limberly; he was still quite a young man. 'If Sara was a *Chorny* squire in a previous war, her eidolon may be black, not white.'

Adama was showing signs of distress. 'How could Chorny have substituted her? Without us realizing? Sara must be a semblance. Someone possessed.'

'No, madam; with respect. If the king is accurate, Chorny has no hand in this.'

'Let us see, then! Clear the chequerboard!' This was addressed to me.

I complied, but said, 'Sara hasn't made a magical move here yet. Not really. She only *showed* us the dagger.'

'That's true,' agreed Meesa. 'Let her make a pawn-jump, a brief one out and back again. She could leap to the Samostan – and fetch some documents which I inadvertently left on my desk.'

'To prove exactly where she went.' Vax nodded to his fellow bishop. 'You remember leaving some papers, which will certainly be found on your desk . . . yet those papers had no prior existence. How hard to accept! But I accept. Provisionally.'

'If I jumped free,' suggested Sara, 'I might bump into Albertini. We've been through three worlds together. I'm sure I have an instinct for where he is right now. I could bring him back with me.'

'Jump *free*?' Vax protested. 'You must conceive your destination clearly, young lady.'

Sara shook her head. 'I'll concentrate on Albertini. Failing that, I'll visit Bishop Meesa's residence.'

'Why should an ex-Chorny squire be familiar with destinations in Bellogard?' demanded Prince Krasno.

'Those will be part of the memories she inherited a short while ago,' said Vax.

'Not entirely,' Sara told him. 'During the last war I infiltrated Bellogard secretly to lay the groundwork for an attack. That's how I met Pedino.'

'Too much, too much!' Adama wrung her hands.

'If you can jump free,' said Vax, 'then do so. Bring back your witness. At least she's being honest,' he observed, for the general benefit.

Sara spoke journey-magic and vanished.

Within a short time she was back again on a square of the chequerboard. In her arms she clutched a squirming, kicking Albertini. She dumped him unceremoniously.

'Phew. Found him in Piazza Market. In a scrape. Traders caught him filching fruit.'

Albertini took in the face above the royal livery. 'Why, it's you!' He leapt up and hugged Sara.

She patted him. 'Hullo there, Albertini.'

'A word of caution!' I said to the courtiers. 'Don't *ever* abbreviate his name.'

Recognizing me, the boy beamed and waved. 'Hi, Puddino! Where's Koko?'

'Somewhere or other.'

'Where's *this* place?'

'Royal court of Bellogard, lad. I'm the king.'

His blithe expression changed to one of consternation.

'Yer's wun already? World's comin' to an end again?'

'No, nothing like that. The war's only beginning.'

220

'Is it? Is it?' cried Adama. 'Not if we stand around for ever. Clear the chequerboard! I shall sing.'

Sara hustled Albertini to the side-line as Adama's voice soared, pitched to summon the eidolons of our enemies.

A trio of ghostly figures appeared. Two were pawn-squires garbed in black suits with obsidian buttons. One occupied the queen's pawn square, the other a prince-pawn square. The third figure was a young bearded knight in black armour.

'Three!' exclaimed Sir Brian. 'Three have already moved!'

'They're probably just exercising,' said Sara. 'See: the queen's pawn frees Queen Boola and her bishop to move. The prince's pawn frees the prince. The knight has leapfrogged out for a canter.'

'Young lady,' said Roque, 'we can hardly rely on the diagnosis of a Chorny renegade! Their queen and prince and bishop are now free to advance, as you rightly point out.'

Adama appeared to have recovered her poise. She spoke crisply. 'We must immediately advance my own squire to free myself and Vax. Also, Prince Roque's squire.'

'She *has* made a move,' said Roque.

Quite true: *Sara* was squire to Roque – I recalled this fact – falsely but indisputably.

'Maybe not *far* enough,' said Adama.

'Hang on,' broke in bluff Sir Brian, 'oughtn't we to check the white eidolons, Majesty? To confirm Sara's move?'

The queen sang again, more slowly in a lower key. Our side of the chequerboard remained totally bare. No eidolon of Sara appeared.

'*How* do you account for this, Vax?'

Vax pursed his lips. 'Hmm. Sara jumped to Piazza Market and back. She possesses pawnmagic. We all saw that. She certainly isn't a black squire. So she must somehow be of neither side – or of both sides! No eidolon can adequately represent her. Magically she's invisible.'

'That's useful,' said Roque. 'The enemy can't identify her.'

'A simple test should settle the matter, Prince. You yourself should jump. Jump anywhere you wish. If Sara is truly your squire, your leap won't be blocked. If she isn't, you'll remain here.'

'Right, I'll do it.' Roque spoke journey-magic and promptly disappeared.

He returned a few minutes later clutching a handful of white powder.

'Snow,' he announced, 'from the top of Mount Planina.' He cast the evidence aside to melt on the floor.

'Now, Majesty,' urged Vax, 'sing the white eidolons once more.'

Adama sang, and behold: Prince Roque's eidolon stood on its proper square.

Sir Brian rubbed his hands gleefully, as though it was he who had handled snow. 'When Queen Boola next summons our eidolons, she'll know that a pawn-squire moved – because the prince is on show. She'll assume the squire met some fatal accident. Ha! Damn it, now we can learn how that previous war went. We can avoid mistakes, if any. Who won, anyhow?' Evidently Sir Brian accepted my revelation pragmatically.

'Chorny won,' I told him. 'Really, neither side won. Both kingdoms lost everything. They lost existence itself. Do we have to fight this wretched, repetitious war all over again?'

Albertini chipped in unwelcomely. 'We mus' fight yer war. Can't not fight. You two said it's magic war sustains a world. Gives i' energy. No war, no world. World goes stale, dry as sticks, no blood in its veins. Rots.'

Unfortunately, so far as we knew, Albertini was spot on.

Vax came to my aid. Perhaps. 'To all intents, Majesty,' he said to Adama, 'the war *has* begun. Moves have been made, though no blood has yet been shed. Surely sufficient has been accomplished for one day?'

'No, it hasn't. I want my own squire to move, to free me. Squire Peterlin.'

'Hmm, that seems a reasonable request.'

'A command, Vax. It's a command.'

'Ah. Yes. Of course. But then let's call a halt. We do need time to analyse the previous war. We must also focus our wits on the magical nature of existence, to which we now hold a key. It may be ages before Chorny moves again. We shouldn't act precipitately. I'm sure you'll agree.'

'Oh very well.'

Consequently Squire Peterlin jumped to Bresh Hill, and returned exhilarated.

'*I* shall nobly refrain from jumping,' said Adama. 'My eidolon would be visible afterwards. Chorny might panic.' She sailed towards me and offered her arm. 'Come, husband mine.'

'But . . .'

'Are we not married? Are we not man and wife?'

'Yes. No.'

'*Yes!* Bishop Vax, you wedded us. Are we not doting husband and faithful wife? Arbitrate!'

Vax licked his lips – while Sara stared anxiously at him. 'I recall so, madam. On the other hand . . .'

'What other hand? A wife in one hand, a second wife in the other? Two wives in the same bed with a single husband?' Adama uttered a laugh of derision. 'What would our loyal subjects think of such an arrangement? I ask you, is this Chorny?'

'In point of fact,' I remarked, 'Chorny is – was –

distinctly strait-laced. Almost repressive! Apart from Queen Babula, whom I happen to have *met*, in Chorny itself! Queen Boola, that's to say.'

'Whom you wish me to emulate?'

'No, she wasn't particularly likable.'

'Come along then, Peddypoo. The bishop has spoken.'

'He didn't say much. Whereas I just said that I visited Chorny. I've been there. Aren't you interested?'

'It will make a pretty bedtime tale.'

Vax spoke again. 'Might I suggest a compromise? King Pedino could stay in bachelor accommodation while we, er, consider his exact marital status.'

'Live as a bachelor? What a ridiculous arrangement! How should I trust it? Shall we employ chaperones? Do *I* not have legitimate desires?'

Sara darted me a desperate glance but I was fresh out of ideas. Adama was such a glamorous, overpowering woman. I experienced a brief phantom glimpse of myself sinking into Adama, body and soul, forgetting my real past, maybe taking to wearing pantoufles and puffing a magic pipe. One of the bubbles which I blew would imprison Sara. She would implore me to release her. Later she would threaten me with her knife so that I would feel glad she was safely locked inside that bubble . . .

'Yer Majesty!' chirped Albertini.

'What is it, wee sprat?'

Albertini glowered but checked his temper.

'Mebbe yerself an' Sara should share a bed. Getta know each other like sisters. Leave Pedino outa it.'

Squire Irina began sniggering, and the queen rounded on her, freezing with a glare. Adama's gaze drifted onward, musingly, to her 'rival'.

'Yer'd be sure nuthin' woz goin' on behind yer back. Yer might getta like each other. Yer might even . . .'

'Yes, yes, I follow your drift. The wisdom of Suleiman,

224

no less! Why not? Why not indeed?' Adama regarded me with rueful amusement. 'Why should I share my sheets with someone who doesn't honestly adore me? Yet to share them with the object of that adoration . . . there's an equation that almost makes sense. Sara and I must have much in common. We could cultivate our mutual interests.'

I could see it clearly written on Adama's face: she intended to *seduce* Sara. I directed a helpless shrug in Sara's direction. To my consternation she smirked at me. Something in the proposal attracted her!

Recollecting her former life on Groody Lane, it struck me forcibly that Sara had *chosen* that particular role for her cover as a spy and saboteur. It was a role which must imply a cynicism about men, a certain contempt, even a measure of hatred. Her choice was surely not unconnected with the fact that Lovats had fathered her as a magical exercise on a mother bought by coin and rank, as much as by joy. Then her father had abandoned her to the state, and only acknowledged her because she was a success – only to commit experimental incest with her.

Had Sara told me the truth about her stepfather, that metallurgist at the Chorny Mint? Such a fellow must have been comparatively young and in good health. How could he and his wife both have *died* of flu? Now that I thought back, this part of Sara's story seemed implausible. A lie. A fantasy. Those two 'decent' parents, one of whom happened to have a pre-marital affair with a bishop . . . no, no, no. But who both conveniently died . . . no. Sara never did have a stepfather who died of flu. She never had kindly foster-parents, thoughtfully provided by Lovats, which of course made her special amongst the army of orphans.

Lovats wouldn't have risked farming out his experiment to strangers. He would have wanted the baby – and any other sibling products of his flesh – reared from the outset in his orphanage where he could keep an eye on them, be sure they were cared for efficiently. In Chorny there were no regular 'ladies of Groody Lane'. Nevertheless! Something along such lines had surely been the arrangement.

By allying with me Sara had turned her back on her fatherland as surely as her own father had turned *his* back on her during her formative years. (Or, if not his back exactly, he had only presented an official face.) True, Sara had seemed fond of Lovats – 'he isn't evil!' she had begged me to believe – but how could she have denounced her own father, even to herself? Did she decide to love me, not because I loved her and spared her life – not for myself alone – but because by loving me, a squire of Bellogard, she avenged herself on all forms of fathers, whether biological or political? And fathers, of course, were men.

My mind and heart churned. I felt lonely and betrayed. Punished, for circumstances which had nothing to do with me (beyond the fact that I'd chosen to stroll down Groody Lane and tap on a window). Now that Sara had saved my own bacon by magicking me back to Bellogard, perhaps we were quits.

The next time I saw Sara – the day after – she was arm in arm with Adama. Both women greeted me gaily, with the complicity of those who share a private joke which excludes outsiders.

Disconsolate, I spent the best part of the day closeted with Vax in the Bibliotek. A restless Albertini was also corralled with us for a couple of hours. Vax plied us with questions about the other magic worlds while a silent amanuensis – possibly dumb but certainly not deaf – wrote our answers into one of the blank books. After Albertini was dismissed – given his leave to caper around the palace poking his nose into kitchens, courtyards, galleries – a cold mutton salad was served, and Vax's questions turned to the subject of the previous war. Periodically one or other of us paced the room to stretch our limbs. The amanuensis seemed professionally immune to cramp.

Later that afternoon a flunkey brought ham sandwiches and wine. Vax kept harking back to my description of old King Karol's magic bubbles.

'So the king could create whole landscapes . . .'

'Twisted ones.'

'Twisted by his own mentality! I repeat: whole landscapes, with eidolons, imprisoned inside a magical bubblesphere. Our own world seems reminiscent of one of those bubbles, albeit on a vaster scale. Far grander, to those of us who dwell within! Tell me: did King Karol concentrate intently? Or did he let his fancy roam so that images welled up unbidden? Did he ever nod off with his pipe still in his mouth, and *dream* a magic bubble? To awaken and find it there before him, nestled upon the blankets?'

'I doubt if his valet let him smoke in bed!'

'Ah, but a bubble is made from soapy water, not tobacco fumes.'

'Sorry, I'm tired.' I gulped some wine, which was hardly the best medicine.

'Did Karol's imagination ever produce a bubble while he was busy with something else entirely?'

'I've no idea. Why?'

'I wonder whether magic worlds might be bubbles which someone dreams *contingently* – as a by-product of some other activity? Maybe the dreamer is a great magician; I don't know. I wonder if soapy water is the *best* substance to use? Did King Karol fix on soapy water by trial and error? Or did he happen to drop his pipe in the royal bathtub one day? Did he discover the efficacy of soapy water by sheer accident? And never try to improve on it? Never experiment. How about milk?

Milky bubbles might be too opaque . . . How about various *oils*?'

'What are you getting at, Vax?'

'I think you should commission a royal pipe of the design you mentioned.' The bishop took the book which the secretary had almost filled and flipped through earlier pages. 'Here we are. The arc of a hyperbola. The bowl, a fractional ellipsoid. Et cetera.'

'With what aim, Vax? To turn me into a double of the old buffoon? That silly prospect already haunts me.'

'Does it indeed? One should heed the promptings of hunches. You ought to blow some bubbles, using a variety of substances. You should try to dream a bubble showing the true origin of our world. A bubble which contains, and captures, the dreamer who dreams us. Or at least an eidolon of our benefactor/malefactor.'

'Shall we worship the image of our creator and destroyer?'

'No, we *examine* it. Paradoxically that bubble might *enclose* our universe – even though to us it seems the other way around. I have the germ of an idea, Sire. We might . . . be able to break through into that bubble. We might open a gateway.'

This project distracted my attention to some degree from the galling affair of Sara and Adama.

Vax and I decided to organize a royal progress for myself the following afternoon, which was the first day of the Jubilation. *En route* to the Samostan we would visit a certain pipe-maker's in Chalk Street – if the said establishment existed in the present world. Our discreet amanuensis – who could speak perfectly well when spoken to – would be sent that very evening to find out, and to forewarn the proprietors.

As soon as the man set out, Vax and I hastened to consult Adama – who appeared delighted by my spontaneous show of regal responsibility. This would keep me out of her hair at a sensitive time and give her more opportunity to dally with Sara in the delicate early stages – the honeymoon period – of their relationship. The queen promised to put in a similar appearance on the streets the day after, no doubt with my love by her side, dazzled by applause and pomp.

We took our leave of the queen; and Vax took his leave of me, to make all the necessary arrangements.

Tired out by talking all day long I retired early to a lonely, if splendid bedchamber. My sleep was interrupted once, by the guard outside my door admitting . . .

. . . no, not Sara. Of course not. It was the amanuensis, lantern in hand. He looked as tired as I felt.

'Excuse me, Sire.'

''S all right.'

'The shop is there.'

After lunch the next day Vax and Albertini and I set out in an open, gilded carriage drawn by four fine white geldings ridden by grooms. A second carriage conveyed Prince Krasno and Sir Jerebet, as our magical escort. A company of guards in scarlet tunics and plumed helmets rode along with us.

Our two carriages were soon purling through the streets, to loyal, often tipsy outcries of excitement and much waving of flags and streamers.

Bellogard was as I remembered it, give or take petty differences. The Spomenik Monument celebrated our frothy, vivacious composer of champagne-music, as ever, from a shifted vantage-point. Cafés around Terga Square were doing a humming, if elegant trade; however, I saw no flower-beds. The square was paved with cobbles. In the centre a fountain sprayed red wine as if from a severed artery.

I muttered to Albertini, 'That wasn't a very bright idea of yours, Sara and the queen bedding down together.'

'Wozn't it?'

'Not really.'

'Sorry, Yer Majesty.' Albertini sounded like the soul of innocence. But if it came to a choice did he owe real allegiance to me – or to Sara?

Our carriage and escort crowded along Chalk Street. We halted outside my old home, my former birthplace. While a groom unfolded the carriage steps for me I was gazing at the shop-window. Much the same display of briars, clays, and lulus, jars of shag and ambershred, snuff tubs, boxes of cheroots. Trepidation filled my heart. Who would I find inside? My mother and father? My kid sister? Myself?

When the groom thrust the door open a familiar little bell jangled. As if in sympathy mightier bells began clonging from campaniles all around the city. I walked in . . .

A merry, fresh-faced woman and a gaunt man stood blushing with pride, embarrassment, and eager awkwardness. The woman curtsied. The man bowed jerkily. Both were in their middle thirties. They were strangers to me.

Total strangers? Their faces looked unfamiliar but in an evocative kind of way – as though this couple might be my grandparents, or great-grandparents, in their youth. Early days, yet, in Bellogard!

'Excellent fellow,' I addressed the pipe-maker. 'We have come in person to commission a very special pipe; and to bestow our royal warrant upon your establishment.' Nothing like supporting home industries.

Bishop Vax had followed me into the shop, increasing the delight and confusion of the couple.

'That's a *purchase*,' I emphasized. 'Paid for in good crowns; I insist.'

I realized that my pockets were empty. A king doesn't

carry money. Fortunately Vax had anticipated this. He jiggled a purse quietly. I took it, loosened the drawstring, and pulled out a gold coin. On one side was my own silhouette; on the other Adama's, with words in the magic language: *Kreditna Banka*.

I placed several gold coins on the counter and proceeded to describe the sort of pipe I needed. My 'grandfather' took pencil notes. He vowed to begin work at once; he could deliver such a pipe the very next day.

'No rush, fine fellow! Feel free to enjoy the Jubilation.'

The man shook his head emphatically. 'This job will be *our* Jubilation, Sire!'

Vax and I left, to board the carriage and continue onward to the Samostan.

A marquee had been erected on one lawn to dispense wine and special celebration ale and wholesome delicacies. The aroma of barbecued eel with hot sauce, sizzling spiced sausages, fried puff-balls teased my nostrils. On another sward a chair o'plane and a carousel were to be found, also side-shows: a fire-swallower, a knife-thrower, an equilibrist. Quite a few women were wearing carnival attire, disguised as vamps and cocottes, odalisques and pierrettes. It was as if Seveno District had spilled into Bishop Meesa's grounds. Some of the men wore brigand or gypsy costumes. Kids rushed about, squealing. The undecapitated peacocks had taken refuge atop the box-trees to scream their pea-brained protests.

What better place to find a clown than at a carnival fête? I soon spotted Koko, grinning and weeping, tottering about on his stilts while clutching an outsize sausage. Kids hooted at his wobbly efforts to balance and bite.

I ordered my carriage to be driven slowly through the crowd in this direction. Voices acclaimed, 'The King! The King!'

I rose. 'Ho, clown! Stagger over here!'

At first Koko didn't recognize me in my natty ermine regalia and modest workaday coronet. In the carriage behind, Prince Krasno looked every inch the monarch in his generalissimo's purple and gold uniform, braided, ribboned, and epauletted; he wore that with considerably more nonchalant aplomb than fat King Mastilo ever mustered.

I beckoned. 'Here, clown!'

Koko collided with the side of our carriage. His feet on their wooden wedges overtopped the vehicle. Blithe and wretched, he peered down at me.

'Hullo, Koko. It's Pedino. Step aboard.'

'*Pedino!*' Koko did as I said, pulled the stilts after him, and rested them like oars along the gilded gunwales of the carriage. He collapsed into a vacant seat. His actual expression seemed to be one of profound relief.

The crowd cheered enthusiastically. A highly popular gesture, this, welcoming a clown on board the state carriage! I had honoured the carnival in the best possible style. Much popularity was gained.

'Can I get on eating?' Koko brandished the giant, gnawed sausage – just as if he was offering the king a mouthful. Cheers redoubled.

'I take it that this gentleman is your other witness?' asked Vax.

'The very same.'

'It might be a shade undignified to continue gobbling *kobasitsy* at the moment. There's a feast in preparation inside. Meesa always caters lavishly. Your friend can have early pickings. After that, I'll pick his brains.'

'I'm half-starved,' protested Koko.

Albertini was jittering with pent-up excitement.

'Solve yer problem! Gimme.' He slapped Koko sociably on the knee, snatched the sausage, vaulted the side, and ran to join in the fun.

* * *

Stuffed with first fruits from the banquet-to-be, Koko sailed through the brain-picking process with flying colours; though he shed other colours. Vax insisted he remove his face paint. It's hard to judge someone's answers when you can't make out their true expression. Koko agreed. He'd been wearing the same paint for days; the waxy pigments were curdling.

With his features newly spruced, Koko's was a round, flat pan of a face. Now, the gaudy tent-suit became a bizarre oddity. This was exchanged for the off-duty duds of a Samostan flunkey: brown cord pants and jacket, yellow shirt, spotty orange cravat. Dismounted and divested, Koko seemed a slight, short, anonymous figure.

By the time the questioning was through, to Vax's satisfaction, it was time for a concert in the Fuchsia Chamber of the Samostan. We sat through overtures by Spomenik, Maximilio, and Shinkovets in company with worthy burghers and their wives, and other guests.

After the concert, I led everyone into the grand Hyacinth Hall, where the feast was laid. Meesa, a late arrival out of deference to my position as senior host, seated himself with dominies from the Gymnasium, his protégés. I summoned the Astrologer Royal, Mr Astrisk, to sit by me during the guinea-fowl course thinking that he might be a prototype of Mr Matyash, but I found his conversation strained and farcical. The astrologer explained how his night's work would be hopelessly aborted by the fireworks display which was scheduled to follow dinner. Therefore he intended to divine a horoscope based on the gunpowder and chemical lights in the sky. He would inscribe this fantasy in gold ink on vellum and send it to the palace for my delight – as a laureate might compose a ceremonial ode. I found him fatuous.

Afterwards I watched the pyrotechnics from the Samostan balcony in the company of Vax and Meesa, Prince Krasno and Sir Jerebet, Albertini and Koko. Golden stars burst in the sky; silver comets raced with the *whoosh* of a cushion suddenly sat upon; emerald meteors descended; red fire dripped down the night.

We returned to the palace, with Albertini sound asleep, Koko nodding off, and Vax deep in thought.

'Perhaps a *mixture* of oil and milk,' Vax confided to me as we were crossing the bridge over the Rehka.

'The doctrine of *necessary existence!*' Vax said to me.

Vax and I were together in the Bibliotek, where no trace of dust had yet had time to settle.

Adama was in town that day, showing herself off to our loyal subjects – with, yes, Sara at her side. Sir Brian and Prince Roque were riding escort in the second carriage.

How secure the people of Bellogard must feel, how blessed and protected by so much courtly presence yesterday and now again today. Not a whiff of revolutionary discontent or worry soured their tiny little souls which were like so many blades of fresh green grass given life by the sunlight of the palace. A whole field full of such souls was equivalent to one royal soul.

Why should our citizens fret? Bellogard would continue to prosper for a century, or two. The majority of the magical war would hardly touch the common folk at all. I myself would slowly – oh so slowly – grow older as their king; their one and only. Only when the time approached for me – or King Martel – to be checked and mated, would Bellogard wither.

In another sense Adama had checked *me*; and I definitely remained 'unmated' by Sara. The prospect of a century or two of frustration made me weary. It was early days but already I could foresee the pattern . . . unless I managed to blow a certain magic bubble.

The escape route might prove to be a malicious trap of fate. I might be fulfilling – voluntarily! – the destiny of any Bellogardian king who blew imaginative bubbles with high hopes at first, but who then grew whimsical, even cynical, the initial bold impulse diluted in parody, mannerism, and a frivolous coarsening of consciousness.

I was a young man yet I felt old, poisoned by an angry sadness.

'Necessary existence, Sire!'

'Yes, what's that?'

'I'm trying to explain. Anything that is magically imagined can achieve a phantom existence somewhere, somehow. This existence in turn breeds a whole population of subsidiary, dependent ghosts. Suppose you imagine a dragon. In the wake of this initial act of the imagination, an entire world must come into being where dragons are possible and actual. A world of fields and forests, of towns and people. Those people generate ancestors. The towns breed history. The farms and fields create a natural history and a geography. The sky above causes astrology, the very stars in the heavens. A million, million collateral items are implied. They emerge willynilly. Yet *you yourself*, imagining a dragon, remain oblivious to this process!'

'Dodgy business imagining things, eh Bishop? Does a world of dragons exist now?'

'Of course not. Neither of us concentrated magically. Indeed I suspect that only a *king* can actively create.'

'As compensation for his other deficiencies?'

Vax ignored this. 'Whereas a bishop can divine. Or can blow a murder-bubble, as you once did at the Razval baths. My point is that somewhere far beyond our world some intelligence or intelligences may be engaged in an activity which involves great concentration. Our world is a by-product of this, due to the doctrine of necessary existence. Normally this doctrine is used to solve the conundrum: "How can I be sure that objects exist when no one is observing them?" For example, how do I know that a certain courtyard persists in housing a willow tree and a water-butt when the yard is deserted? *Necessary existence* is the answer. I simply extend the doctrine.'

Tracing an invisible line on the table with my fingertip I remembered – I anticipated – how dust would give rise to more dust. I nodded, half convinced.

'Once the morphic pattern is established,' continued Vax, 'we can expect close generic similarities between one cycle of activity and the next . . . Will you tell me some more about Bishop Veck's conduct as head of security? I'm intrigued by that trait in my character.' Frustratedly Vax cudgelled his brow with a fist. 'What anamnesis will assist me to remember? None, I suppose. Your Majesty leapt from the last world to this present one. I didn't.'

A bell tinkled; Vax went to the door.

'Pardon me,' reported a guard, 'but a pipe-maker from Chalk Street has delivered a small parcel addressed to the King.'

I sat on my ivory throne in the crowded Ex-Chequer Chamber, feeling like a fool.

The floor – as ever – was white marble. At this hour of the morning bars of shadow patterned it. Brass-bound doors led to the Chequer Chamber. Guards wore their scarlet tunics and plume helmets.

Amused, anticipative, Adama lounged in her throne. Sara dawdled by the queen's side. The two women whispered. They touched fleetingly, communicating incomprehensibly in the language of the fingertips. Sara smiled at me pleasantly enough.

On a japanned table before me stood bowls of milk and oils and mixtures, with soapy water as back-up. The 'perfect pipe' of briar trimmed with silver rested in a sandalwood box lined with blue satin.

Vax made a short speech to outline our intentions.

Then he blessed all the bowls, using the very same divination spell that Bishop Slon had used when he tested my boy's soul once, long ago in an earlier world.

I lifted the perfect pipe solemnly and rinsed it in milk. I spoke magic and puffed gently. A white bubble swelled and swelled, then burst. A droplet of milk flicked into my left eye; tiny splatters hit my face like sticky raindrops. Adama simpered sympathetically.

A flunkey took the pipe, washed and dried it on best linen, and handed it back. I dipped into oil of terebinth and tried again. A fairly foul encounter.

Next I dipped into . . . no, I shan't say which particular liquid. After I invoked, I tried to keep my mind blank by thinking of empty, magic space. I blew steadily.

A shimmering bubble swelled. A trembling rainbow sphere the size of a basketball was balanced upon the bowl of the pipe. I jerked my head aside and barked the well-remembered spell to glassify and clarify.

The bubble crystallized, then cleared.

What did I see?

Why you, my reader!

You who are reading this tiny (but not indecipherable) book. You with your magnifying glass. Or is that a microscope?

You sat deep in thought confronting another brooding individual across a chequerboard. On the board stood wooden carvings of ourselves, lifeless caricatures of a queen, a king, princes, bishops, knights, squires. Facing those were figurines of our black-souled foes in Chorny.

You and your opponent were as motionless as two waxworks. Almost. You breathed as slowly as the sun sets. You blinked the way a lazy cat yawns. Did your right hand move? 'Twould take it a fortnight to grasp one of the carvings.

* * *

It cost Bishop Vax almost a year to devise the right magic to insert an object into a bubble without bursting it, fracturing it, destroying its efficacy. As yet, only a smallish object: about the size of a baby's fingertip. Numerous experimental bubbles were destroyed in the quest. The original bubble, we kept under permanent guard in the Ex-Chequer Chamber.

During that year Squire Dennis was killed in a magical attack by a prince of Chorny. Squire Ben succeeded in wounding the black attacker slightly. Sara continued to consort with my consort. I slept alone. I had a new obsession to occupy my mind. As soon as Vax was sure he was on the right track I started to dictate this account to a secretary.

A whole team of amanuenses is labouring over enormous magnifying glasses copying the text on to dissected pages of a tiny, blank volume from the Bibliotek. These copyists use magic ink and ingenious pens with nibs thinner than a human hair made for us specially by a horologist.

When they have finished their work the miniature pages will all be carefully glued back on to the spine. That will occur soon. Very soon. My account is almost complete (and obviously it cannot include its own logical climax within itself).

Tomorrow or the day after tomorrow I will accompany Vax to the Ex-Chequer Chamber. I shall be holding the minuscule volume – the *opusculum*, as Vax likes to call it. Vax will open a little magic hole in the bubble. Using a pea-shooter scrounged by Albertini I shall blow the midget book through on to the black and white board where you sit cogitating.

Might you mistake the *opusculum* for a fly? (Of peculiar build!) Only at the risk of knocking your own queen over. (And what would happen to Adama *then*?)

Will you have the wit to fetch a magnifying glass?

Surely a deep thinker like you will have enough hot porridge in his head.

Perhaps now you can appreciate a certain reticence on my part about the magical language and my refusal to disclose the *exact* mechanism of spells. There's no percentage in my teaching you magic.

But I give you fair warning: there are whole worlds you have never seen, which you have brought into existence – you and your kind.

In Bellogard we're on the brink of a 'magical revolution'. We're beginning to make real strides. Vax has racked his brains about Sara's 'othermagic', the strange-magic which extends beyond any single restricted set of rules, and given all the clues he has come up with real solutions. We'll be grand masters, and mistresses, of magic. Tomorrow: one little hole through which my *opusculum* leaps, by way of a visiting card. Next year (that's *decades* before Chorny could disable us) we're going to expand that bubble in the Ex-Chequer Chamber. And we'll open a hole through which a courtier or a king can crawl, armed with knife and magic.

Despite psychological factors rooted in Sara's upbringing I think she'll tire of the queen's loving embraces. I hope she'll be intrigued at the idea of squeezing through a hole, with me, to elsewhere. I still love her.

Would you like to meet Albertini too? We'll see if it can be arranged. Though unmagical, he's conveniently small. Maybe we'll send him ahead of us. If you see a little boy behaving oddly, watch out. He's an ambassador from Bellogard.

Yet perhaps, as Vax hinted to me barely an hour ago, *yours* isn't the original of *our* world after all. Perhaps ours is the original of yours!

In which case, I come to rescue you from tedium – from the automatism of moving models on a flat board.

In any event, prepare to meet Pedino! Pedino wishes to play. With you.